STEVEN MOORE

The Condor Prophecy

A Hiram Kane Adventure

Contents

XI Epilogue

A Quick Note

At the back of this novel you'll find a link to the first instalment in the Hiram Kane series, absolutely free.

If you enjoy this book, just follow the link, sign up to my newsletter, and I'll deliver 'The Samurai Code' directly to your inbox.

For now, sit back, strap in, and enjoy 'The Condor Prophecy'.

A Prophecy

Now it is time for the uprising.
The prophecy must be fulfilled.
Revenge is not just expected, but demanded by Incan gods.
And the once mighty condor must take flight again.

Prologue

Lima, Peru
Summer, 2011

Light wind lifted dust from the dry grounds of the park, swirling it through the cool air, like memories drifting through time. Centuries of painful memories.

Parque de la Muralla was almost silent in the hours before dawn, the only sound the nattering of stray dogs aroused by the intruders. It was still night, but it wasn't very dark, Lima's garish street lights casting crazed shadows everywhere, one in particular, prominent across the ground; a Spanish conquistador astride his horse.

They didn't have long. Soon the park would bustle with early morning joggers, eager to exercise before the sun rose too high. Four men stood silently beneath a street lamp. They were young men, tough and wiry, their faded shirts tight over sinewy muscles, their dark, chestnut skin and narrow eyes indicative of Quechuan mestizo men in Peru.

The gathered men were proud of what they had done and what they were going to do. Nevertheless, they didn't want to be caught, and had a lot more to achieve. They ran to that vast shadow and stopped, taking a moment to gaze up at the massive statue before them. It was tall, some twenty feet, its bronze glimmering in the darkness. The rider sat mounted on a powerful horse, he and it both heavily armoured. He had his sword raised, and the stern glare in his eyes would intimidate any enemy.

The statue's striking profile was a dark and dominant silhouette against the faint hint of dawn. Impressive. But not for long.

The first of the four men, their single-minded leader, clambered up the pedestal with a length of thick rope. He edged high onto the mighty horse's back, where the cast bronze shone under the lamp's orange glow. Two other men laced their own ropes around the front legs of the horse, pulling hard to tighten the knots. In less than two minutes, the statue of horse and rider had three lengths of heavy-duty rope dangling from it.

The fourth man edged their powerful flatbed truck into position, twenty yards in front of the statue. With all the ropes now linked as one, the driver fastened it to the truck's winch. It was time.

The leader, his authority unquestioned, motioned to the others to join him. They stood in line, and with the horse and rider statue before them, the big man said a few words in his native Quechuan:

Across the Andes Mountains, the mighty condor once soared,
Where spirits of the Incas will look down forever more,
And when the name Pizarro, from the history books has gone,
The legend of the Incas, forever and always, will live on.

The the driver then ran to the truck and restarted the engine, revving it to life. He stepped hard on the pedal, the screech of the wheels harsh on their ears. But they didn't care. The driver focused his eyes on the leader's raised arm and waited for the signal. Their hearts raced. The moment was near.

Destiny.

And then the arm fell.

He lifted his foot from the brake, and pressing the accelerator down with all his strength the powerful truck lurched backwards. The ropes resisted, the truck wheels skidding and swerving on the concrete, but it didn't retreat. The thick bronze of the statue groaned under the pressure as the eerie sound resonated across the empty park.

Then the rider's head shifted just a few inches forwards as the statue began to yield. The driver gunned the pedal, straining the engine to its limit. And as if in slow motion, one of the horse's knees buckled, the entire statue tilting to the left. The screaming of tyres and twisting metal sounded deafening to the men standing close. Yet still the horse and rider didn't fall, but clung on as if their immortality depended on it. After long, nervous seconds, the men shared doubtful looks. But finally the second leg buckled, and the colossal sculpture fell to its knees. It left the rider leaning precariously forwards and the tip of his lance mere inches from the ground.

The leader looked at his driver, an instinctive message passing between them. His build was solid, and tall for an Andean native at six foot. The man commanded obedience. He was the eldest, but despite his relatively young age his weathered face was scarred and his eyes had already seen a lifetime of pain and disappointment.

The driver slipped the gears back into first, and as the truck edged forward a few yards the ropes fell slack. A heavy silence now haunted the empty park, the street dogs long since retreated in fear. After all the noise they'd made, the park wouldn't be empty for long.

This was it. The final effort. Their leader nodded, his wild eyes alive with anticipation. The driver took a deep breath, slammed the gears once more into reverse, and accelerating backwards the ropes pulled taut and the huge statue was unceremoniously hauled to the ground. As bronze slammed against concrete and sparks flew like an exploding firework, the horrific sound of warped and scraping metal was a fitting welcome to the dawning of a new era.

The driver left the truck and joined the others as they walked to the head of the fallen rider. They didn't speak, but they didn't need to. Their duty was done. The prophecy was being fulfilled.

The men turned toward the truck, but the leader paused. After a moment's thought, he walked back to the rider's caved in head. Unzipping the fly of his jeans, and with utter calm, the big man urinated on the upturned face. Satisfied, he rejoined the others.

Without a word they drove away into the dawn, just as the day's first locals began entering the park. And the men left safe in the knowledge that the despised Spanish conquistador Francisco Pizarro would never cast his dark shadow over Inca lands again.

Pachamama

May 7th, 2012
The Andes Mountains

Hiram Kane swatted half-heartedly at a mosquito. It's not that they didn't drive him insane. They did, the very bane of his life. But something else occupied his thoughts in that moment, and not even the buzzing of a million mosquitoes would distract him.

He sat on a flat rock, the ancient stone warmed from a high, midday sun. A nearby waterfall churned white, gravity sending it cascading into the valley below, its constant white-noise roar transcending all other sound. But Hiram heard nothing. He sat still and focused, his mind tuned into something the few people sitting nearby couldn't have known. Squinting against the harsh light, he stared into the jungle before him, narrowed eyes penetrating the impenetrable.

He was close. He knew it, could feel it in his bones.

The quest of a lifetime–the quest of several lifetimes–would at last be over. Kane had found what he and so many others before him had sought. It was within his grasp, and as electricity tingled his fingertips Hiram knew he'd found the real lost city of the Incas.

Vilcabamba.

Kane and his team members were deep in Peru's iconic

Sacred Valley, far from the overused hiking trails between Machu Picchu and the city of Cuzco. Few foreigners in the modern era ever laid eyes on the wild terrain in that unexplored area of the valley, which meant the scenery was untainted by humans, thus remained magnificent. Mountains towered off at impossible angles in every direction. Some peaks were covered in snow, despite the warmer season, while others lay shrouded beneath an almost perpetual mist. It lent them a mystical quality always so alluring to Hiram. The steep, jungled slopes fell away to the mighty Urubamba River, where its dark and dangerous waters raged in violent brown rapids.

Kane had been close to the area before. The last time was twelve months previous, when he'd led another expedition of archaeologists and wide-eyed treasure hunters far into the depths of the valley. Most people didn't really believe they would find the genuine lost city of Vilcabamba, but it didn't stop them dreaming of success, and groups dedicated vast amounts of time and money every year to try. It was Hiram Kane's job, and pleasure, to lead them.

But Kane differed from the others, and always had. Hiram truly believed the legend of Vilcabamba was real, and not only that, but he would be the man to find it. And he had an advantage over all those others.

Hiram Kane had a map.

A contemplative frown pinched Kane's face as he pondered his decision, his eyes darkened by deep thought and his mouth set in what looked like a scowl but was more a study in concentration. He had a big choice to make, and he would not take it lightly.

Considered average looking by most, and not least himself, Kane possessed a rugged, outdoorsy quality admired by many. At a modest five feet eleven but with a physique that hinted at his years of competitive sport and outdoor living, Kane cut a commanding presence. Kane was reserved by nature, yet his cropped and slightly greying brown hair and perma-stubble added a tough edge. But his rich hazel eyes–eyes that faded to jade green under a bright sun–were sharp and wise and painfully honest. With a few hidden tattoos and a collection of well-earned scars, Kane's was a body that had seen and felt a fully lived life. He'd even lost half a finger, destroyed by a bullet when he found himself confronted by ruthless Yakuza men in Japan last year. It still hurt sometimes, a painful reminder of that horrific episode on Miyajima Island.

Yet, Kane would be the first to tell you he was only now getting started. *Life's short,* he said often, *seize it by the horns.* On his expeditions, he led by example.

But Kane felt torn. The group of six people with him, resting in the shade of a native *polylepis* tree after a long and arduous hike up the valley, had all invested a lot to join this expedition, and every one of them had the same ambitions as Hiram; locate the lost city of the Incas. They all wanted to be there when history got rewritten, wanted to be there when the true Vilcabamba was discovered.

They deserved to know the truth, of course. All six were successful in their respective fields, and among them were two archaeologists, two art historians, an eminent professor of antiquities, and a photographer. Completing the team were three porters, four mules, and a cook. Despite the heat and the harsh conditions, the native Quechuan fellows had barely raised a sweat. They sat away from the group, quietly savouring their rolled cigarettes while chewing wads of bitter coca leaves. In contrast, the foreigners' clothes were soiled, their bodies drenched in sweat, and their overworked lungs gasped for rarified breath in the high altitude air, the very epitome of exhaustion. Yet, no matter their physical state, all eyes were wide with wonder at the imposing panoramas that very same altitude granted them.

He should share his thoughts with them. They had that right. Kane though had always worried that if the wrong people found out about Vilcabamba, then the world's press would descend upon the site too soon and before the proper provisions and precautions were in place. Yes, these guys were all professionals. But that didn't guarantee they would act in a professional manner. In fact, Kane believed in many cases it almost guaranteed they wouldn't.

Kane was just being cautious, and he understood he had to tell them what he was thinking. After all, they had each paid him a small fortune based on the reputation of his integrity.

Now rested, a lean, middle-aged archaeologist from Cornell called out to Kane. "What do you see in there, Hiram? Not a mountain lion, is it?" He chuckled at his own joke. No one else did.

Kane swivelled to face them. It was time to tell them what he believed was true; that beyond the near jungle, just a few hours hike from where they were sitting, lay the place that had ruined so many fortunes, shattered so many dreams, and over the last century, had cost many, many lives. Yes, they were just a couple of miles from the fabled lost Incan city. Vilcabamba.

"No, it's not a puma," Kane said with a smile in his deep, confident tone. "That would be exciting though, wouldn't it?"

"Well, what is it, man?" the archaeologist asked, impatience lacing his voice. "What's kept you so rapt for the last fifteen minutes?"

"When we set off on this mission," said Kane, "we each dreamt of what we'd find. Well, it's my honest opinion that a few—"

Suddenly, the docile mules began braying while straining hard at their tethers, causing a commotion among the Quechuans. Something was wrong. The mules knew it, and hearing their ominous cries, so did the porters. In thick, accented Spanish, their leader, a short but commanding figure, shouted, *"Carrera! Carrera!"* Run! Run!

A low roar emanated from deep within the very ground they sat on, a grinding rumble, like far-away thunder. The hairs on the back of the archaeologist's neck stood up, his intuitive fear instant. The tree above him swayed, its papery red bark trembling. And then the ground shook.

Earthquake.

The ground shook with violence–left to right, up and down–and those who'd jumped to their feet were thrown to the hard earth like scarecrows in tornado alley. Boulders of all sizes came tumbling toward them from high up the slopes, a loaf sized rock striking an unfortunate mule on the head and killing it on the spot. The polylepis creaked, the thick trunk splintering, and it fell, the Cornell archaeologist diving clear with inches to spare.

Without a moment's hesitation, Kane and his Quechuan leader sprang into action. They darted across the rocks and grabbed the two nearest members of the group, shoving the stunned senior art historian and the young photographer to the safety of a ledge. But with a deafening roar the ledge shifted, and like a slow-moving tsunami, it crumbled down the slope. "Landslide!" Kane shouted, "Move. NOW!"

Two of them leapt clear, the professor of antiquities and the younger archaeologist. The French art historian immediately followed. However, her young PhD student companion Claude froze in fear, rooted where he stood. She shouted, "Allez, Claude, se dépêche!" Come on! Hurry!

But Claude didn't move.

In the dozens of expeditions he'd led before, Kane had never lost anyone. There'd been many earthquakes, a common event in the Andes, and plenty of landslides, and Kane had witnessed stronger ones than this. But he knew things could worsen, and probably would. Using all his athleticism he scrambled down a few yards, almost riding the loose debris, until he straddled the fallen tree, and leapt across the crevice that opened between Claude and the group.

"Claude," he yelled. "You need to move."

"Ce n'est pas possible! I… I can not!" Terror shook his voice and tears streaked his dusty cheeks. But at that moment the sliding ledge came to a shuddering halt, the horrifying rumble fading to a direful growl. Kane took his chance.

"It's okay, my friend. You can do it. You have to move. Take my hand."

Claude shook his head, still unable to move. Then, just twenty yards away, a boulder the size of a small Citroen crashed past them, slamming trees aside like dominoes until it disappeared into the misty valley below. Claude was a sitting duck, and it was all the inspiration Kane needed.

Without pause he launched himself out onto the precarious ledge, only just finding his balance in time to prevent plummeting to a certain death. Then, and with some not-so-gentle physical persuasion and a few choice expletives, he hauled the young Frenchman over the crevice, almost certainly saving his life. The others, huddling under a tree and thanking their God or the universe that the earthquake had somehow stopped, stared at Hiram Kane in speechless awe.

Kane and his head guide, Sonco, hustled around the group checking for injuries, relieved to see they'd all escaped with little more than a few scratches and scrapes. They'd been lucky, Kane knew. He also knew they weren't out of trouble. After a quick deliberation with Sonco, who understood the terrain better than any man alive, they agreed another landslide might happen at any moment, and in fact they expected it. Kane addressed the group.

"We've had a narrow escape, but the danger hasn't passed. Earthquakes often have after-shocks, and it wouldn't take a lot for the whole side of this mountain to collapse. We have to go. Now! We'll backtrack as fast as we can in the direction we came for an hour, and there we'll make camp. If nothing drastic happens during the night, we can return tomorrow, and depending on the trails, try to continue on."

Every member of the group agreed without hesitation, especially Claude, whose tear-stained face nodded rapid approval. Even Mr Cornell didn't complain.

As they retreated to a safer distance along the trail, and both the real and proverbial dust had settled, Kane recalled he'd been on the verge of telling the others they were close to Vilcabamba.

He was not a religious man, far from it, but the rituals and traditions of the world's diverse civilisations fascinated Kane. He was also a touch superstitious, though he wouldn't admit it, and Hiram couldn't help but wonder if the landslide was a sign from the Incan Earth Goddess, Pachamama. The ancient Incas believed if they upset Pachamama, she had the ability to destroy the land with violent earthquakes–like the one they'd just witnessed. Hiram gave little credence to such archaic superstitions himself, but there it was. On the hike to camp the thought lingered with him.

Kane settled into a restless silence as he walked. After another consultation with Sonco, they believed they were now beyond any immediate danger, which meant tomorrow they could continue with the expedition. But it somehow didn't feel right. Kane was an instinctive man and had learned the hard way to trust those instincts. The one occasion he hadn't trusted them had haunted him for almost three decades. Shaking his head, he dismissed those dark thoughts and pushed on.

After arriving at their new campsite, Kane spent a couple of hours deliberating his options whilst the porters set up camp and the team members tried to relax after their harrowing near miss. It was a tough decision, but after once more conversing with his most trusted friend, Sonco, he made it. Kane was terminating the expedition.

It was a big call, but now he'd made it there was no backing down. Whatever had caused the earthquake and the subsequent landslide–whether an act of nature, or the supernatural whim of Pachamama, as Sonco suggested–Kane took it as a sign that one way or another he should keep the surety he felt about their proximity to Vilcabamba to himself. If confronted–if some of the party insisted they push on–he would inform them the terrain was too unstable, that it was too dangerous to proceed, and that he as expedition leader had a responsibility for their safety. If necessary, he'd remind them it was also in the contracts they'd all signed.

Kane was sorry it was over for them–he was sorry for himself, too–but there was no other choice. He would also tell them about Pachamama, about Incan superstitions, and hope they were superstitious enough to read into it the same inauspicious warning as him; that the Earth Goddess had chosen to keep the Inca secrets a mystery.

And though he himself didn't buy into it, Kane knew exactly how Sonco felt.

Anyone would be foolish to challenge Pachamama's will.

Ringsfield, Suffolk

January 25th, 1992

Hiram relished the wide-open spaces of White House Farm, the Kane family estate in the English countryside. It's where his grandparents still lived, and he looked forward to his infrequent visits. His grandfather had always been an excellent storyteller, entertainment guaranteed, and he was soon regaling Hiram with anecdotes about the pair's first trip to Peru together. It was two years previous, and Hiram's maiden trip to the Andes. Though he hadn't quite grasped it yet, it would have him hooked for a lifetime.

It was in the Andes that his great-grandfather, Patrick Kane, served as chief assistant to celebrated explorer, Hiram Bingham, and as a child young Hiram listened in rapt attention as he heard tales passed down over several generations about the most famous of all Andean expeditions, the search for the lost city of the Incas, Vilcabamba.

It was during their mission that Bingham, with the help of Patrick and the native Quechuan Indians, rediscovered for the outside world the ruined Inca citadel known as Machu Picchu–Old Mountain–and though it turned out to be one of the greatest discoveries of the twentieth century, they'd failed to find what they set out for.

Their search for Vilcabamba was a bitter-sweet failure. Despite giving Bingham and Kane world renown, Patrick still felt like a fraud. It was because of Patrick's perceived failure that the youngest Hiram, and his grandfather before him, shared a passion and a desire to find what their honoured forebear could not.

And he could not extinguish the fires of that passion until he at last located Vilcabamba. Hiram and his grandfather left the warmth of the blazing fireplace and approached a large bay window, looking out onto a picture-postcard winter scene as a cold, bitter wind swept swathes of snow into deep enticing drifts.

Today was a big day, a day the young Hiram was to become an adult, at least in a legal sense. It was his eighteenth birthday. Beneath the studious exterior and athletic, sporty frame, however, beat the heart of a child. Today the snow was just too tempting. It was a passion for the outdoors shared by all the family, and his grandfather's eyes exuded the same youthful glow.

With a disapproving look over her tiny spectacles, Jan turned her face to conceal a joyous smile as she waved the two kids off. That they were a combined age of almost ninety mattered little, and the elder Hiram was no more restrained than his grandson.

After donning their wellies and wrapping up in scarves and hats, they made their way out into the vast expanse of land stretching away from the house. *He'll never grow up*, Jan thought with a warm heart as they disappeared out of view. She too was excited. Today, on his eighteenth birthday, Hiram was to receive something very special, something her husband had waited patiently to pass on to his grandson when the time was right. That time had come. He was ready.

"It's good to see you, laddie. Your grandmother and I miss

you."

"I miss you both too, Grandad," replied Hiram.

There was a pause, a moment of reflection between the two of them. The last time they saw each other was a sad occasion for all the family. Hiram's mother Melanie had died the year before, having succumbed to cancer after a short but agonising bout of chemotherapy that had ultimately failed. The family was distraught, Hiram's father still undone with grief. They had all taken a train north to Melanie's native Edinburgh for the funeral, but because of school commitments, Hiram hadn't seen his grandparents at all since that day.

"It's been almost a year since your poor mother passed. How are you coping, lad? And how's your father doing?"

"I'm okay. It's hard sometimes, and I get angry, wishing there was more I could've done. I have good friends on campus, which helps. I know dad is struggling. He misses her. We all do."

Hiram's grandad put his thin arm around his shoulders as they walked. "I know, my boy... such a terrible loss for everyone. I feel for your father. He's never really recovered from when your brother went missing, so it's no wonder he is the way he is. Of course, we sympathise with our son. But I can *not* forgive him for blaming you the way he did. It wasn't your fault. You do know that, don't you?"

Hiram fell silent for long seconds, gazing out into the wintry day as they ambled on. His grandfather gave him all the time he needed. After a considerable while, Hiram stopped.

"I shouldn't have let Danny leave school with me that day. But... He would've gone with his friends eventually, so I—" Another long pause. "I just thought it was better he came with me."

That's the story Hiram had convinced himself of, anyway.

Hiram tried to keep his tears of guilt bottled up, especially around his father. But his grandfather had always been understanding and had never once apportioned any blame.

"You know," he said, "if your father possessed even a quarter of the adventurous spirit you and I have, he would've seen that whole terrible event differently. Of course he felt devastated about Danny's disappearance from the house that day. We all were. But no one can attach any blame, especially not to you." Now Hiram's grandfather fell silent, as if trying hard to remember something lost to time. He shook his head, bewildered, still in disbelief. "Something that's always troubled me is that there was no body. No evidence of any struggle. No footprints leading out of that old house, only yours. Nothing. Just so, so strange."

And it was strange. Apart from the shock and confusion and obvious devastation for the Kane family to have lost its youngest member, none of what happened made any sense to anybody, including the police.

The two lads had broken into the abandoned Old Rectory, a building that had lain empty for more than two decades. Though harmless, it was unwise, but that's just what curious kids did. That part at least made sense. What didn't add up was that there was never any evidence of foul play, not a shred. Hiram was adamant Danny couldn't have snuck past him out of the Old Rectory. And even if he had done, surely he'd have just gone home.

Of course, after again searching the entire structure until convinced Danny wasn't there, Hiram sprinted to where they'd left their bikes, expecting to see Danny's gone. It was still there.

Hiram rode to the nearest house in a panic and raised the alarm. The police arrived five minutes later, and ten minutes after that had broken open every window and door of the Old Rectory and turned the entire building upside down. And yet they found nothing, not one single clue as to what could have happened to Danny. It's a mystery that remains unsolved to this day.

Hiram and his father were never close. His dad had in no way inherited his own father's adventurous spirit, and though he'd travelled a little, he'd never ventured further afield than Spain. Emotionally, Hiram was much closer to his spirited grandfather, so when Danny went missing and his heartbroken father began searching for answers, it was inevitable when Hiram became an outlet for his father's blame.

Hiram had always maintained he hadn't encouraged Danny to bunk off school that afternoon, but that just wasn't true. The real truth, that he had teased and cajoled Danny until he agreed to skip school and go with him to the Old Rectory that afternoon was a secret that burned him, a curse and a burden he'd carried in all the years since, and probably always would.

It was unfair of his father to blame him, based on what he knew, yet he still did. With the cold truth hanging like a rock of penance around his neck, Hiram just accepted it. They'd not spoken more than a few sentences since that time, and now his mother was dead, the relationship between father and son had devolved into a haunted wasteland.

Hiram and his grandfather shuffled on through the alabaster snow until they reached the crest of a hill. It was the most beautiful spot at White House Farm, far from the house, and as the crow flies, more than a mile from any other buildings. It's where his grandfather spent a lot of his free time, especially in the warmer months, but he was an old man now, and though healthy and full of life, he had never liked the cold. What he did enjoy was spending time with his grandson, and a notion shared only by himself and Hiram's grandmother, Jan, his protégé.

Their elevated position–it was the highest spot in the entire county of Suffolk–afforded them panoramic views over the estate and the countryside beyond. To their left, a forest which started within the boundaries of the property but spread west several more miles, was rich in wildlife. They spotted tiny muntjak deer regularly, along with multiple species of birds, and their particular favourite, a beautiful barn owl they never tired of seeing, and who visited every dusk. To their right arable farmland spread as far as the eye could see and brought to mind the early nineteenth century paintings of John Constable. Ahead of them, the gently undulating hills synonymous with England stretched all the way to the coast, and while green for most of the year, today lay hidden beneath a dazzling blanket of silky white. It was a spectacular view, and an appropriate spot for Hiram's grandfather to at last hand over his secret heirloom. But not, however, before a spirited snowball fight that left the old man wheezing through a broad smile.

It took a few minutes, but once he'd recovered enough he sat his grandson down on an ancient stone bench that he had hand carved himself to mimic classic Inca masonry. "Hiram, both Jan and I are so proud of you, and we couldn't wish for a finer grandson. You're a perfect son, too, though your father doesn't see it that way. But that's just his mistake. Your mother was also very proud of you, and as for Danny—" The old timer paused for a moment, and looked deep into Hiram's eyes. "You were a hero to Danny, the best older brother a kid could have. You must never feel any blame for what happened to him. Never."

Hiram's eyes glazed over as he fought back tears that would sting his face, despite the freezing air. His guilt was a constant nemesis.

"Hiram, you're an exceptional young man, and you've proven that often over the last few difficult years. That's why I've chosen to give you something today... something special."

Taken aback, Hiram blinked away his negative thoughts. His grandfather sensed the confusion, and paused, heightening the anticipation.

"Well, Grandad, what is it? Not that mouldy old explorer's hat you used to wear, is it?" He thought it might be.

"Wouldn't that be an acceptable thing to hand down to a grandson with the same passions as me?" He smiled, and it was a smile that held in it more than six decades of curiosity and adventurous spirit. "No, lad, it isn't my old hat. I'd never part with that, not even to you." He winked at the hearty declaration. "But what I am giving you today is no joking matter. It's an object of the highest cultural significance, and I'm giving it to you because I believe it could not be in more appropriate hands. However…" He paused again, making sure his grandson was paying attention.

As ever, Hiram was.

"However, it comes with a heavy burden… you are *not* to take this lightly." It was a sombre speech, but failed to hide the excitement that laced his voice and sparkled in his eyes.

Hiram had heard whispers of something like this when he was younger, when the older members of the Kane family got together on special occasions and discussed the adventures of their famous patriarch, Patrick. He also recalled rumours of an old map, but believed it was just a fanciful story for the kids' enjoyment. Now though, because of the serious manner in which his grandad was addressing him, he had to wonder: *The map?*

"Hiram, what I'm giving you must remain secret. It's too important not to take serious, and I know you will. Do you understand?"

Hiram nodded.

"There're only a handful of people who know about it, and I trust each of them. I need to ask: can I trust you?"

Hiram's heart raced. *Whatever is it?* "Yes, Grandad, you can," he answered, his voice hushed. "You can trust me."

"I know, laddie." He removed the backpack from his shoulders and opened the zip, and with great care removed a small, fine leather package, his pale eyes shining with excitement. "Take, it lad, and open it up. Be gentle, mind."

Hiram took the package, unconsciously holding his breath. Slow, and with the utmost care, he opened the folds of the package and gazed in disbelief at what he saw inside.

In his hands was something that perhaps held the secret of one of the all-time greatest mysteries of exploration. Next to a large X, its blood-red shade in stark contrast to the faded brown and green cloth, was the one word that had forever occupied his thoughts and dreams, just as it had those of his grandfather and his great-grandfather before him. In small but clear writing, was a single word;

Vilcabamba.

He was holding a map to the Inca's most famous lost city.

In Hiram's excitement he didn't notice the shadow that passed over his granddad's eyes. The old timer had mentioned the map came with a burden, but that burden was a million times more important than he could let on now. There was still time to explain all of that to his grandson, and although that time could wait, just how much of it he had was an answer beyond even his vast knowledge.

The old explorer knew only time itself would tell.

Time, and the ticking bomb of a five-hundred-year-old prophecy.

New York City

October 4th, 2013

Early autumn in New York meant the city's trees had started their annual display of colour, the vibrancy of the reds and gold and blazing oranges in stunning contrast to the diluted grey drabbery of the concrete jungle. Kane wasn't a big fan of large modern cities and felt more at home in the narrow crumbling streets of atmospheric Cuzco. But the air today was crisp, and carried on it the myriad scents associated with the Big Apple: coffee, donuts, freshly toasted bagels... and traffic fumes. Despite the latter, it was enough to make a grown man hungry, and Kane's stomach grumbled a protest. It would have to wait.

It was only to be a short stay in New York, but one Kane had been anticipating a long time. He was there to meet a select group of individuals, men and women who would form the team of his next expedition into the Andes. Kane had led several such expeditions over the last decade, but the focus of each had become more and more refined every year. This expedition would be the most focused yet, and they would set out with only one objective: locate Vilcabamba.

Within the world of extreme adventures, Kane has garnered an almost legendary reputation. Renowned not only for the safety of his team and the diligence of his preparation, Kane has long been respected for his conscientious affinity with local cultures and traditions, wherever he is in the world. During his career, he has led groups across the Arctic, traversed the Sahara and the wilds of the Mongolian Steppes, and has completed several circuits of Nepal's notoriously difficult Annapurna Range. And though those adventures are not without their unique and often dangerous moments, Kane has never lost a single person. It's an incredible track record he is rightly proud of, but his reputation is no more than his skill and integrity deserve. There is no doubt about it; Hiram Kane is the best in the business.

Born of the old school, Kane also relies upon his own research and abilities, and the expert on-the-ground teams he puts together. Making use of all the high-tech gadgetry and communications available was not an option to Kane, who would rather follow in the footsteps of the great explorers of the past. To Hiram it felt almost akin to cheating to haul along the latest equipment, and though his modus operandi got mocked by some in the expedition world, many others admired him for it. It had served him well. If he was going to find Vilcabamba, Kane was going to do it his way.

He turned up to the noon meeting twenty minutes early, as was his custom. But, looking through the restaurant window, he was a little ashamed to see he was last to arrive. Still, the looks of admiration and excitement on the faces of the attendees as they spotted him both embarrassed Kane and put him at ease. Such was his reputation, those guys would've been happy to wait hours, if not days, to secure their place on the proposed expedition. Kane pushed his way through the doors of the famous *Tavern On The Green* restaurant along Central Park's western fringe, and approached his waiting guests. All those seated at the table stood.

"Good afternoon," he said, with a serious look on his face. "And congratulations. You've all passed the first test."

After a moment of confused looks shared among the others, Kane smiled, putting them at ease. "Relax, guys, I'm joking. Actually, I'm only half joking, because for what we're planning to do, punctuality is crucial. And you are all early, so well done."

One by one Kane introduced himself with a quick hand-shake and a few words of welcome. He also expressed his gratitude for their attendance. There were some impressive, successful people gathered, including A. J. Waters, a world-renowned archaeologist. Equally well-known art historian Professor John Haines was there, along with his protégé, Katherine Edgewood. Lesser known were the Spanish Professor of Religious Studies, Angelo De La Cruz, and an American writer named Howie Hooper. Completing the eclectic mix of adventurers was Kane's old friend and expedition photographer, Evan Craft and Kane's soul mate and on/off lover for most of the last two decades, Alexandria Ridley, herself a Professor of Antiquities.

Kane had studied under Professor Haines at university, and they were old friends. Also, Haines had vouched for Katherine Edgewood, which was good enough for Hiram. He'd met A. J. Waters on numerous occasions and the two shared a mutual respect for each other's work, and he knew Evan and Alexandria well, and considered them his closest friends.

Kane knew little about the Spaniard, Professor De La Cruz, except that he taught at both the obscure Catholic University Saint Vincent Martyr in Valencia, Spain and the Universidad Nacional de Trujillo, in the west of the country. He seemed like a decent, unassuming man. Kane had always planned to have a writer on the expedition, but if little was known about the Spaniard, Kane knew even less about Hooper. But, he'd paid a significant fee to be the party's official writer, and in Howie's own words, he was proud to be the one to document *a history making expedition.*

The two-hour meeting came to a close. Each member of the group had contributed to the discussion, and none were under any illusions at what a difficult mission it would be. A genuine buzz of excitement drifted among them, and Kane felt more confidence about success than he ever had.

So, this is my team, he thought. Kane stood up and said his last words to them in person before they came together in Peru the following May. "It's not all going to be fun," he said. "We need to become a well-drilled unit. Forming a tight-knit team will be crucial to our success, and there must be trust and transparency between all of us, and of course between the local team and my guide in Cuzco. If we can achieve that, then come next May, we'll trek deep into the Andes mountains on the trail of one of the great undiscovered places in the world of exploration." Kane paused, and with a big smile and his glass raised, he said, "Here's to the lost city of the Incas, and may we be the ones to find her."

As the group clapped in appreciation, Hiram felt certain that at long, long last, the Kane family would have their success.

I

And So It Begins

An Ancient Capital

Cuzco has long been considered by many scholars as the archaeological capital of the Americas, and sits nestled high in the Andes. The air is so thin at the head-aching altitude of 3,440 metres above sea level it sucks the breath from your lungs and makes walking up small hills feel like hiking impossible mountains. Yet Cuzco is spectacular, and not only for its setting in the heart of the sacred Huatanay River Valley. Because of its sublime mix of Spanish colonial and ancient Inca architecture, and historically important archaeological features, it's already unique. But add to this the myriad cultural festivals and the wide range of locally made handicrafts sold by smiling Indian vendors, it's no wonder Kane fell in love with his adopted city.

The name Cuzco itself is controversial. The ancient city was the political and religious centre of the Inca Empire, known as *Tawan-tin-suyu*, the Four Quarters of the Earth. That gave it its name, *Qosqo*, meaning centre, or navel. But to demonstrate their power and humiliate the conquered Inca, the early conquistadors altered the name to the similar sounding Spanish word, Cuzco, meaning hunchback, or small dog. Only as recently as 1990 did the local government restore the city's official name to Qusqo, though it's still known internationally as Cuzco, a permanent issue of contention to the city's native Quechuan population.

Though Kane loved his city, it had one negative element he couldn't deny: the altitude was terrible for a sharp hangover. Kane could handle his drink, but he'd been dry for weeks leading up to this expedition and had resisted the urge for a beer until last night. He wasn't expecting the few small Cuzqueñas to develop into a party, but Alex Ridley had a habit of doing that to Kane, and he should've known better. Despite her high IQ and brilliant career, no one who knew Ridley would say she wasn't a party girl at heart, and if she wanted someone to drink with, she rarely took no for an answer. And it was often Kane. But, after a cold shower and some hot Peruvian coffee, he was ready to face the day.

As instructed, the other members of the expedition had arrived in Cuzco over a week ago in order to make a gradual acclimatisation to the crushing altitude. If a person was unaccustomed to such dizzying heights, not only was it uncomfortable for them as individuals, with harsh bouts of debilitating nausea and diarrhoea in tandem with crippling headaches, but it could be dangerous, and even undermine an entire expedition. This group of adventurers had taken Kane on his word, and all bar none had proven themselves dedicated to a successful trip. He showed his gratitude by treating them all to dinner at his favourite Quechuan restaurant.

Kane was both relieved and honoured. It meant they were showing both him, and the physical demands needed, the respect required for a successful expedition.

To acclimatise they'd spent ten days walking Cuzco's cobbled streets, admiring the architecture and learning of the city's rich yet troubled history. Led by Kane, the group also took a few mini-hikes into the hills surrounding the city, soon appreciating just how tough the conditions would be so high above sea level. One such hike led them to the magnificent Inca UNESCO site of *Saq-say-huamán*. The megalithic fortress was vast, the hundreds of tourists swarming among the ruins as insignificant in size as city ants. Most scholars agree ancient Cuzco was designed in the shape of the sacred puma, the fortress of Saq-say-huamán forming the puma's head, and it took little imagination for the group to see the gargantuan stone blocks that formed the terraces as the ferocious teeth and jaws of a mountain lion.

Two days before their departure on the expedition, Kane led the group to the famed Santa Domingo Church and the *Qorikancha*–the gold enclosure–an Inca temple dedicated to their Sun God, Inti. After the Spanish conquistadors defeated the Inca, in another deliberate show of their might they built their church right on top of the temple using its existing foundations, and what can only be described as an architectural palimpsest could not have been a more disrespectful insult. But as Kane explained in his most serious tour-guide tone, Earth goddess Pachamama and Inti the Sun God could not and would not accept the horrific insult, and have lain waste to the church with violent earthquakes on numerous occasions since. The most amazing thing about it, Kane told them, was despite the Catholic Church being destroyed multiple times during the subsequent centuries, not a single Inca stone was ever dislodged, demonstrating not only the power of Pachamama and Inti, but the skill and mastery of the Inca's stone construction.

Right now, though, an ugly steel skeleton of scaffolding and a skin of blue plastic sheets concealed serious damage to one section of the church. Three months previous in the early hours of the morning, an unknown group of men had thrown a series of small, homemade bombs at the church, causing significant mutilation to the façade. Local inhabitants were shocked, but it was yet another incident that echoed reports of similar occurrences in Lima and other cities, where statues of conquistadors and various Christian buildings had been attacked and vandalised. While national media suggested organised terror activity, no group claimed responsibility for the violence, though notorious communist terror group *The Shining Path* were quick to distance themselves from the attacks. Whoever it was, the events had caused Christians nationwide to take notice. Kane, however, did not notice the anger raging beneath the façade of one of his expedition members.

He would learn about it soon enough.

The Night Before

Tuesday, May 1st, 2014

Hummingbirds flitted in and out of the draping crimson bougainvillaea, and from below the tantalising and familiar smells of roasted alpaca and guinea pig drifted Kane's way. Relaxing with his feet dangled over the ornate iron railing, the view across Cuzco's pretty Plaza de Armas from his apartment balcony remained as satisfying as ever. With some reverence, he watched the dusky blue sky fade first to pink and then a fiery orange, while sipping his third ice cold Cusqueña beer.

It was moments like those, on the eve of a grand adventure, when Kane felt most alive. All the necessary preparation for the expedition got done with the utmost diligence and meticulous detail, and because of his wealth of experience at such undertakings he'd left nothing to chance. As he always did Kane recruited a highly skilled team of local support, from the best Quechuan guide in the Andes to a team of the strongest and most reliable porters and pack mules. When possible Kane used the same locals, one in particular whom he considered essential: his long-term guide, and good friend, Sonco Amaru.

Sonco, meaning *of good and noble heart*, in Quechuan, was a remarkable man. He stood just 5' 3" tall, and weighed in at a little less than fourteen stone (196lbs), yet the man had the strength of an ox and the stamina of several llamas. Whether or not he had the agility of an Andean goat depended entirely on the quantity of Cusqueñas he'd downed. With dubious validity, Sonco claimed to be forty-two years old, and when anyone queried his age, he always replied with a mischievous wink; *"Si. Quarenta y dos,"* he'd say. Yes, forty-two. Yet according to Kane, Sonco had been claiming he was forty-two for the last seven years. Regardless of his real age, what Kane couldn't deny was his incredible knowledge of the area and his unrivalled skill as both a guide and porter in the unpredictable conditions and terrain of the Peruvian Andes.

Somewhat of a local legend, Sonco once held the record for the Inca Trail Annual Race, clocking an unbelievable time of three hours and twenty-nine minutes. To put that into context, Kane always told his travelling parties that the average tourist took four days to cover the same twenty-six miles. Quite simply, Kane could not run his operations in the Andes without his pal Sonco, and nor would he want to. They were good friends, and Kane trusted the man with his life.

Kane put down the empty beer bottle and contemplated a fourth when his mind drifted to the past. In much the same way that during those moments before an expedition he felt energised and happy, the opposite was sometimes true. Negative, guilty thoughts crept up on him from the Andean darkness to threaten his positive mood, and it was a common theme, the physical highs and lows of an Andes trek matched by their metaphorical emotional counterparts. It was a theme he didn't deal with at all well.

The guilt, that's what got to him. A guilt that his brother Danny wasn't sharing his adventures, or not out carving his own history somewhere else in the world. Danny had been denied that opportunity by what was very likely foul means, though no one had ever discovered the truth. Yet here Kane was, loving his life, and with a new adventure always on the horizon. With the world at his feet, he was the lucky one, and it galled him every single time.

But it also inspired him. He was on this mission to Vilcabamba for himself, but also for his family, and not least Danny. It would be the discovery to heal several generations of hurt and disappointment.

Hiram and his father weren't close. It's true that when he was a very young boy their relationship was better, but it had taken a steady downturn over the years. To begin with, the young Hiram never understood why, other than it being a simple case of a father having a favourite son, that there was a greater fondness for Danny than for him. That was okay, he guessed. Hiram had always enjoyed a fantastic relationship with his mother, and if he was honest he supposed she had her favourite too. So he understood it a little, and his dad had a point.

Hiram and Danny, however, were very close. They fought and bickered, just as all siblings did, but did it with sly grins and always stopped short of genuine angst. Just two years separated them, but Hiram was a natural athlete and far more physically developed, nearer four years Danny's elder in terms of physical prowess. Not that he ever showed off to his brother. If they raced, Hiram often let him win, and in an arm wrestle it was always a close match but shouldn't have been. Kane adored his little brother, always ready to punch the nose of anyone who picked on him at school. He assumed Danny looked up to him, just as he would've, had he been the younger of the two. Danny teased Hiram about being the family

9

favourite, the stronger, smarter, more handsome brother, he the runt of the two child litter. But Hiram dismissed it as nothing more than friendly banter and good-natured jealousy. Sibling rivals, just like all brothers.

Kane had always clung to the notion Danny was adventurous like him and had wanted to go to the Old Rec' that day. But he was only kidding himself, and in doing so, Hiram was betraying his brother's memory. His father was right. *I should never have let him bunk off school with me, should never have left him alone. He wouldn't have gone missing, and he... He'd still be here.*

Those are the thoughts that haunted him then, and always would.

Hiram didn't kill his brother, but harboured enormous guilt about his disappearance. Regardless of the details, it had ripped the family in two. Kane opened the fourth Cusqueña.

Thousands of dark nights had passed since that tragic and fateful day in the spring of 1989, but the pain of the loss never lessened its grip. It was guilt. And worse, whether justified or not it was a truth he would always know.

Unless...

Kane believed one of the only things that might someday slacken his disabling noose of guilt was to find the thing that had eluded his family for so long. He thought if he could at last lay claim to discovering that elusive lost city of Vilcabamba, he would be laying many ghosts to rest, not least his own. His great-grandfather, Patrick. His own grandfather, Hiram. Perhaps even his father might forgive him. And, of course, Danny. In his heart he knew if Danny was still around he too would be as committed to Vilcabamba as he himself was, and their forefathers before them.

The answer to his emancipation was simple. Kane had to find Vilcabamba, and cast both his own, and his family's, demons aside forever.

He knew he was close last year. If it wasn't for the earthquake that forced them to abandon their quest, he was certain he would've found the lost city. So close, and yet in hindsight he believed it was a good thing. No one was seriously hurt, and all members of that group felt relieved to have left the Sacred Valley alive. This time Kane was even more prepared. He'd assembled an exceptional group of dedicated professionals, some known personally, others more or less strangers, but he believed all would prove great assets to the expedition.

The only one who perturbed him slightly was Howie Hooper, the writer. He didn't know what it was about the man, but something had begun to niggle at Kane now their departure was so close. To be fair, Hooper was healthy and strong enough, and he talked a good game. Besides, Hiram needed a writer with travel experience, and Kane had confidence in his own abilities as a leader. He had dealt with almost every situation and scenario possible in the Andes and led many successful adventures around the world. And he had alongside him Sonco Amaru.

"Howie Hooper." Kane found himself muttering the name aloud, as if it would deliver some profound insight about the American. Then, "Silly arse," he said, lips curling into a wry and crooked grin, as if to prove his point.

With a final look over the famous plaza below him, the square alive with the sounds of market vendors and tourists no doubt drunk on the potent mix of altitude and pisco sours, Kane yawned, and was just about to call it a night when a gentle double thud at his apartment door grabbed his attention. It could only be one person, and the thought of her raised another wry smile. He swung open the apartment's aged, squeaky door, fully expecting to see his friend, old flame, and long-time travel buddy, Alexandria Ridley standing there, but the gloomy corridor was empty. *Strange*, he thought. Ridley was a feisty one, no question, and a practical joker, too. She was probably sneaking into the room over his balcony at that very moment. Kane closed the protesting door and returned to the balcony, yet was just as surprised not to find her there. He decided it was just neighbourhood kids messing about and prepared for bed.

He needed the early night. Tomorrow was a big day.

Kane tugged at the lamp's chain and plunged his cosy bedroom into darkness. But there it was again; a quick double knock. *What now?*

He raced to the door, and this time it was Ridley. And as always, Alex Ridley looked ravishing. "Care for a nightcap, Kane? I've brought the pisco if you'll add the sour?"

Before he could answer, Ridley breezed right past him, and with a knowing smile, Kane closed his door on the night for the final time.

The Time Has Come

After a long year of careful planning and organisation the day of departure had finally arrived. Thrilled, Kane grinned. His hangover was history, and he was about to make some of his own.

At 8:15am Kane met the others in the lobby of their hotel on the Plaza de Armas, happy to see them all in great spirits as he entered the hive of activity.

Self-appointed patriarch among them, A. J. Waters, hustled about the group to make sure they were prepared. He was a touch bossy, but it was good-natured and they met his demands with a smile. Known as 'Muddy' to his colleagues, the notorious Waters wasn't afraid to do what it took to locate a find. Credited for a plethora of important cultural artefacts across the world, native Boston-ite Muddy was as passionate as those half his age, and his impressive physical stature was more than matched by his larger-than-life personality. Decked out in his ever-present field fatigues, khakis that looked as if they hadn't seen a washing machine since his last dig, Muddy was a legend in the world of archaeology. The tatty, ever-present straw hat and ruddy round cheeks completed the familiar look.

John Haines watched his old colleague and smiled, more than happy to let his friend take centre stage. Haines himself was beyond retirement age, but his heart beat like a twenty-something and the sparkle in his grey-blue eyes left no one doubting the adventurous spirit that still burned within. Tightening the laces on his expensive hiking boots and smoothing down his shirt–tailored, despite heading into the jungle–the classy, dapper and classically handsome professor was ready for action.

Equally ready was Evan Craft, expedition photographer and Kane's old friend. Though he and Kane had undertaken many adventures together Evan had never been into the Andes before, and Hiram saw genuine excitement in his mate's eyes. A tough cookie, his wit and humour would be crucial on the long and arduous hikes, his personality as colourful as his range of shirts. Today's choice, a kaleidoscope of parrots.

Despite the lateness of the previous night, Alexandria Ridley glowed as she strode into the lobby. She'd spent the night at Kane's apartment, but agreed to keep their unique friendship hidden from the others. Of course, their mutual mate Evan knew the deal. Kane just preferred a more professional working relationship in public, but in truth that's really what it was. Kane and Ridley's moments of fun were seldom, not often enough to consider themselves an item. It suited Ridley more than it did Kane. She moved on from each encounter with less emotional traction than Kane, and each time they departed his heart ached just a little more.

Attired in her typical outdoorsy wear, Ridley wore tight-fitting khaki trousers and hiking boots, khaki long sleeved shirt, the sleeves rolled up, and her trademark red bandana, a throwback from her Guns N' Roses concert days and which kept her long, mahogany hair out of her face. Kane didn't know how she did it, but despite the rugged gear Ridley somehow seemed glamorous. He shook his head, and Ridley gave him just the hint of a wink.

Making last minute adjustments to her backpack, Kate Edgewood squatted nearby, her slight frame looking as though a stiff breeze might blow her over, and that an Andean expedition would just about kill her. But she'd managed the acclimatisation drills with relative comfort, and Kane believed she was tougher than she appeared. She glanced up and caught his eye, giving him a confident nod.

Loitering adrift from the group and speaking quietly together were Howie Hooper and the Spanish professor, Angelo De La Cruz. Hooper was an athletic man, lean yet toned, and if Kane didn't know better he'd mark him down as ex-military. The buzz-cut hairstyle added to his no-nonsense appearance.

By comparison, De La Cruz was inconspicuous by definition. Just 5' 8" tall and slim, his passive face marked him as a straight-laced and serious man. His plain clothes were a good match for his countenance, simple yet durable, and Kane sensed an inner strength he guessed few people ever witnessed. Yet, although the man moved about with a distinct calmness his eyes were watchful, constantly scanning his surroundings. Kane assumed the man never missed a trick.

There was something not quite so subtle about Hooper. The man fidgeted, as if on edge, and as Kane looked over at him then, something made him instinctively uncomfortable. Sure, he looked capable enough, and like the others had proven himself very able during the preparation.

Hiram had done what research he could on the members of his expedition team, but you never really knew how a person would react when the actual adventure started. *Maybe he's just nervous,* Kane mused. He hoped he hadn't misjudged the man.

Standing in the centre of the busy lobby, Kane stood tall and clapped his hands loud to get their attention. They responded in an instant.

"My friends," he said at volume, "My friends. Are you ready to make history?"

"Yes, sir," shouted Evan.

"Me too," bellowed Muddy Waters, and before long the entire group were cheering, unable to contain their excitement. There was a palpable nervous tension among them–they were about to enter the wild terrain of the Andes, after all–but there was an equal sense of anticipation and relief that they were at last about to get started. Even the dour Hooper cracked a grin.

Kane thought they looked ready. They *were* ready. And so was he.

"Okay then, mi amigos y amigas, vamanos. To the mountains we shall go, and history we shall make."

Much like a teacher ushering a bunch of excited school kids on a field trip, Kane led the group out onto the cobbled walkway that skirted the Plaza De Armas. With several taxis already waiting for them the twenty-minute drive to *Poroy* Station was soon underway. From Poroy they'd ride the train to its furthest station, the dusty yet picturesque little town of *Aguas Calientes* that lay in the shadow of Machu Picchu Mountain.

Aboard the train they relaxed into the rhythm of the journey, absorbing the majestic scenery of the Andes and mentally preparing for the physical and emotional tests to come. There was little chatter to begin with, each taking time to consider the enormity of what they were soon to undertake.

From his seat at the rear of the carriage Kane took a moment to appraise the expedition members, and knowing he had done all he could to motivate and prepare them, he knew they were ready. Some of them he'd known a long time; Ridley and Evan, and Professor Haines, whom he'd studied under at university. Kane had only met Muddy Waters twice but was well aware of his towering reputation as a tenacious archaeologist and keen adventurer. In regards to those four Kane had no worries about the gruelling days ahead.

The others–Edgewood, De La Cruz, and Hooper–were the unknown element of the unit. But despite his lack of knowledge about the trio, Kane believed it was time one of his Andean expeditions had a run of luck, and he was more than prepared to put some trust in his own judgement. Besides, it was a little late to start second guessing himself now.

Descending from the dizzying heights of Cuzco to the lower altitudes deeper into the Sacred Valley seemed to energise the group, and it wasn't long before Evan was sharing his limited repertoire of jokes. And they were atrocious.

"What do you call a slug wearing a crash helmet?" he asked with an impish grin.

"Don't know," replied Muddy, chuckling at Evan's enthusiasm.

"A snail."

Groans all round, except Kate Edgewood, who emitted a rather embarrassing snort. "Not bad," she said, then hid her blushing face with her hands.

"Okay, what do you call a pig with three eyes?"

Blank looks as they tried to work it out. Nothing.

"A pi-i-ig," Evan said with a defined stutter.

Haines liked that one, his shoulders jiggling in time with the jolting train. Ridley, who'd heard these jokes too many times before, just shook her head in dismay.

"Okay, one more. What do you call a deer with no eyes?"

"No idea," said Kane, taking a seat opposite Evan. "Do you get it, Muddy? No-eye-deer?"

"Spoilsport," scolded Evan, mouth curled in a smirk, "How about this, then? What do you call a deer with no eyes *and* no legs?"

Kane grimaced at the follow-up. No one else had a guess.

"Still no-eye-deer. Get it? With no legs, it can't move. It's still? Don't worry, fans, I'm here all week."

"They might just be the worst jokes I've ever heard," said Haines, laughing, "And they'd better improve over the next few days, or you'll be sharing a tent with a burro."

"You old-timers just don't know classic comedy, that's all. Wasted, I tell you, totally wasted."

And that's how the remaining two hours of the journey passed for the familiar members of the team, Kane and Craft mocking each other like old friends did, and Ridley mediating the banter and explaining it to the confused American, Muddy.

A few seats away, both sitting alone, were Angelo De La Cruz and Howie Hooper. Flicking through the pages of a book on the conquistadors, the Spaniard was scribbling on the page margins. More than content sitting by himself, Kane had learned over the last ten days in Cuzco the man relished his privacy. On the other hand, Hooper had a pompous look of superiority about him, as if demonstrating he was too smart to listen to Evan's childish jokes. It wasn't lost on Kane, and just one more thing he made a mental note of. Hooper–doesn't play well with others.

A high-pitched whistle pierced the white noise of the rumbling train, soon followed by the unearthly screeching of overused brakes reverberating through the valley as the old train ground to a halt at the equally old Aguas Calientes Station. Within seconds of stopping eager tourists streamed out onto the platform to be accosted by cheerful ladies selling everything from coca leaves, to soup, to bamboo walking sticks. After buying last minute supplies they headed out in search of the hot springs, or embarked on the short but calf-busting hike to Machu Picchu.

Kane stood and stretched. He allowed the rush of tourists to depart the platform first, then grabbed his backpack from the overhead rack and stepped down from the train. A second later someone gripped him in a crushing bear hug. *Sonco!*

"Hiram, my friend," roared the human barrel, pinning Kane's arms and lifting him off the platform. After a moment he released him and stepped back, casting his eyes over the expedition leader. "Did you get fat?"

Kane laughed. "It's good to see you too, Sonco," he said, and returned the friendly banter. "You didn't get any thinner."

It really was good to see Sonco, his long-time friend and trusted guide, and although they'd spoken on the phone almost every day during the last couple of months, in order to organise the local team and discuss logistics, they hadn't seen each other in the flesh since the last aborted attempt on Vilcabamba the previous year.

Kane and Sonco chatted while corralling the others and their gear and were soon free of the tiny station's bedlam. A little way down the road, away from the hustle of Aguas

Calientes' main drag, Sonco led Kane and the group to where his own team waited. After the briefest of introductions, they were on the move again, headed west into the relatively unknown terrain beyond the infamy of Machu Picchu. Unknown to most people. For Kane and Sonco, it was familiar ground.

Completing their party was Sonco's team of porters and mules. The Quechuans were proud men, and had always been excellent on Kane's expeditions, and Sonco always chose his team with due care. Kane was often a little edgy on the morning of a big expedition, not only because of the nervy excitement of what they were setting out to discover, but more because of the responsibility he had to guide and look after the people under his charge. Knowing he had Sonco with him, calm and proud, and ready to do anything Kane needed of him, filled Hiram with a confidence he simply couldn't muster without his friend alongside.

With all that in mind, Hiram was ready. Today was the first day of what he believed would be a fourteen day round trip, the day which he truly believed marked the start of his greatest adventure yet. Very soon–about a week, if all went well–he would be standing in the genuine lost city of the Incas.

Vilcabamba.

Aguas Calientes. The exotic name means hot water in Spanish, and for Kane the small town had often been the start and finishing point for many serious expeditions. He knew well the joys of taking a long and restorative soak in the thermal springs that bubbled up from beneath the mountains, though they are always crowded with weary but jubilant trekkers after completing the four-day Inca Trail to Machu Picchu. He was almost sad they didn't have time for a dip in the baths now. Almost. But not quite. He could wait for his celebratory soak.

If Aguas Calientes seemed exotic, then Machu Picchu simply oozed evocative myth and legend. In 1912, Harvard archaeologist and freelance explorer, Hiram Bingham and his assistant Patrick Kane rediscovered Machu Picchu. They explored the Andes searching for the last Inca stronghold, in the region fated ruler Atahualpa allegedly led his people in a desperate attempt to save the Empire from the Spanish conquistadors, themselves led by Francisco Pizarro.

Legend has it that in that remote location, the Incas had hidden their remaining treasure from the Spaniards, including gold, jewels, and knowledge. Bingham had made finding the lost city his life's ambition. Travel weary, and on the verge of giving up after months of gruelling exploration, Bingham and his team stumbled upon a village of native farmers on the jungled mountainside. After a series of negotiations, the villagers led Bingham's men to what he believed with all his heart was Vilcabamba.

They had indeed rediscovered a beautiful lost city. But, in what turned out to be a devastating blow for Bingham and his assistant Kane, they found no treasure. It certainly bought them fame, despite the lack of Inca gold, and Bingham maintained for most of his life his stance that he'd located the lost city. But Patrick Kane never accepted it, and lived with his disappointment in perpetual sadness.

In simple terms, Vilcabamba remained a mystery.

Fifty years after Bingham's failure American Gene Savoy and his team declared they had discovered the real Vilcabamba, at the site known as *Espiritu Pampa*. They also suggested that Bingham's team had passed through that location themselves, but dismissed it as the wrong place and moved on, stumbling rather fortuitously upon Machu Picchu instead. Other scholars still dispute the claims of Savoy, stating he'd made his declaration in haste and without sufficient scientific evidence. And what's more, there was still no treasure.

Ultimately many people, including Hiram Kane and his grandfather, remained steadfast in their belief that the true Vilcabamba was out there, the lost city still undiscovered in the wild mountains of Peru. The Kane family believed they'd be the ones to unravel the greatest of all archaeological mysteries.

The Trail

Half an hour after leaving the village Kane and the group were moments from taking their first steps on the trail. At this stage it was Hiram's custom to pause and say a few words.

"Gather round, everyone, and listen up," he said, waiting until they were all close enough to hear. "What we're about to embark on will be both a physical and emotional challenge, make no bones about it. I don't want to scare you, but you all know by now that underestimating these challenges is both futile and dangerous. However, we're very well prepared, and we're lucky to have along with us the best guide in all Peru." Kane waved his hand in Sonco's direction. Sonco responded with a bashful nod. After a quick round of applause, Kane continued. "But despite our best preparation, I always feel it's prudent to make an offering to the Earth Goddess, Pachamama. Regardless of your faiths, or lack thereof, I hope you'll humour me in honouring both Pachamama, and the sacred Condor, to protect us on our perilous journey."

One of the young Quechuan porters handed each member of the team, including the other porters and Sonco, a cup of corn beer.

"Please, close your eyes, and repeat after me. *Pachamama,*" Kane said, and they all repeated, eyes tight shut, "*we give you thanks, as your children, for holding us so sweetly in your womb of love and life, as we heal all of our stories, our shadows and our fears."* Kane paused a moment, before continuing. "Now, open your eyes, take a gulp of the beer, and pour a little into the earth as an offering."

They all did.

"Now close your eyes again and repeat.

> *Great Condor. Thank you for taking us on your wings to our highest path of destiny. Thank you for showing us the holy mountains, and reminding us to envision our lives from this place."*

Again, they repeated each line. "Okay, guys, another swig of beer, and pour the rest into the ground."

"Are you sure?" Evan chirped up. "What a—"

"I know, I know," Kane cut in with a smile. "Ev, before you say anything, to you it must seem like a waste of perfectly good beer, right? But believe me, if it makes Pachamama look with favour upon us, then it's no waste at all."

Nods of agreement all round, and with the short ceremony over the animated expedition members took their first real steps in the mountains. All were animated, that is, except one.

Angelo De La Cruz thought no one had seen him, but Sonco Amaru possessed the eyes of a condor himself, and had spotted the Spaniard not joining in the solemn prayers. More than that, he saw a scowl on the professor's face as he silently mouthed different words to those Kane had said. To top it off, he even made the sign of the cross once he'd finished. *Hmm*, thought the bullish Quechuan guide. Saying prayers to your own god was fine. Sonco respected that. But not taking part in Kane's traditional prayers and offerings to Pachamama?

Well, that was rude. Sonco knew it was also damn stupid. But De La Cruz was Spanish, after all, and Sonco's sympathies towards the Spanish were understandably slim. He also knew that if Pachamama was watching there would be a whole lot of trouble ahead for this particular Spaniard.

The sun was already high, and on a clear, late spring day, the air was hot. As it was, they were well prepared and making good time on the gentle ascents of the first day, but despite their preparation Kane wouldn't push them too hard. Giving them an early false sense of security could be dangerous. Trekking in the Andes was demanding, and the suffocating altitude had been deadly before and would be again. But not on Kane's watch.

Kane wasn't surprised to see Howie Hooper surging ahead of the group. He'd witnessed it before in younger men, pushing on to demonstrate their strength. Kane knew how stupid that kind of machismo could be. Yes, the first few hours and miles on the trails were benign, gently ascending slopes and lots of flat stretches. But that was the problem. Whether a hiker felt it or not, they were still at serious altitude. Time would tell if Hooper would regret his bravado.

Hours later, as the Andean sun began its daily descent beyond the distant horizon, the now weary hikers rounded a long bend, surprised to walk right into a pre-set camp. The native porters had raced ahead of them and raised the tents, the bright red fabric luminescent in the setting sun.

No matter how many times he'd worked with Quechuans, their efficiency and ability to operate in the thin air impressed Kane every time. He smiled and shook his head. The big Quechuan cook had already prepared their evening meal, and less than an hour later, with full bellies and exhausted bodies,

Kane's group settled in for an early night.

It was a successful first day in the Andes Mountains, and in the privacy of his tent Hiram Kane breathed a long sigh of relief and said a silent prayer of thanks to Pachamama.

II

Day 2

Progress

Until the day's sun infiltrated the valleys, Andean mornings were crisp bordering on glacial. The group hovered around the campfire, warding off the chills whilst feasting on a simple yet sumptuous breakfast of omelettes and rice, and either tea or coffee, depending on their taste. Or, it seemed to Kane, their nationality. As an Englishman, Kane's choice of tea was an easy one.

Breakfast, on what was now their second morning in the mountains, had been prepared as always by Yupanqui, the rangy and well-built Quechuan cook whose size and surprising agility combined to form an impressive man. Yupanqui said little, not even to his fellow Quechuans, and often sat deep in thought while focusing on something with great concentration. An air of mystery hung about the powerful man, a certain aura, as if his mind was truly aligned with the surrounding landscape. He was, after all, a descendent of the Incas, and this was his land and his history. People like Yupanqui formed the very fabric of the Sacred Valley.

Hiram sat on his rolled up sleeping bag and sipped tea while observing the group from afar. Other than Hooper and the Spanish professor, who remained aloof from the others, they were a good bunch, and Kane was now confident that, at least in a physical sense, they were up to the challenge. The trekking had been reasonably straight forward until now, and he'd kept their pace slow and steady to ease them into the demands.

Today, however, the difficulty would ramp up from intermediate to formidable. Departing from the more mellow trails, they were heading into thicker, deeper, and steeper terrain, the likes of which all members of this group beyond Kane and Sonco had never attempted. But Kane was excited. It was what he lived for, what he loved to do, and with a confidence born from their progress over the first few days he was itching for the challenge ahead.

Finishing his tea, Kane stood, and tapped a stone on his empty tin cup. All eyes turned towards him. "I'd like to say a quick well done to you all this morning. You've made it through the first stage of the trek, and although it hasn't been too difficult so far many people drop out at this point and head back to Cuzco, wilted tail between their worn out legs. But from here it gets more difficult. A lot more. The jungle is thicker, the trails narrower, and cliff edges where one slip could cost you your life come along often." Kane reached into the top of his fleece, pulled out the necklace that held his beloved golden sun disc, and raised it up so everyone could see it. Even in the early morning gloom it shone with almost magical intensity. His mind flitted back to when his grandfather had first given it to him in the summer of 1988.

"Close your eyes, my boy," his granddad had said. Hiram did.

He placed something in his hands, and said: "Open your eyes. Go ahead, open them."

Threaded over a long leather necklace was a dazzling disk

of gold, two inches across. In the dusky, late August sun the disc absolutely glowed. Hiram was enamoured by the tiny object.

"Well, put it on then," said his grandfather, his delight clear.

Hiram lifted the shiny talisman over his head, the shimmering disc coming to rest in the middle of his chest. It was beautiful, and though he cared nothing for its intrinsic value, to Hiram it was priceless. It became his pride and joy.

"My own father gave it to me a few years before he died, and now I want you to have it. He found it on an expedition with Bingham in the Sacred Valley way back in 1911. It's an Incan sun disc, made to honour the Sun God, Inti."

"Is it real? I mean is it really Inca gold?"

"Yes, my boy, it most certainly is."

"Kane?" Evan said, bemused.

Hiram's moment of reflection had lasted no more than a dozen seconds, and he refocused on the waiting listeners.

"Sorry... This is an artefact from the Sacred Valley. Genuine Inca gold. It's out there somewhere, the rest of Atahualpa's hoard, just waiting to be discovered. If Pachamama and Inti wish us well, maybe we'll get lucky."

Kane turned his gaze to the rising sun in the east. He knelt down and scraped a handful of earth from beneath his feet. Inti and Pachamama. The sun and the earth. A God and Goddess.

He eyed the team, their eyes fixed on his. "And I believe they do wish us well." Kane raised his cup, and even the sullen Hooper joined in the toast.

Kane checked his watch. Quarter past seven. "Good. We have a big day ahead, so eat, and eat well, as history waits for no man... or woman."

Conspirators

Finishing his rice and eggs and grabbing a third mug of coffee, Howie Hooper returned to his tent. Hooper was an athletic man, tall at 6' 2". Lean and with wiry strength, his hard face and shaved head suggested a tough life while his gruff countenance did little to soften his appearance. He had few friends and didn't care. He was his own man, and that was just how he liked it.

Kate Edgewood gave Hooper a minute, and looking around to check no one was watching she made for his tent. "Howie? It's me. I'm coming in."

Twenty-three-year-old Kate Edgewood was a graduate student at The University of East Anglia's School of World Art Studies and Museology, or WAM, as it was affectionately known. She'd enjoyed studying under Professor Haines so much as a bachelor's student that she'd followed that through into a graduate degree. Haines expected a bright future. He knew she had both the talent and a keen passion for the arts and their history, and though he had doubted her credentials for this type of adventure he'd been more than a little impressed so far. He knew she hailed from a wealthy background, but what he didn't appreciate was just how driven to succeed she was.

Haines didn't know it–couldn't have known it–but Kate

Edgewood had many secrets, and only three people alive knew her agenda. Dutchman Dr. Ferdinand Benedix, another professor of some renown at WAM, with whom she'd being having an affair since her second year of university, knew everything. Hooper also knew. The third was the Spaniard, Angelo De La Cruz.

Benedix was a professor of art history who specialised in pre-Columbian cultures, and had gained some prominence at WAM for his passionate speeches on the legends of Aztec, Mayan, and Incan treasures. It was common knowledge he was a big admirer of the history of the conquistadors, which to some of his peers and students seemed at odds with his admiration for Old World cultures. He brushed the contradictions aside with comments like, "Well, art is art, and culture is culture, and religion is religion. In the end, history shows us the strongest of those cultures and religions always prevailed." It was a sentiment difficult to argue with. He was popular and well respected among his peers, but what they didn't know was Benedix harboured secret fundamentalist religious beliefs. For many years he'd known of the ancient Incan Condor Prophecy, and knew that one day the Inca would rise against their European Catholic oppressors. The Dutch professor had plans in place to not only quell that uprising, but turn it back on the Incas, striking at the very heart of their people.

The strongest would indeed prevail, and he would make sure of it.

What Benedix needed was another accomplice. Benedix and Edgewood had been sleeping together ever since they'd met, and Benedix firmly believed he'd convinced her to take part in his nefarious scheme. In wooing the delightfully naïve–and not to mention, attractive–Kate Edgewood, he'd taken the first step. He thought Edgewood was oblivious to being used as a mere pawn in his game, believing she was infatuated by him, a handsome, confident scholar.

But Edgewood wasn't as naïve as he thought, and she had her own agendas. Needs must, she knew, and she had skillfully forged a friendship with many mutual benefits.

One question remained, though neither realised it. Who was using the other better?

The harsh sun had at last crept into the valley, steadily burning away the morning mist as Edgewood zipped up the tent behind her.

"Are we still on target with our plan?" she asked, her gaze at Hooper firm. The man was integral to their scheme, though she didn't like him one little bit. Benedix had recruited Hooper, and with some reluctance she would just have to trust his judgment.

"Yeah," he grunted, "of course we are. Relax. Everything's under control."

But Edgewood was far from relaxed. She'd dreamed about these next few days for a long time, and was so close to fulfilling that dream she could taste it. If everything went according to Benedix's plan, in mere days she would be richer than she'd ever imagined. She wasn't comfortable with some of the things she'd have to do to achieve her goals, but that was the nature of the beast. And she could handle it. Her father hadn't become rich by being nice, that was for sure. She figured he had taught her well. When all was said and done, not only would she be rich, but she'd be world famous. She saw the headlines now:

Lost Inca Gold Discovered by Graduate Student Kate

Edgewood

Just a few obstacles ahead, a little collateral damage that she'd have to accept, and it would all be hers. She knew she'd be betraying many people to fulfil her dreams. But Inca gold had a history of betrayal, stretching all the way back to Atahualpa and Francisco Pizarro's conquistadors, and who was she to break with tradition? Atahualpa himself had stolen it from his own brother, before Pizarro stole it from him. She almost chuckled at the thought.

After all, as an art history professor, Ferdinand was all about tradition, wasn't he? She doubted he'd appreciate the irony once he realised he'd been double-crossed.

III

Day 3

An Accident

After an uneventful evening, and some much needed rest, the group had made a good and energetic start to the day. But now, two-thirds through its daily arc the high sun took its toll on the weary trekkers.

Sonco noticed the pace had slowed and sidled up alongside Kane to suggest a half-hour rest, to which he agreed. Kane had to look after his group, and knowing Sonco's instincts rarely failed him, if the Quechuan said they needed a break, that's what they'd have.

Yupanqui set about boiling water for afternoon drinks, then handed around pre-cooked snacks of rice and vegetables wrapped in banana leaves to the grateful hikers. There was little chatter among them, each taking the time to rest their limbs while admiring the wild surroundings. The rumble of a nearby waterfall cascading into a ravine was loud enough to drown out the sounds of the jungle, and though they couldn't see it they knew it was nearby. Muddy Waters stood up, looking about for a convenient jungle loo. Keen to check out the falls, he made his way towards their thunderous roar.

"Be careful, Muddy," called out Kane, to which Muddy responded with a casual wave of the hand as he disappeared around a bend in the trail.

A moment later Kate Edgewood gave Hooper a subtle nod.

He nodded back, stood up and stretched, and strolled off in the opposite direction to that of Muddy. De La Cruz, anonymous but aware, saw it all. Nobody else did.

Once beyond the view of the group, Hooper changed pace and direction, scrambling almost vertically up the jungle slope, moving swift and silent, like a trained solider. In less than a minute, he doubled back past the camp below, taking great care to remain unseen. It was time for stage one of his personal mission.

Muddy was having a grand old time. He'd been on plenty of archaeological adventures before, but with age at last catching up with him, this was likely to be his last. And what a way to bow out, he thought as he ambled along the overgrown trail; to be a part of the team that at last discovered the lost Inca treasure. *Something to tell the grandkids,* he mused, standing on the edge of the trail and admiring the waterfall, oblivious to the dark shadow that crept up behind him, its sound drowned out by the raging torrent nearby.

And then all the world went black.

Stealthy and smooth, Hooper scaled down the last patch of rock that led to the waterfall, and saw Professor Waters standing with his back to him and about to relieve himself. Hooper couldn't help but smile. *Too easy.* He edged up to the old professor, and without a moment's pause, smashed a rock down on his head.

Hooper watched with chilling apathy as Waters' knees buckled and he crumpled to the floor. With a cursory glance back along the trail, he bundled the lifeless body over the edge, watching with indifference as it vanished beneath the water below. Dead! Hooper's heart rate didn't raise one iota.

Hooper cast his gaze to the heavens, and with two deft

movements, made the sign of the cross over his chest. Then, retracing his steps, he hustled back up the rock face and circled back around to camp, and with a quick dust-down of his clothes, Hooper strolled into camp and retook his seat against a fallen tree trunk. He was gone less than five minutes.

"Hey, Kane," called over Ridley. "What'll you do when you become the world's most famous explorer? Will you remember your friends once you're labelled the new Indiana Jones?" she bantered with a not-very-subtle wink.

"That depends who the friends are," he returned. "Are we friends, Ridley?" Kane always had trouble concealing his fondness for Alex Ridley. It wasn't any different now.

"Yes, I suppose we are. But don't get any other ideas." She knew how much Kane admired her. She felt the same about him. But for her it was enough to keep it that way. And although she teased Kane about it, she appreciated his reasons for keeping their unique friendship on the down low in the company of others. She believed she was doing a good job.

"Kids, kids," said Haines with a knowing look. "When are you two going to get married, anyway? Imagine the adventurous offspring you'd produce."

Kane grimaced, mortified, and even the unflappable Ridley flushed with embarrassment at the comment. But nobody else seemed surprised, and Kane at once knew their ruse was futile.

Sonco just shook his head as if it was old news. But his smile was broad, and he'd always wanted the two to be together. Alongside Alex was when his friend Hiram was happiest. "Okay, Hiram," he said, "Need to go now. Night coming."

Draining the last of their drinks, the others stood up and stretched out their worn muscles. It was Evan Craft who first

41

noticed Waters' absence. "Muddy seems to be taking a while," he said. "Must be one hell of a leak."

"The old timer probably fell asleep on a rock," replied Haines, chuckling.

De La Cruz looked on, impassive, almost invisible to the rest.

"I'll run and look for him," called Ridley as she trotted out of sight around the bend. But she'd been gone less than a minute, when even above the roar of the waterfall, an unmistakable cry for help reverberated through the valley.

Kane froze, then sprinted after Ridley, and soon found her clambering down a precarious rock face parallel to the waterfall. *What the hell is she doing?* Kane's gaze drifted below Ridley to the foot of the falls, and straining his eyes he saw a hiking boot sticking out of the water.

"Muddy?" Kane was over the edge of the rocky cliff in an instant, negotiating the terrain like the expert climber he was.

"What happened?" he bellowed over the thundering cascades.

"Don't know. I couldn't find him. Then I saw the boot."

They both made it down at the same moment, and hustled to the professor, each expecting to find a dead body. Kane reached down and hauled Muddy's head above the frothing natural pool. As unlikely as it was, he was breathing, and blood streamed down his face from an ugly wound at the back of his head. Together they dragged the professor out of the pool and sat him upright against a rock.

Muddy opened his eyes, and he choked, wrenching the water out in violent spurts. After a few seconds he recovered, his eyes darting about in wild confusion.

Muddy had no idea either who nor where he was, until

at last he looked up at Kane. After a deep, calming breath, he seemed to relax. He looked around, and nodded in comprehension.

"I was–" He paused, frowning, as if trying to recall something. "Yeah, I was standing up there, admiring the water fall, and… And that's the last thing I remember. I guess I must've gotten dizzy and fell."

He reached his hand to his head, his eyes widening in shock to find his fingers covered in blood. "Oh, shit," was all he could say, and he promptly vomited.

"He's in shock," said Ridley, urgency lacing her tone. "We have to get him back to the trail. He'll freeze down here." She looked up and saw Sonco and a porter scrambling down to assist.

By combining ropes with the strength of two pack mules, they carefully raised Professor Waters up to the relative safety of the trail. It was amazing he'd only suffered minor injuries. The head wound was nasty, but the ageing professor would live.

The group gathered round, worry etched on all their faces.

Except one. What might have looked like concern to those nearby, Hooper's gaping jaw was evidence of the shock he felt at seeing Muddy alive. He didn't believe it was possible. However, a sharp word from De La Cruz straightened him out, and with difficulty Hooper feigned a look of concern.

Edgewood made a concerted effort in assisting Muddy, but when the chance arose she shot Hooper a look, her eyes blazing with anger. Fortunately for them, the bedlam of the moment had kept their attitudes hidden from the others. Only de La Cruz knew. The Spaniard closed his eyes. *Patience,* he thought. *God's work will be done.*

Aside from a sore head and the dozen stitches needed to close the wound, expertly administered by Ridley, over the course of the next hour Muddy Waters made a good recovery. He still felt like shit, and he had certainly suffered a concussion. It was a harsh reminder of the hangover he'd endured after the famous Boston Red Sox World Series win in 2004, their first victory since 1918. That was a worthy headache, at least.

"You're a lucky man, Muddy," said Haines. "Whatever happened?"

"I just don't know, John. One minute I stood on the rocks admiring the view, and the next... Well, everything went dark. I guess I must've slipped and bashed my thick skull." He grimaced. "It's gonna hurt in the morning."

It was a plausible explanation. John knew Muddy was getting on in years and that he'd been struggling a little with the heat and the terrain. But his concern wasn't enough to mention it to Muddy, or Kane. Hindsight was a wonderful thing, of course, and now it was easy to imagine the old professor becoming faint and stumbling.

Kane, though, felt troubled. He *had* noticed when Hooper discreetly left the group at the same time as the professor, though he thought nothing of it, assuming Hooper was also visiting the jungle bathroom. Kane had no reason to consider any foul play, and he didn't want to accuse anybody of anything without evidence. But what should he do? He'd felt a little dubious about Hooper from the moment they'd arrived in Cuzco, but he could think of no reason the writer might have for harming the harmless old archaeologist.

Kane knew the discovery of Vilcabamba–and the potential unearthing of untold Inca gold and treasure–would be the archaeological find of a lifetime, and there were many people around the world who'd die for a share of its riches. Indeed, many people had already lost their lives over the last century chasing the alleged myth. But to think people might have hijacked his expedition for some ruthless archaic ideology was abhorrent.

Kane was in it for the adventure and the pure joy of genuine discovery, and sought no personal fame or wealth from whatever success he found. To even consider that others were willing to kill for it tormented him no end. But the more he thought about it, the more Muddy's incident seemed premeditated, almost as if it was a case of waiting for the right moment. *Attempted murder? By a writer?*

It made little sense, and Kane was awash with an un-accustomed feeling of helplessness. He hoped it was just imagination getting the better of him, and Muddy's fall was nothing more than an accident. But Kane would watch Hooper with refocused attention.

He recalled something his grandfather had once said to him on the day of his eighteenth birthday–the day he received the map. *This map comes with a great burden,* he'd said. Those words had stayed with Hiram ever since.

And now he couldn't shake the horrifying thought a killer might be among them, that burden was looming very large indeed.

IV

Day 4

Suspicions

"Morning, handsome," said Ridley, catching up to Kane on the narrow trail and giving his bum a playful tap. "You seem distant." She stepped ahead and paused, assessing him. She knew Kane well and sensed he was troubled. "Everything okay?"

"Just tired, that's all. Didn't sleep well," he said, rubbing his eyes. But he knew the reason.

Mid-morning and progress was slow and steady, inevitable given the treacherous terrain. The narrow path was barely a path at all, uneven due to the dirt and loose rocks, and the constant tangle of vines and low-hanging branches. Every step was taken with extreme caution, and more than once they had to clamber over fallen trunks and under rocky outcrops. Most of the team had banged their head at least once.

Ridley had a point. Kane was a little aloof. He was in his element, hiking in the beautiful mountains in pursuit of the one thing he prized above all others, yet he couldn't shake his disquietude about Hooper and Muddy. Whether guilty or not, Hooper gave him too much to think about.

After breakfast, while helping to dismantle the camp, Kane spoke to Professors Haines and Muddy about his concerns. Both men believed he had nothing to worry about.

"He's just different from you, that's all," said Muddy, a man who'd seen and done it all in the field. "He's a city boy, not used to the great outdoors. Perhaps he's just caught up a little with the fever of the adventure?"

"I agree with Muddy," said Haines. Professor John Haines was a world-renowned art historian and had published multiple books across a variety of disciplines, with great success. He was often a guest speaker at art conferences around the world, and when he spoke, people listened. "Look, Hiram, I've been studying art and artefacts all my life. For an old man like me to feel as excited as I am, despite all the treasure hunts I've been on, imagine what it's like for a first-timer like Howie. He's probably thrilled just to be here, and who knows, perhaps on the cusp of one of the greatest discoveries of the last hundred years?" There was definite fire in those wizened eyes, and Kane had to agree he was probably being a touch sensitive.

He nodded. "Maybe you're right, John. You usually are."

"However," added Muddy, "how about we keep a close eye on him, let you know if we see anything dodgy?"

"Yes, do that. Thanks." Kane still wasn't convinced, but he trusted those men.

A few hours later and Kane finally relaxed into the day's hike, cruising along behind Ridley. It was a view he'd long admired. His mind drifted back to the autumn of 1997 when they'd met at a tae-kwon-do class they both attended.

Kane admired Ridley from afar for weeks. He adored women, yet always took a passive approach to dating. It wasn't arrogance. It was more an innate shyness and reluctance to get involved, and he didn't expect the opportunities that came his way. But they often did, and after being upfront about his complete inability to commit he often took up those opportunities.

And so it went with Ridley.

Kane & Ridley

Autumn, 2003
Lowestoft, Suffolk

Paired against each other in a pre-tournament sparring bout, Kane and Ridley faced off. He had no qualms about sparring with girls–the fact they practiced tae-kw0n-do in the first place meant she could handle it. But not all women were as sexy as Alexandria Ridley. She circled him around the mat, encouraging him forward. *Shit,* he thought, grinning. *I'll have to be careful.* After a few half-hearted lunges, all which missed by a mile, Kane thought he heard her whisper, "I'm taking you home tonight."

If it was what she'd actually said or just his imagination playing tricks, it completely caught him off guard. The next thing he knew Ridley flattened him with a no-holds-barred roundhouse kick to the temple. Dazed, he looked up as she pulled off her red bandana and unleashed a mane of hair the colour of mahogany. She looked down with unsympathetic eyes, and for a moment held his gaze. But with a wink more at home in the Moulin Rouge than on a fighting mat, she said, "Hank's Bar, seven o'clock."

A second later she turned and left.

I'll probably regret this, Kane thought, entering Hank's at exactly six forty that evening. He looked about, took a seat at the bar, and ordered a pint. The mysterious Ridley was nowhere to be seen. A little nervous, he'd almost finished his first beer when he heard the roar of a powerful motorbike pulling up outside. He checked his watch and smiled. Six fifty-nine.

Moments later Ridley was occupying a seat next to him and had already ordered a beer. A minute later, and after two long gulps, she was halfway down her pint.

"How's the skull? Looks like you survived well enough." She smiled.

And just like that Ridley had broken the ice. They settled into easy conversation, skipping the mindless small talk Kane usually endured on first dates. They discussed China's heinous occupation of Tibet and their hopes for its eventual freedom, moving onto the less serious but no less animated topic of who had the best voice between Vedder and Cornell. After each claiming the virtues of their choice, they settled on a magnanimous tie. Coupled with that a shared interest in the wider arts and outdoor pursuits, and of course their favourite wines and beers from around the world, within an hour Kane knew Alexandria Ridley was a special person. Despite himself, Kane felt enamoured.

Both aged twenty-six, they learned each had an inborn and insatiable thirst for adventure. Kane's need to travel had led to an experiential life, and he had enjoyed many foreign trips even before finishing high school. He credited his adventurous grandparents for that.

Ridley's tale was no less interesting, yet it was a tale laced with tragedy. An only child, Alexandria was orphaned after her parents died in a boating accident. She was just sixteen, but was at least fortunate that life insurance had paid off her parent's mortgage. Not only that, but her parents' estate had left her considerably wealthy for someone so young.

Lacking few close relatives and any real guidance the young Alex went off the rails, drinking too much and blanking out her misery and despair by any means possible. The bottom line was, Alex was wasting not only her inheritance but her vast academic potential, and that was more important.

However, by the time she turned twenty and after almost a year backpacking around south east Asia, most notably in Vietnam and Laos, Alex developed a passion for different cultures and spent a lot of her time volunteering in a series of desperate orphanages. It was a moment at one such orphanage in the sleepy northern Laotian town of Luang Prabang that Alex regained her lust for life.

On one of her daily visits to the Children's Centre, in a dusty street behind the town's main temple of Wat Xieng Thong, she witnessed an act of kindness so humbling it restored her fractured faith in humanity. A tiny five-year-old girl named Alamea, and her friend, four-year-old Pep, were found wandering alone in a village several miles outside town and were collected and deposited anonymously in the early hours of the morning several weeks previous. They were both starving, dehydrated, and sick, and their immediate prognosis was that they'd be lucky to live out the week. Hungry and dangerously weak from malnutrition, Alamea refused to eat until her friend, Pep, his health even more precarious than hers, was fed. With care and affection, and a course of antibiotics, over the three weeks they'd been at the Children's Centre their health steadily improved. They would now survive, thanks to the help of the orphanage. Alamea meant *precious* in Laotian.

Such selflessness in such a young child forced Ridley to question everything she thought she knew about herself. She realised then she had become selfish while feeling sorry for herself and was wasting the good fortune of being born and raised in a wealthy, powerful nation such as England. Yes, she was helping out in the orphanage, both with time and money. But she could do so much more for these poor, underprivileged kids. It was a major turning point in her life, and a moment she would never forget.

With some hard work and serious soul searching, and plenty more world travelling, Ridley came through those traumatic few years, and in order to put her money to good use and give her life some meaning she donated a vast sum of money, enough to support the orphanage in Luang Prabang for the next twenty years. Next, she enrolled in the University of East Anglia's Art History degree program. She'd finally found her calling and was revelling in her new life.

There was no doubt about it, Kane and Ridley had much in common, not least their shared love of a few adult beverages. As the night wore on and the beers continued to flow, Kane kept trying to ask a question that had troubled him ever since she'd humbled him on the tae-kwan-do mat. When his Dutch courage had sufficiently lubricated his reticence, Kane asked his question.

"I've been meaning to ask… Erm… Did you really say—?"

Ridley raised her hand, silencing him. She knew exactly what he wanted to know. "Yes, I did say that. But I didn't know if I meant it then."

"Then?" Kane asked, incredulous.

"Yes, then. It depends on you."

"On me?" He couldn't help it. It didn't happen often, but Kane flushed with embarrassment. "How?"

"Depends whether you'll pay for our taxi home?"

And since that day forth the two of them have been the closest of friends and often more, which is how Ridley knew, looking into Kane's eyes as they walked along the Andean trails, that he was having a rough day.

"It's that Hooper, isn't it. You've been eyeing him like a hawk. What is it?"

Kane contemplated telling her what he thought about the American, then thought better of it. For now, he didn't want to worry anyone if it was a false alarm. He turned to face Ridley. "Listen, Alex. I'm okay. Honest. Everything's fine. Trust me."

Ridley shook her head in mock grumpiness but followed up with a smile. Kane knew that smile. It meant, *I'm here if you need anything.* Hiram knew she would be.

"Now," he said, "You know I'm not sexist, but how about you get back ahead of me. With all due respect to Muddy, yours is a much more attractive backside."

Scheming

Kate Edgewood couldn't help but be inspired by both the beautiful Andean scenery surrounding them and the history she sensed as she hiked in the footsteps of the Incas. Despite her heinous ulterior motive, Edgewood's passion for art history and the myths and legends of the ancient world was genuine, and she was so spellbound by the magnificent views that an element of doubt about her intentions crept unbidden into her conscience. If they actually succeeded in finding Vilcabamba and the Inca treasure–and she was confident they would–there would certainly be mixed feelings about claiming the glory herself.

All the world had heard about the legendary lost Inca gold–there were movies and dozens of novels written about that very thing. But if they were the ones to finally find it, didn't they have a moral obligation to return it to the Incan descendants? Of course they did. And could she handle the fact people were almost certainly going to get hurt, even die? Yes, she could.

Yet, those thoughts were fleeting at best, and Edgewood chided herself for the moment of weakness. Ultimately, her desire for the Inca riches surpassed all else, and continued to grow with every passing mile.

"Stunning, isn't it," said Evan, snapping another image of

the wild scenery. "Totally inspiring."

"It really is," replied Kate. "More spectacular than I even imagined. Photos online and in books could never do justice to the real thing. No offence." She smiled an apology at the good looking photographer.

"None taken," replied Evan, "and I couldn't agree more." He meant it, too. Evan Craft was cajoled into coming on the expedition by his friend Hiram to shoot a photographic record of what he believed would be their successful quest for Vilcabamba. Craft had his reservations about a two-week trek in the Andes, more comfortable photographing animals on the plains of Africa, where he could spend long hours sitting on his arse in a jeep. But Kane convinced the notoriously lazy bloke it might just be the defining work of his career, and he agreed to come.

"Do you think we're going to find it?" she asked. "The treasure, I mean."

"Well, after Hiram told me how close he came last year, when only the earthquake got in the way, if anyone can find anything out here in these mountains it's my old mate, Kane. Especially with his map." Evan leaned in close, a conspiratorial gleam in his eye, "And between me and you, Kane said it'll be more amazing than anyone could imagine."

Edgewood believed it, too. To hear it from someone so close to Kane only solidified her determination. It also gave her an idea. She knew she could use Craft to her advantage, and began right away, all moral doubts forgotten. "What will you do, you know, when you become the famous photographer of Vilcabamba?" She hated flirting with infantile characters like Craft, but given Hooper's inadequacies she thought she'd need a backup plan. With coquettish abandon, Edgewood began making an ally of Evan. It seemed to work.

"Well, I thought… Once all the fuss has died down, maybe I could, you know, I mean… Maybe we could go to Hawaii." Craft was jabbering. "I, um, I know this great place on Maui with the best pizzas, the beaches are perfect, and as for the sunsets…"

And for the next hour, Evan was undone by the charms of Kate Edgewood, rambling on and oblivious to the fact that after just a few flattering words, she had him exactly where she wanted him.

Up ahead, Kane and Sonco were in deep conversation. "Very soon we have to leave trail and cut deep into jungle." Sonco's English, mostly learned from Hiram, was decent, but an exotic mix of Quechuan and Spanish accents were unmistakable. "There was small avalanche one month ago. Normal pass is closed. Other way is good."

Kane recalled his last expedition, the one which took him closer to Vilcabamba than he'd ever been. He and his group were lucky to escape with their lives, and he had to abort the attempt. Regarding their routes, Kane trusted Sonco completely, and if he suggested an alternative route for safety reasons, then that's the way they'd go. "Okay, my friend, lead the way. Let us hope Pachamama is kind this time."

Sonco nodded. Internally, though, he cursed the ignorant Spaniard, De La Cruz, for daring to disrespect Pachamama. Only time would tell if it would cost them.

He steered the group on a north-easterly tangent deeper into the jungle and set them on a course that would test their physical capabilities more than anything until now. Dense trees closed in around them, the hanging vines a knotted tangle. Within the sweating jungle, the humidity seemed to rise with each passing moment.

Ahead of them, one of Sonco's men literally had to blaze a trail with expertly vicious swings of a razor-edged machete. Their already slow progress became ponderous by necessity, nature dominating human endeavour. Nevertheless, spirits remained high, and Kane sensed a growing determination, necessary to match the increasingly difficult conditions.

The sun had reached its zenith yet little light filtered through the low jungle canopy, the dappled darkness adding more treachery to their every step. And though they'd moved away from the dangerous cliff edges, other perils awaited them. Ruined stone walls, built half a millennium ago by skilled Inca masons, were hidden, reclaimed by a greedy jungle. Unseen, any false step could topple you ten feet down an invisible drop. Breaking a leg or neck would be easy.

Unpredictable terrain wasn't the only danger, and native wildlife was now a serious issue. Venomous spiders, scorpions, and aggressive snakes lurked beneath those ancient stones. Though rarely fatal, one bite or sting could bring a swift end to the victim's expedition. And then there were the bugs. Winged insects of all shapes and sizes fluttered here and there, human eyes and ears their preferred target. Infuriating, the constant waving necessary to keep them at bay caused many to stumble on the rocks.

But when it came to swarming insects, Kane's personal nemeses mosquitoes were causing utter chaos, inescapable due to such immense numbers. They didn't carry malaria like their African cousins, but nonetheless, their incessant droning had been known to drive men insane. Kane thought he might be next.

Aside from bugs and snakes and a multitude of unseen dangers, one menace, though diminutive in size, was more feared by locals than anything else; the Bot Fly. After one bite, Bot Fly larvae like nothing more than to feast on human flesh–from the inside. No amount of squeezing can remove its barbed, spiny body, and the nasty, gruesome creature is paralysingly painful.

The dreaded Bot Fly was just another of the many perils Kane's team faced in the damp and dangerous darkness of the Andean jungle.

Hooper

If it was possible, Howie Hooper was distancing himself further from the others. After their chat with Kane, both Haines and Muddy had attempted to engage him in conversation, but with little or no success. He'd replied to their morning greetings, grunting a few words to tell them he was fine. But as the day wore on it became increasingly obvious that he was against conversing with anyone. That combined with his agitated attitude had aroused their suspicions, not least Hooper's American counterpart Muddy. He made it a point to get Hooper talking.

"How're ya holding up there, Howie? Me, well I'm as tired as a Spring Break clean up crew." Muddy had dropped back and fallen into step just ahead of the writer.

"Fine," came the curt reply.

Muddy probed. "You don't say a lot, do you?".

"I'm focusing on my steps, that's all. It'd be dumb to fall now and miss out on victory."

Muddy noticed a sudden flash of passion in Hooper's eyes, though he quickly blanked his expression. Writer? Didn't seem likely. "Kane tells me you write. Who d'ya write for?"

Hooper had his cover story worked out, though he hadn't yet needed to use it. He was unprepared. "Um, well, I write for, you know… various magazines. In the States." He wasn't convincing, and Muddy pounced.

"Oh yeah. Like who?"

"Why the fuck do you care, anyway? Can't a man trek in peace?" Hooper shoved his way past Muddy on the narrow trail, done talking. But the bulky professor placed a surprisingly strong hand on Hooper's shoulders and spun him around.

"You wouldn't be lying now, would ya? I know a liar when I see one."

Hooper's eyes narrowed with sudden rage as if he was about to strike the older scholar. "Back off, old man," he snarled. But just as quick as it came, he regained his composure and backed down. Now wasn't the time, and he closed his eyes for a second. "Listen, I'm sorry. This is a big story, an opportunity to make something of my writing career. I'm nervous, nothing more."

Muddy removed his hand from Hooper's shoulder and glared at him. It was plausible, but–

Howie offered up his hand. "No hard feelings, Professor?"

Muddy looked deep into Howie's eyes for long seconds, but saw nothing sinister.

He shook the hand.

The atmosphere in camp that evening was as cool as the falling temperature, in harsh contrast to the draining humidity of the day. Understandably it seemed as if Muddy's accident had aroused in the group a heightened level of respect for their undertaking. Muddy was okay, more or less recovered, but a new edginess drifted about the team as they came to terms with the reality of the many dangers they faced.

It's not that the team members weren't getting along. On the whole, it had somehow brought them together. Edgewood, who'd disguised her anger over Hooper's failure with cold efficiency, was cosying up with Evan as they sought the warmth of the campfire.

He couldn't know it, but Kate had certain agendas that needed fulfilling, and always a soft-touch with the ladies, Craft would be a useful ally. Kane teased him about his obvious attraction, and warned Kate off with banterous tales of his friend's long list of disappointed conquests. Ridley and Kane, their special friendship now in the open, no longer sat apart, while Haines chatted amiably with Angelo De La Cruz, finding mutual ground with talk of Valencia's rich history and splendid architecture, not least its Roman ruins, one of Professor Haines' many specialities. And in order to rest his aching joints and a sore head, Muddy hit the hay early, as he called it, but not before assuring them he'd be ready to rock n' roll come first light.

Though the others were oblivious to his anxious fidgeting, Hooper remained distracted. Of course he was. He'd failed in his first assignment and now feared his boss Benedix would cut him from the deal. Sure, he was supposed to answer to Edgewood while in the Andes, but it wasn't her that worried him. In fact, he doubted Benedix was too concerned about her, either. All Benedix cared about was success. If that meant removing Edgewood from the equation, Hooper wouldn't hesitate to do it.

His immediate worry was the Spaniard, for it was De La Cruz overseeing their mission on the ground in Peru. Hooper wasn't sure who wielded more power, De La Cruz or Benedix, but he knew the Spaniard was a dangerous man, driven by blind faith and guided only by God. Hooper knew he could deal with Edgewood. But Angelo De La Cruz was an entirely different prospect. He said little–at least not to him–but he knew without a doubt the man did not miss a beat, almost as if he was omnipotent, like God himself.

Howie couldn't deny it: the seemingly innocuous Spaniard unnerved him.

Umaq

Away from the main camp, Sonco and his men sat in a tight cluster around their own fire. Smoke drifted above them, curling from their delicate stone pipes in wispy trails. They spoke quietly, at peace with the world.

But one among the Quechuan contingent was less at peace than the others. Their youngest member, Umaq Huamani, was troubled, and he hated himself for it.

Hailing from a poverty-stricken farming village, to get assigned on an expedition like this was akin to winning the lottery, the family on the verge of financial ruin. Due to injury, his father could no longer work as a porter on the Inca Trail, a job he'd done with pride for two decades, and his mother was weak from ill health, unable to shift bronchitis she'd suffered with for several years. To top it off, Umaq's elder brother was killed in a landslide while working in the mountains five years previous. At just eighteen, Umaq was barely a man himself, and yet he'd already endured a tough life.

But luck had finally shone on the Huamani family. His kid sister, Miski, attended the same school as Sonco's daughter, Quri and their families had become friends. As a favour, Sonco invited Umaq to accompany him on two previous treks. The boy had acquitted himself well, and Sonco trusted him enough to employ him for Kane's latest expedition.

On the first day of the expedition, however, Umaq was approached by a young woman in Aguas Calientes. She was European though Umaq didn't know from which country. The woman had a proposal for him—a proposal worth ten thousand dollars, and an opportunity to secure his family's financial security forever. The money was an absolute fortune for a destitute Quechuan family, enough that he could get the medical help his parents needed. Not only that, it would ensure his beloved sister Miski could stay in school. Umaq could even follow his dreams and go to university in Lima.

Ten thousand dollars. He still didn't know why she'd approached him. All he needed to do, she said, was one thing. One simple act that, when she gave him the signal, he did it without hesitation.

Umaq said no at first. He was a nice kid, raised with high morals and a solid notion of what was right and wrong. But he also had a strong sense of duty to his family. Umaq was the man of the house, now, and the responsibility to care for his family sat heavily on his young shoulders. That's what troubled him most. Because of that responsibility he found himself considering the bizarre offer. Ten thousand dollars would change their lives. He didn't know what she expected him to do, but ultimately Umaq had little choice.

The cook Yupanqui had been watching Umaq like a hawk since day one, enough to unnerve him. Though he couldn't be sure what it was, Umaq knew there was more to Yupanqui than met the eye. Yesterday the big Quechuan had taken him aside, and with a firm grip and a dark expression, had asked him a surprising question.

"Are you a Quechuan man, Umaq?"

"Quechuan? Yes, I am."

"Yes, I know you are." Yupanqui's eyes softened just a little. "You are Quechuan, which means you are also Incan, like your ancestors before you. Like me. Do not forget your history, boy. Understand me?"

"Yes, Yupanqui," Umaq replied, his voice weak.

Without another word, the cook left him there. It was another strange encounter. But Umaq soon turned his attention back to the woman, his mind made up. When he got a chance he would accept the offer and do whatever Kate Edgewood wanted him to do.

V

Day 5

Tension

Dawn announced itself with an ethereal golden glow.

First to emerge from the sanctuary of their tent was Muddy Waters. He rubbed his sore head and winced while stretching the stiffness from his bones. A collection of nasty scrapes on his arms and legs stung, and if he wasn't mistaken he'd cracked at least two ribs as evidenced by the difficulty he had breathing. However, he was a tough character, and despite everything he felt good. It would not stop him continuing, and eager to show the others he was fit to carry on, the faux-bossy patriarch returned.

"Rise and shine, kids." Muddy's tenor-like voice echoed across the valley. "Breakfast is imminent."

And it was. Yupanqui was busy scrambling eggs and prepping tea and coffee, and roused by Muddy's call, one by one the tent flaps opened, the weary campers struggling to leave the relative warmth of their tents. But lured by the tantalising aroma of strong, hot coffee, they were soon milling about the welcome heat of the central fire.

"How do you feel?" asked Ridley, stifling a cavernous yawn. After a quick stretch, and after gratefully accepting a cuppa from a porter she took a seat next to the professor.

"I feel great, Alex, thanks. I'm ready for the day. It'll take a lot more than a clumsy slip to set this rugged old adventurer back." He beamed a smile, and she knew he was right.

Sat on his haunches in the doorway of his tent and listening to their conversation, Hooper couldn't keep the scowl from his face. A moment later Edgewood approached wearing a look of such disdain he was momentarily taken aback. "One more chance. Don't mess it up."

Hooper swallowed his anger. He hated being spoken down to, especially by a woman. But a lot was riding on this job and he would rather proceed as planned than take it into his own hands. At least for now. Howie would play Benedix's game, and he would complete his mission.

On the outskirts of the camp Umaq leaned against a tree, observing and waiting for his opportunity to approach Edgewood. He was reluctant, but he had a duty to his family to secure that money.

Sonco was also watching, but his eyes weren't on the group. He was appraising Umaq. Sonco had noticed the young kid hadn't been his usual self since leaving Aguas Calientes, and though he had no inclination why, something didn't sit well with the experienced guide. His loyalty to Hiram was fierce, and as always wanted everything to go well for his friend. Sonco had known Hiram since he was a teenager on his first adventure in the Andes, on a trek to Machu Picchu with his grandfather. Sonco, just a couple of years older, was working as a porter on that trek, way back in the late-eighties, and despite their limited ability to communicate back then, they'd remained friends ever since.

Since Kane's career as an expedition leader took off he'd worked hard trying–and failing–to convince Sonco to travel beyond Peru and work with him on other adventures. But that would mean flying, and though he'd always admired the mighty condors that had graced the wide Andean skies since before the days of his ancestors, he knew that if humans were meant to fly he'd have wings instead of arms.

Turning his attention back to the boy, Sonco made a conscious note to keep a close eye on the kid he considered his protégé.

"Buen día, mi amigo," said Kane as he approached Sonco. "Everything okay?"

"Si, Hiram, esta bien," replied Sonco. Yes, everything's okay.

"You sure? You look worried."

"The kids today. We give chance," he said, tipping his head towards Umaq. "They take for granted. The boy, there. I give job when family need, but always sulking. Everything difficult. Too lazy."

Kane cast his eyes at the boy, Umaq. He'd seen no evidence of the young Quechuan's laziness, in fact he thought the opposite was true, and Kane had him pegged as a diligent, competent porter. Sure, he looked distracted, worried even. But Sonco was prone to exaggeration.

What is it with this expedition? thought Kane. His concerns over Hooper wouldn't dissipate, Muddy's accident, and now a young porter looking as if his world might end that very day. Even Sonco was out of sorts. Kane slapped his friend on the shoulder and shook his head. "You worry too much, amigo," he said. Sonco just shrugged, and Kane left him to it.

Kane walked off and looked around him, into the jungle and then above, catching a glimpse of the little sky visible through the dense canopy. It didn't look good. The morning glow was gone, smothered by clouds a dozen shades of grey that had crept up the valley, threatening and inauspicious. Kane smiled, but it wasn't a smile borne of confidence.

"Pachamama," he whispered. "What do you have in store for us?"

He wouldn't have to wait long to find out.

Nature

Kane and Sonco were buoyant, happy with their progress so far, despite the looming weather. They'd covered a lot of ground and were on schedule for the seven-day target Kane set for reaching their destination. That meant they were more or less half way, and with a little luck and if no further incidents hampered their progress, by mid-morning in a few days they would pass the point he and Sonco had reached last time out. Kane knew if they reached that point it was just several hours further until the location of the big X on his map. That single mark, allegedly drawn by the shaking hands of Hiram Bingham himself on his deathbed some fifty-five years earlier, had driven Kane for a decade, and he was once more getting close.

Without thinking he reached into the neck of his shirt and clutched his golden sun disc. As he did he saw images of his grandfather's pale blue eyes encouraging him. Next to him stood his great grandfather Patrick, that old explorer's assistant who'd gone down in history as part of the team that re-discovered Machu Picchu. In his mind, their smiles willed him on, and that golden Inca sun disc, the artefact he'd had worn every day since receiving it so many years before, seemed to radiate power. Not in a supernatural sense, but more of a confidence boost that he was nearing Vilcabamba, and in doing so, fulfilling what he'd long believed was his destiny: locating the real lost city of the Incas, and with it, Lord Atahualpa's legendary lost hoard.

They broke camp and bore south, even deeper into a jungle that now arced downwards into the valley, and toward the wild and rampaging Urubamba River below. Known as the Willkamayu in Quechuan, the ferocious sacred river had claimed many explorer's lives over the decades, notably that of English geologist John Walter Gregory, in 1932. After assessing the sky, Sonco and Kane knew they were in for a fearsome Andean storm, just a matter of time until it hit. With a wry smile, Kane hoped he or any of his team wouldn't become the latest additions to the long list of the Urubamba's victims.

To begin with just a few raindrops penetrated the tree-line, nature's brolly serving them well. But within mere minutes the rain hit them in torrents the likes of which those unfamiliar with the Andes had ever seen. The drops fell like stones, and the trail became a lethal quagmire. *Okay, now we'll be tested*, thought Kane, and with nowhere obvious to wait out the deluge they had little choice but to press on. In reality, Kane wasn't that concerned with the storm. It meant they were forced to proceed slowly, and by default, carefully. He made sure to stay close to the older, less agile guys, but not too close as to give Muddy or John a complex. They were tough. Shit, Muddy just survived a twenty-foot fall, almost unscathed bar a few scratches.

If it was a fall. Since that moment there had been no evidence of any wrong doings by Hooper. In fact, Kane had even seen Howie helping Muddy pack up his things earlier that morning. Still, thoughts of Hooper leaving the camp just moments before the accident seemed too much of a coincidence. Or did it? Maybe Hooper simply needed the bathroom too? *Am I being paranoid?* he thought. *Maybe.* Kane couldn't be sure.

Through the raging storm visibility fell to only a few yards, and the single file procession had inadvertently spread out over a quarter of a mile. In a dangerous jungle that is far. Too far. The terrain was testing enough, but in those conditions, they were hardly moving. Howie Hooper was to the rear of the group, plotting his next move. He didn't know who was next in front, but it was Edgewood, who suddenly turned to face him.

"You have until tonight to dispose of Waters. No excuses. If you fail, the deal's off. Use the storm."

For a split second, Hooper had the urge to get rid of Edgewood, strangle her with one hand right there and then. It would be easy, what with his military background. But that would mean dealing with De La Cruz, and later, more explaining to Benedix. He clenched his teeth, then nodded.

"It will be done." He glared at her a little longer than he meant. And then he smiled. "Ma'am."

Edgewood didn't miss the antagonism in his eyes, but she knew he'd succeed. There was both a victory and a fortune awaiting, and though she knew his motivation was in part religious, she also knew he needed the money. After his dishonourable discharge from the U.S. Military for multiple drug misdemeanours, Hooper became somewhat alienated from society in the United States, and found his way to England in search of a new start. He'd written and published some articles about life and the widespread use of drugs in the military, as well as a few travel articles, and had received some minor success. She wasn't sure how Hooper and Ferdinand Benedix became involved, but that wasn't of any concern to Edgewood.

She knew Benedix was using her, as she was using him, and they were both using that idiot Hooper. That she was going to betray Ferdinand troubled her. She admired him for his passion and his vast knowledge, and had enjoyed their romance, as fabricated as it was. But it only troubled her a little, and she had more important issues than her feelings. She needed to keep Evan by her side, and maintain her facade as a weak but keen graduate student on an adventure, in the eyes of Kane and the others. And she had to dominate Hooper. That was under control. He wouldn't fail again.

Unseen by them Umaq Huamani had witnessed the hostile exchange between the woman and the ugly American. He hadn't yet spoken to Edgewood about his decision, but he couldn't help wonder if she wanted him to make the American go away. Umaq was a gentle kid, and had never hurt anyone or anything. But the thought of his impoverished family, his sick father and weak mother, and of Miski's disappointment when they'd pulled her out of school because they couldn't afford the fees, well they were hurting, and it broke his heart, and Umaq knew he'd do anything to improve their lives. He didn't like the American. It seemed to Umaq that nobody did. Perhaps he'd be doing them all a favour, if that was what she asked of him.

Quechuans were spiritual by nature, and since the arrival of the Spanish in the fifteenth century their religious beliefs had assimilated certain Catholic values. Thus, they worshipped both the Holy Father *and* pagan Gods such as Pachamama, the Earth Goddess. They believed she controlled the destiny of the Quechuans through her power over the land and the weather. Reaching down, Umaq grabbed a handful of the mud from beneath his feet, and now on his knees, said a small combined prayer to both God and to Pachamama, asking for forgiveness for whatever it was he had to do, and that his beloved family was not punished for his sins. He kissed the earth before tossing it to the ground, then crossed his chest in the Christian tradition. Umaq was no fool. He knew, that before this expedition was over, his life would never be the same again.

Just then a giant hand clutched his shoulder with enormous strength. He turned his head to see the thunderous face of Yupanqui looming over him.

"Stand up, boy," he growled. "You are Quechuan, with Inca blood in your veins, yet you pray to that false God, the God of the invaders that raped our land and killed our people."

"I… my family… we are Quechuan, but we believe in the saviour Jesus Christ, and Inti the sun God and the Earth Goddess, Pachamama."

"Why do you believe in that false Catholic idol, when you know what the Catholics have done to our people, torturing and killing, and devastating the mighty Inca empire?"

"I… it's just what we do, it's what my…" His voice failed him.

"Enough. It doesn't matter what you believe, or thought you believed, because the time of the prophecy has arrived. The Inca are rising once more, and you will obey me, Pachacuti, your master, for if you do not, you will die with the rest of the heathen Catholics in our land, and your family will die too, sentenced as traitors in legion with the conquistadors. We will kill them, as they once killed us, and expel them from the land of the Incas once and for all. Make your decision Umaq, or the prophecy will see you as one of them." Yupanqui turned and left the young Quechuan shaking with fear.

Doubts

The weather deteriorated even further by mid-morning. Thunder reverberated all around a valley lit up every thirty seconds by tremendous explosions of sheet lightning. If it wasn't so dangerous it would have made a spectacular show. From what had started out as a mild Andean storm, they now faced the very real threat of deadly landslides. Worry etched Kane's face as Sonco hustled them on. Leading the way, he huddled them into a small cave, hunkering down and waiting for the stragglers to emerge from the downpour. John was next, and then two porters and their mules, soon followed by Evan, drenched through but somehow managing a smile. He was more worried about his precious camera equipment than his own safety, it seemed, and hugged his pack to his chest. Two more porters soon emerged from what was becoming a series of waterfalls cascading down the slopes, and next came Ridley and Edgewood, faces taut and grateful for the respite. And then, to Kane's horror, the last two of the Quechuan porters, who's primary duty since the first minute of the expedition was to bring up the rear of the party. Shit.

"Where are the others?" Kane bellowed at the surprised porters, immediately fearing the worst. "Are they behind you?" The two young men shared a surprised look, and lacking English were unsure of Kane's meaning. They were last, as instructed to be. Weren't they? Kane didn't wait for an answer, and dashed back out onto the trail, Sonco close behind.

They didn't get far. Out of the gloom emerged Hooper, rushing to meet them. "It's Waters," he shouted. "Come on."

Kane's gut tightened, his instincts screaming that Hooper had done something bad. They ran together, the American leading the way, until blocked by a fallen tree. Hooper pointed over the trail edge, and Kane saw Muddy. He wasn't moving. The three of them scrambled down the scrubby bank to Muddy, who groaned in pain. Assessing the situation, it didn't look good, and Kane saw straight away that Muddy had broken his leg.

"Muddy, it's me, Hiram. Can you hear me?"

Muddy stirred, and rolled over onto his side.

"It hurts, Hiram… It hurts so much."

"Don't move. Lie still and we'll get you out of here. Sonco," he yelled over the thrumming rain, "Run back to the others and get the first aid kit. Bring Ridley back and assemble the stretcher." The second Sonco left Kane dragged Hooper away from Muddy. He stared hard at the American, searching for any sign of guilt. He saw none. "What happened, Howie?"

"I don't know. We were walking together, then the lightning struck that tree and the next thing I knew the old man was gone. I guess he tried to dodge the tree and slipped." Howie's features remained passive. *Too calm,* thought Kane.

Kane turned back to Muddy and found the professor now sitting up and resting on his elbows. There was a look of pain-filled anger in those blue eyes, and it was as if he was trying to give Kane a message.

"What is it, Muddy? Are you trying to tell me something?"

The old archaeologist looked from Kane to Hooper, eyes hard, then back again to Kane, and started to say something when a wave of unbearable pain overtook him, and he passed out, slumping to the ground.

Kane was about to confront Hooper when Sonco and Ridley came scrambling down the bank. Ridley immediately sensed the friction in the air, but their first concern was Muddy Waters, and she unfurled the stretcher pack and laid it out next to Muddy.

"He has a broken tibia. He fell down that bank. Apparently." The look in Kane's eyes was venomous, now totally convinced Hooper was responsible. But he had to focus on Muddy. Over the course of the next thirty minutes, they gave Muddy some powerful painkillers, put his leg in a cast, and made him as comfortable as possible. Sonco had found a nearby route back up to the main trail that was a gentle slope, and in an apparent act of mercy from Pachamama the rain had eased to a light drizzle. Kane and Sonco carried Muddy to the cave, and Hooper seized the moment to speak to Ridley.

"Hiram has some doubts about me, and I think he believes I'm somehow responsible. But I'm not. I promise I'm not... why would I hurt Muddy?"

"Why would Hiram think that? I'm sure you're wrong. It's true, you act distant sometimes, even arrogant, and you don't join in with the others, but..."

"I'm just shy, is all. I'd never hurt anyone." It was a convincing grovel, and Ridley bought it.

"Look, just stay out of the way for now, and I'll speak to Hiram. He's under a lot of pressure on these expeditions and hates to see anyone get hurt."

"Okay. Got it. Please tell Muddy I'm sorry he's hurt."

Muddy, now comfortable on a makeshift bed in the cave, was in no doubt his expedition was over. The pain had ceased, and he sat alone with Kane. Kane looked at the aged professor with a mixture of compassion and questioning eyes. Muddy Waters looked both sad and confused, as if now unsure what happened.

"Muddy, I have a question, and it's blunt. Did Howie Hooper push you over the bank?"

Muddy seemed to think hard, his eyes scrunched up in both pain and concentration, and after a full minute he looked at Hiram, slowly shaking his head. "I'm sorry, Hiram. There's some fuzziness, and Howie's face keeps popping into my head. But I don't know. I can't remember... I only know that..." The old man started sobbing. It was clear to Kane the man was struggling. Muddy wouldn't want to accuse anybody of something so heinous, in fact, couldn't believe anybody was capable of it. But mostly he felt an overwhelming sadness his adventure was over. Kane let the old man have a few moments to compose himself before speaking.

"Look Muddy, something very strange is happening here, and I don't like it. But unless you're sure I'll have to let it slide. And I think you know we're going to have to call an end to your expedition... I couldn't be sorrier."

"Hiram, the last few days have shown me that my trekking days should have been over long ago. Aside from the first accident at the waterfall, I realise I'm slowing the group down and adding an extra worry to you, when you already have so much to think about."

"You're not slowing us down, Muddy. You're doing great."

"Of course you'd say that, and I'm grateful for your apathy. But I'm not stupid. My heart tells me both falls have been my

84

own dumb mistakes. Maybe you think so, but the bottom line is that this expedition is over, and I'm going home to Boston, to put my feet up and spoil my grand kids. And don't you dare consider stopping this trip on my behalf, or out of concerns about Howie. Continue on without me. You have to."

Kane looked with great empathy at Muddy, and he knew the man was right. They had to push on, despite his reservations about Hooper and his sadness about the big professor. "You're right. But you'll be missed, Muddy, and you will share in this expedition's success, whether you're here or not." Kane leaned over to give the man a hug, then called for the others to come in and see how he was.

Kane stepped out of the shelter as some of the others walked in, but Ridley caught him by the arm. Edging him out of earshot, she asked him about Hooper. "What's going on with Howie? He thinks you hold him responsible for Muddy's accidents. Why would you think that? What evidence do you have?"

"Listen, Alex, I've had a bad feeling about him since we first met. I couldn't be sure why, but something niggled me about him. I didn't mention this before, but at the waterfall, Howie left camp right after Muddy. He snuck out and snuck back, and in that time Muddy nearly died. And this today? The coincidence is pretty big, don't you think?"

Ridley pondered it for a second. "I agree, it seems strange, but it doesn't mean there's anything in it. Why would he want to hurt Muddy? For what purpose?"

"I don't know. I really don't. But there is something going on, and I will find out what."

First Man Down

Kane and Sonco arranged for two of the porters to escort Muddy Waters back to their starting point at Aguas Calientes and continue with him back to Cuzco. Muddy would ride one of the mules, and Sonco had given them strict orders to go easy. He trusted them, and he knew they wouldn't let him down.

Muddy felt devastated, of course. This was to be his last adventure into the wilderness, and it had ended in personal failure. He only hoped that the rest of the expedition was successful for the others.

At long last the rain had stopped and dazzling sunlight pierced the jungle canopy. After some fond farewells and promises to stay in touch with Kane, Ridley and the others helped Professor Andrew 'Muddy' Waters onto a mule. Keeping his sadness hidden he addressed the group, and with his customary stoicism.

"My friends, I know I can seem a touch bossy sometimes, but since you already know that I'm going to be bossy one more time." He winced, his broken leg reminding him it was broken. "My last order to you guys is to not feel sorry for me. I've had an amazing, adventurous life, and even though my last treasure hunt into the wilds is cut short, it's still been memorable. But do not let my failure stop you from your success. You must complete this mission. You must succeed in your goals. Do not be disheartened. Do not fail."

This last harsh command did not disguise the twinkle of excitement that remained in the old explorer's eyes. He wanted them to succeed, wanted them to find Vilcabamba. But more than that, he knew they must. The impoverished Quechuan people had a right to the wealth of Atahualpa's lost hoard. Whether it be direct cash handouts, or simply from a boost in tourist dollars that the discovery of Vilcabamba would ultimately bring into the economy, Muddy firmly believed that it needed finding and he had no doubt this was the expedition to do it. With a hoity wave of the hand the sad procession edged down the trail on the long trek back to civilisation. Howie grabbed the moment.

He rushed over to Muddy and extended his hand. "Mr Waters, I'm very sorry you're leaving the group, and I'm sorry you're hurt."

Muddy looked at him hard, trying to sense any scheming, but found no trace of anything but sympathy. He turned his eyes on Kane, whose jowls clenched and eyes narrowed. The American's show of compassion didn't convince him, but with reluctance, he nodded at Muddy as if to say *okay, Howie will get the benefit of my grave doubts.* Muddy returned the nod and took Howie's hand.

"Thank you, Howie. And good luck to you." And with that, they were gone.

Sonco motioned to Kane to follow him. "Rain so heavy. Path dangerous. We camp here today and start again tomorrow."

Kane was keen to push on and put the sad image of Muddy

leaving behind him. But as always he trusted Sonco, and they set up camp in the shelter of the cave area.

Hooper walked away and smiled to himself. He had tried to kill someone and failed. Twice. Yet that person was now out of the way, and his first mission was complete. Though Hooper was Catholic, and technically on a Catholic mission, his faith was not as strong as it once was. He looked skyward, peering into the now bright clear sky. Could it have been divine intervention? He wanted to think so. It seemed God was on his side, and it instilled in him a confidence rarely felt. Regardless, he would not be so careless next time, and was now free to focus on part two of his mission; the swift removal of Professor Haines.

VI

Day 6

Plans

After leaving the temporary cave shelter, Sonco led them on.

"So… how about that date on Maui?" purred Edgewood as she hustled up alongside Craft. "I've always fancied Hawaii. But why should I go with you, Evan?"

The mood had been sombre since Waters' departure yesterday afternoon, but now the weather had improved and with it the atmosphere.

"Well, it's a good question, and I have no better answer than to say why the hell not?" Craft wasn't known for his skills with the ladies but, as his oldest friend Kane would say, *it's not for lack of trying.* But Evan really did fancy Kate and was keen to secure a date after the expedition. To cover his nerves, Evan put on his poshest English accent. "My dear, in my favour is the fact that as a photographer I know all the most beautiful spots, and as someone who adores food I've frequented many spectacular eating establishments on Maui."

She chuckled. "That's a good start. I heard there's a nice drive somewhere on Maui, to a waterfall?"

"Yes, my lady, that would be The Road to Hana, and yes it is stunning. We could rent ourselves a convertible, partake in a splendid road trip around the island? Or would madam prefer a horse and carriage?"

This was going well, thought Edgewood, and it was just

what she wanted. To pull this off she needed the trust of someone close to Kane. But she was torn. Evan was a nice guy, so too Kane and Ridley. However, that one or more of them would get hurt was just collateral damage, and she could deal with that. Her only decision was whether to cut Benedix out of the equation. She believed she could do it. That naïve young lad Umaq would soon come around, knowing he'd be a fool to turn down that much money. Of course, she would never actually pay him, and he would simply disappear with the others. But, using his help to get rid of any evidence of Hooper's actions, and then to dispose of both Howie and that stuck up Spaniard De La Cruz, she'd be home free to claim the prize and the glory. And she would claim it alone.

Back at the front of the convoy Kane was in deep conversation with Ridley.

"It's been pretty eventful so far, hey Kane?" she said, smiling despite all the drama.

"Sure has. But we wouldn't have it any other way, would we?"

And that was true. They were both born to live adventurous lives, and whether she shared the same notion or not, Kane was always happier when on an adventure with Ridley. He wanted to believe she enjoyed his company as much as he did hers, and he sensed she did. But Ridley was fiercely independent and rarely needed anything from anyone. Kane wondered if part of the appeal was that she came across as so unattainable, unless it was on her terms. It wasn't as if Kane chased her, far from it, but he was always keen to hook up with her when the chance arose. But it didn't always pan out that way. She openly liked Kane and had never been closer to any man than she was with him. But for some reason she just would not commit to anything other than an occasional fling.

In her deepest of hearts she did want more, and she wanted it with Kane. She trusted him more than anyone, and admired him for his kindness, sincerity, and passion for life. But Ridley herself knew she was unpredictable, perhaps unreliable, and she would not forgive herself if she hurt Hiram. She actually believed that in some ways she even loved him, but that was something she'd never tell him. She respected him too much to string him along on false hope. Because of that, she kept her distance. But not always. He was a lovely, considerate man, and when they did get together, the chemistry was undeniable.

"I asked you before, but you avoided the question. Seriously, what'll you do when you find Vilcabamba?" Ridley again asked what was a valid question.

Kane couldn't deny it. Things would change. Once this expedition was over, and he had become the first person to locate Vilcabamba and Atahualpa's riches, he would for sure find himself in the world's spotlight. That he'd been named after Hiram Bingham certainly added an intriguing element to the story, and Ridley's question was a good one. What *would* he do? He wasn't afraid of a little publicity though he didn't crave it like other explorers did.

But what he cared about above all else was regaining some of his great-grandfather's dented reputation, and even more important than that was what would actually happen to the infamous treasure once discovered. Some scholars estimated its worth to be as much as two billion US dollars, an astonishing prediction considering no one really knew exactly what the hoard comprised.

In fairness to Kane, he wasn't at all interested in personal gain. A smidge of glory, perhaps, but he didn't want a cent of any treasure. His priority was to make sure that it ended up, whatever the treasure turned out to be, in its rightful place. Whether that be in the various museums of the Andean nations that made up Tawantinsuyu, the Quechuan name for the four quarters of the Inca empire, most notably Peru, Bolivia, Chile and Ecuador, or divided up between direct descendants of the Incas themselves. He couldn't suppress the wry grin that came when he thought of his trusted friend Sonco being handed a giant sack of gold or a cheque for more money than he could even imagine. Nothing would make Kane happier than helping some of the world's poorest people by simply giving them what was rightly theirs, and it inspired him more than anything else.

And when all that had finished perhaps he could convince Ridley to get serious.

Meanwhile, some of the others were making plans too.

The youngster Umaq Huamani was in tatters. What should he do? He knew he needed to be strong for his family and commit himself to Edgewood. He would not only be securing his family's future, but his own. However, Yupanqui scared him. But more than that, when he searched his heart he found he agreed with the man. His family were typical of most Quechuan families these days. They were spiritual by nature, and weak, and didn't limit their faith to the traditional pagan Gods, but to the Catholic Gods of the European invaders. When he dug deep into his heart he knew that they were wrong. He was Quechuan, as Yupanqui had declared, which meant he was also Incan. Where was his pride? He was suddenly awash with shame. Shame that his forefathers had

94

forgotten their traditions. Shame that their ancestors were beaten and destroyed by the so few Spanish. Shame that they had betrayed Inti and Pachamama. Yupanqui was right.

Umaq had heard whispers of an uprising. There had been incidents in the capital Lima and beyond, isolated cases of Catholic churches and monuments being vandalised, and priests and worshippers being attacked. Even the famous statue of Francisco Pizarro was destroyed, despite being moved to a less antagonising location in the city. They were sporadic and rare events, but little by little they grew in frequency. Something was definitely stirring in the capital, and more so, in the hearts of the Incan descendants.

Umaq had tried hard to find the right moment to talk to Edgewood. He'd thought long and hard about what to do, of which way to turn, but now the choice was an easy one. He was loyal to his family, of course he was. But things had changed. Umaq had seen the light. Now he would be loyal to his ancestry and serve Yupanqui. He would still be doing what it took to secure a better future for his family. But now it would be on the side of his kin, of his Incan ancestors. He would rise with the condor and he would stand with Yupanqui.

By luck or divine intervention, Howie Hooper was lucky Muddy Waters was gone. To Howie it mattered little how. That part of his mission was complete. His next target was the old man, John Haines. He'd made his plan, and he just needed to wait for the perfect moment. He had a deadline of midnight tonight to get the job done, and since it was already late afternoon, time was running out. But he was a professional. He had done this kind of thing many times. *Shit, I'm ex-military*, he thought. *Piece of cake.*

This time there would be no mistakes.

Origins

The sun shone so brightly off the sea Kane had to shield his eyes. The water itself was the most iridescent emerald green, and it mesmerised Kane as he tacked the tiny rented yacht across the wide expanses of north Vietnam's Halong Bay, his old mate Evan by his side. Other than an almost imperceptible swaying, the calm water and silence set Kane's mind drifting to his recent revelation.

In the university summer break of 1994 Hiram and Evan went backpacking in south east Asia. They wanted adventure, and in Kane's case a little soul searching. He'd worked out what he wanted from his life, but his father wasn't pleased. Hiram desired nothing more than to follow his heritage and become, for want of a better term, an explorer. His dad, who had not inherited an adventurous spirit from his own parents, thought it foolish. But Kane was determined, and half the purpose of this trip was to prove to himself–and his father–he could survive in the world alone.

Like so many backpackers, they began their adventure in Bangkok. But they soon grew tired of the raucous parties and loud, obnoxious tourists, and headed instead into the wilds of Cambodia. Kane had wanted to visit the famed temples of Angkor ever since hearing his grandfather's stories about their beauty and mystery, and he wasn't disappointed. The Kingdom of Cambodia was only just opening its borders to tourists in the aftermath of the heinous Khmer Rouge era, and Kane was awestruck.

For several days they peddled rented bicycles from one magnificent temple structure to another. Evan revelled in the unique photography opportunities while Kane spent hours lost amongst the ruins. Imagination running wild, he tried in vain to conceive of what it was like during the 12th century Khmer heyday, and marvelled at the sheer size and splendour of the main temple of Angkor Wat. Clambering among the charismatic stylised heads of The Bayon Temple he struggled to comprehend the foresight to build such enormous artefacts, and how it was even possible so many centuries earlier. It astonished Kane.

But what most struck him was the enigmatic and myste-rious temple in the walled city of Ta Prohm. He had never seen anything quite like it. As he passed through the outer walls of the complex, stepping over and around the giant fallen stones and ducking through low arches, then climbing over enormous roots of trees that paid no respect to human endeavour and had reclaimed the structure for themselves, Kane started to realise what made him tick. There he was in an ancient temple, deep in a wild jungle on the other side of the world and all alone except for one friend, a couple of other like-minded tourists, and a dozen curious macaque monkeys and who knows what other creatures.

He was in his element, and he knew then that it's what he was meant to be doing. It didn't matter what his father thought. He would follow in the footsteps of his predecessors

Patrick and Curly Kane, and would spend his in search of adventure. When just a boy Kane's grandad spent hour after hour telling him stories of his and his own father's adventures around the world, so it was in his mind as well as in his blood, and in his grandfather he saw a man who'd lived a joyful and exciting life without regrets, and who still had a sparkle in his eye to rival the shiniest of Inca gold.

Even though he was young Kane knew he'd never be motivated by wealth. It was adventure he sought, going in search of myths and legends and ancient artefacts, and though they'd of course be valuable, often even priceless, Kane wasn't interested in their monetary worth. Only the historical significance of the places and their secrets would inspire him.

In the dark and moss lined corridors of Ta Prohm's eerie central temple, Kane sat on an upturned stone that had likely lain that way for hundreds of years. There was nobody around him, and he sat in total silence. In his mind's eye, he saw his grandfather Curly, and his great-grandfather Patrick, hacking their way through the dense jungles of Peru. He knew what it was they were searching for and had heard often about their experiences. Peru. The Andes. Synonymous with adventure. Synonymous with lost treasure; Atahualpa's gold... The lost city of the Incas.

Vilcabamba.

He'd been to Peru once before, and he had to return. That was his destiny.

Hiram Kane was going to find Vilcabamba.

"Hiram." It was the second time that Evan had called to his friend. "Kane, are you with me?"

At last hearing his friend's voice, Kane snapped back from his daydream. "Sorry, I was miles away."

Just then, Craft pointed to something on the horizon, and Kane turned to look. He didn't see anything.

"There, can't you see it?" Evan asked, edging nearer his friend.

"See what? I don't…" He didn't finish his sentence. Without ceremony his oldest friend pushed him over the side, and roaring with laughter somersaulted himself into the warm waters of The Gulf of Tonkin.

Kane didn't care. In fact, he didn't have a care in the world at that moment, his wide smile stretching from ear to ear.

"What are you so happy about?" Craft asked, "what's tickled your fancy?"

"The future."

Evan didn't understand Hiram's short and cryptic reply. "Okay, clever clogs, I know you're smarter than me, but what the hell does that mean?"

"It means I've seen the future, and it looks pretty damn good." He paused for effect. "I'm going to become an explorer."

A Heavy Burden

Being in mountainous jungle seemed almost second nature to Kane, and he always felt aware of and in tune with the rugged beauty of his surroundings. He admired with awe the diversity of plant and bird life all around him, and given time he could spend hours gazing into the shadowy trees in the hopes of seeing something new.

Kane was in his element, though that was an understatement as wild as the Andean terrain itself. Nothing made him happier than an extreme trek, especially when in search of something as fabled and mysterious as Vilcabamba. At least in his mind, Kane was always planning a new trip somewhere, his thirst for adventure insatiable. Friends often teased him for his undisguised love of Indiana Jones, and while he couldn't deny the similarities, Kane would retort and say, "At least my adventures are real, and I don't wear a hat."

Fit, healthy, and with rugged determination, Kane was almost as built for the Andean habitat as the Quechuan contingent. He owned lungs that never tired and limbs that walked and climbed forever without fatigue. He was a machine, and like all machines he operated best with no outside influences.

But that's not how he felt today. His physical body felt fine, but something he couldn't see or feel was layering like a fine and darkening mist around the periphery of his mind. The verdant greens of leaves and snaking vines seemed muted, as if they too lacked vitality, and as ever, the sun beneath the jungle canopy filtered to weakness.

He forged ahead of the group, his purposeful strides leaving the others behind as he sought out space and time to consider what perturbed him. From almost the first minute Hooper's presence had occupied his thoughts, and despite witnessing the American help Muddy, and show what seemed to be genuine sadness when he'd been hurt, there had always been doubts nagging at Kane's conscience. But there was something more, now, and the thickening mists in his mind denied him clarity of thought. Were there any signs? Anything I've missed? Edgewood and Hooper seemed close, at least they spoke a lot in private. But so what? That didn't mean anything. Did it? They'd arrived together, but as they told him, they'd met only once before at the Autumn gathering in New York. Meeting again at the airport in London before the flight to Peru was mere coincidence, at least that's what they'd said.

Kane also noticed that Evan had seemed distant for a couple of days, but attributed exhaustion and altitude for Evan's jokes drying up. But now he thought about it, Evan had been spending a lot of time talking to Kate Edgewood, though that wasn't surprising, considering Craft was known as an outrageous yet terrible flirt. It was as if his usual upbeat persona had become sullied by conversations with Edgewood. Very strange, as Kane believed nothing could dampen his friend's spirit.

Figure in Muddy's accidents, too, and Kane had to admit there was a lot on his mind. But there was more, he knew it. If only the mist would clear, then maybe he could work it out. Was it the Quechuans? Were they a little more aloof than usual, less jovial? Even Sonco had seemed out of sorts, the reliable life and soul of any expedition. Maybe Kane was just feeling the strains of the jungle himself. He was past forty now, and perhaps his physical peak was behind him, though he didn't believe that and knew he was in great shape. *Damn, what the hell is it?*

Without noticing, Kane found himself a good ten minutes ahead of the others, and snagged the chance of a break. Finding a rare patch of sun against a rock face, he took a seat, enjoying the warmth on his face and a cool drink from his canteen. Thinking of his friend Sonco, perhaps there had been a little tension between him and his team of Quechuan porters. Sonco was an excellent leader who always kept his men in good spirits, commanding automatic respect because of his unrivalled experience as a guide and his affable, inclusive manner. But for the first time in what must be a dozen expeditions with Sonco, Kane realised his friend had been acting a touch strange. Why was that? Like Evan, Sonco was a fun-loving and happy-go-lucky character, yet also like Evan had appeared subdued. *Why didn't I notice this sooner?* Kane chided himself.

Sonco had recruited a new cook for this expedition, the big fellow they called Yupanqui. Kane had never met him before but, as always, he trusted Sonco's choice. Yupanqui had proven himself an excellent addition to the team, and his meals had gone down well with the group. Sure, he was a little distant, and rarely spoke to the foreigners, but being a friend wasn't in his job description. Now though, as Kane pictured the cook, he had seen a glaring, steely look in his hard eyes.

When Sonco had first introduced Yupanqui, Kane put him in his early twenties, his bulk down to good appetite and his strength that typical of a native farmer. Now Kane knew beneath that exterior lived a serious man, who chose his words with care and whose attitude was that of someone on a mission. Kane hadn't witnessed him undermine Sonco at any point, but the more Kane thought about it, Sonco did appear to shrink a little in his presence, as if the roles were reversed, and Yupanqui was team leader and Sonco the subservient porter.

Kane couldn't understand it. Sonco was the bravest man he'd ever met, and they had been through a lot together. For over twenty years Sonco had been a close and trusted friend of the Kane family, and Hiram had never known anything other than an open, honest and genuine man.

Kane was worried. Sonco's rare change in demeanour meant something was wrong, filling Kane with a sense of foreboding. But Sonco was a proud Quechuan man, and if asked, Kane knew he'd dismiss his fears with a smile.

But something nefarious was going on that Kane couldn't fathom, something festering in the atmosphere that felt bigger than him, bigger than the expedition to find Vilcabamba. Something sinister. He just didn't know what. That comment from his grandfather surfaced once more, slow at first, like a winter sun over distant hills, but as the mists cleared, the sun brightened to illuminate the meaning of those words, and a sudden icy fist clenched hold of Kane's heart.

The words seemed so simple: 'a heavy burden,' and yet nothing back then had suggested their enormity. But now it was closing in around him, Kane saw how prophetic they were. He knew now that it was major, much more important than himself, and that somehow he held in his hands the power to prevent some catastrophe, some act of unimaginable terror, and it was all linked to Vilcabamba. It was all about the lost city, and the hidden Inca treasure unseen for almost half a millennium.

It was a race against time, Kane now knew, and one that if he didn't win, would see the world as he knew it changed for all eternity.

The Eagle Alliance

Angelo De La Cruz was a shy eighteen-year-old when he first met thirteen-year-old Ferdinand Benedix. It was 1982, and the boys formed part of a large group of youths on their first missionary trip. There were other places they could have gone, such as Madagascar or the Philippines, but both had chosen to save souls in the rainforests ofsouth-eastern Peru. And, of course, to spread the word of God.

Ferdinand inspired Angelo, and the reason Angelo was so taken by Ferdinand was an incident he'd witnessed. During an interaction with the native kids, Ferdinand, who towered over the indigenous Quechuan boy he was proselytising to, suddenly got angry. He punched the boy in the stomach, and when his knees buckled, kicked him in the head with his hiking boots. It was a vicious assault and shocking to witness. There were no adults anywhere nearby.

"Why did you do that, Ferdinand?" one of the missionary kids called out to him. "What's wrong?"

The young Ferdinand stood calm and collected as he replied. "This heathen doesn't believe in God, and refuses to convert." He paused, and shouted to anyone that was listening, "He needs to be punished." Without so much as a look back,

106

Ferdinand walked away towards camp.

Angelo De La Cruz, timid around people, had stood unseen nearby. He'd watched the assault with unmoved intent, and watched still as Ferdinand strode off as if nothing special had happened. Something stirred within him, some previously unknown passion for their cause. As missionaries, they were there to share the truth of the one true God to these jungle people. If the natives didn't convert, they were supposed to persevere, encouraging them to choose their God rather than indulge in pagan worship of the sun and the mountains and the surrounding jungle. But those were the adult rules, and they didn't always work.

Angelo knew who his mighty and noble ancestors were, which meant he knew he had the blood of genuine conquistadors flowing through his veins. That knowledge, combined with the passion he'd just witnessed in Ferdinand, instilled in him a new found righteousness, a new sense of power over these backwards, uneducated heathens who still lived in huts and wallowed happily in their degrading poverty and torn clothes. He began to despise them, abhorred their lack of shame in such dirty and hopeless environs, and as he stood there, looking down now at the poor unknowing disgrace of a human slouched in the dirt, he felt something else; Angelo felt hate.

He looked around. All the other young missionaries had left. It was just him and the kid on the floor. The power within grew, his passions rising, and before he knew it Angelo had launched his boot into the face of the fallen boy. Blood erupted from a broken nose, and that power Angelo experienced grew until he felt invincible. He was eighteen, a young man, but in that moment he became a man for the first time. He thought of his name: Angelo De La Cruz. *Angel, or Messenger of the Cross*. He was a man with a purpose in life.

From that moment, Angelo was a soldier of God.

After a few more similar incidents word spread throughout the missionary camp that there were a couple of rogues among them, and very soon the two boys got hauled before their superiors. It didn't take long before they'd been sent home to their countries in disgrace, with a warning that unless they changed their ways, they would be excommunicated from the Catholic Church.

Despite the age gap, Ferdinand and Angelo became acquaintances from that day on, as each continued to develop fundamentalist views. Together they formed what at first was nothing more than a club for passionate young Catholics, each with their own branch in their respective countries; Ferdinand in his homeland of Holland, and Angelo in the heartland of the conquistadors, Trujillo, in western Spain. As the years passed they grew more zealous in their beliefs. On occasion they met in person to organise what was now becoming a more militant faction. But with the advent of the internet in the late 90s, their communications became easier, and the two comrades soon put together a scheme which would define their very lives.

Through research, and their knowledge of history in the Inca heartland, they learned of a growing dissidence among the new generation of Peruvians. This new generation saw what was a distancing of their people from mainstream politics in Peru, and tension was rising. Over the last several years an underground group had performed some minor terrorist activities that struck out at the Catholics in Lima, their most notable act the destruction of a statue of the most notorious of all conquistadors, Francisco Pizarro.

Something had to be done, and led by Ferdinand and Angelo, The Eagle Alliance was born.

Having named their group, they knew that the responsibility for change was now theirs. The Eagle Alliance would crush the Inca insurgents, known now as the Condor Uprising, and not only that, but they would wage war on all the indigenous people of Peru who would not convert to Catholicism.

It would be bloody and brutal.

And it would be magnificent.

Yupanqui

His duties finished for the night, Yupanqui took his fireside seat with Sonco and the porters. They were quiet men by nature, calm and peaceful people at home in the mountains. They chatted together and enjoyed the usual banter among men, meanwhile tuning themselves to the soul and sounds of the surrounding wilderness, drawing comfort from and revelling in their beautiful landscape. The mountains belonged to these people, and these people belonged in the mountains.

Yupanqui watched them, appraising them, looking deep into their hearts and into their minds. They spoke Quechuan like him, and in one way or another they were all descended from the Incas. More than five hundred years ago the Incans assimilated almost all the Andean tribes under one banner, the Inca Empire, and Quechuan became their adopted language. Today, all remaining indigenous Indians in the Andes are labelled Quechuan, an easy blanket term for modern anthropologists and historians.

But in genetic truth, the purest of all Incan descendants are the Q'ero, an ancient tribe of just six hundred people that escaped the conquistadors by hiding out high in the mountains, remaining untouched by the outside world until the middle of the last century. Yupanqui Atoc was Q'ero.

When the Spanish conquistadors destroyed the Inca Empire

in the early sixteenth century, the event was known as a Pachacuti, a great change. Pachacuti was the son of Viracocha, a legendary Inca King named after their creator God, and the name Pachacuti became synonymous with times of upheaval. Since then, the Q'ero elders have preserved the knowledge of a sacred prophecy, that a second Pachacuti would come, the world would be turned the right way up, harmony restored, and chaos and disorder among their people ended.

Their prophecies are positive, a coming together of nations and peace between both the indigenous tribes and their Gods, and better relationships between the natives and what they saw as their conquerors. To the Q'ero, the prophecy also refers to an end of time as they know it, the death of a way of thinking. But Yupanqui knows better than that, and would never trust the ramblings of withered old men, so isolated in their mountain hideouts.

The Q'ero have been waiting half a millennium for the revered condor of the south to fly with an eagle from the north, a sacred union that would spell the beginning of a golden age for their people, and a thousand years of peace. That's not how Yupanqui interpreted the prophecy. Why wait for the eagle of the north to venture south, when he knows that eagle to be the might of the USA, and their arrogant belief they should rule the world with their Christianity based government? Whether the president was Catholic or Christian mattered little to Yupanqui, for they were all false Gods.

But Yupanqui was tired of waiting, tired of seeing so many of the indigenous people living in poverty and squalor while the Catholics, and now the half-breed mestizo Catholics, live comfortable lives and occupy the ruling seats of Peruvian government. The time is right for change, and Yupanqui believes the Q'ero prophecy has chosen him.

In recent decades, since Yupanqui was just a boy, signs that the prophecied great change was coming were evident: the high mountain lagoons across the Andes dried up to little more than ponds, and the once widespread and mighty condor now flies on the verge of extinction. After the earthquake in 1949, the Golden Temple in Cuzco was discovered, a clear sign to him that the wrath of the Sun God Inti had been wrought.

Recent events in Lima and Cuzco proved to him that the next Pachacuti had already begun, and with it, the promise of a new Inca sovereign after the current period of turmoil. Yupanqui was firm in his belief. Not only was the Pachacuti upon his people, but he was its epicentre, its guiding force. Its leader. Now he would educate his Incan brothers.

But would they be with him? They should be. If not, they too would die at his hands.

Yupanqui stood. It was time to reveal his true identity, and declare to the men around him the Inca were rising, and that an enemy was in their midst. Yupanqui was a big, powerful man, and as the glow of the fire danced upon his tough face and massive chest, he cut an imposing figure.

"My brothers," he began, "We are all the same, you and I, each of us carrying within our bodies the sacred blood of the Inca, and in our minds, the sacred spirit of our ancestors." Yupanqui paused, waiting to see if he had their attention. He did. Only Sonco Amaru seemed less aroused by his opening lines. *That's okay,* he thought, *soon I will have him.*

He continued. "But being Incan carries with it a great responsibility, a weighty burden, and the time has finally

112

come to unload that burden." He stalled for effect, just a few seconds. And then... "The Pachacuti is upon us." He stopped, looking ahead but watching Sonco from the corner of his eye. As he knew he would, Sonco had sat up and now listened with intent. "Yes, my brothers, the time of the new great change is here. In fact, it has already started.

"The prophecy of my kin, the Q'ero, states that the condor will one day rise and fly with the eagle of the north. But I say to you, that eagle is a dangerous prey, and will not come in peace. It will come in two forms, an eagle that wears the military insignia of the United States upon one wing, and the cross of the barbaric Catholics upon the other. The first threat is imminent, so listen with care: the Catholics are here, and they are here to destroy us again. That is not in question.

"The real question is, my friends and brothers, are you ready to join the fight against them?"

Amongst the seated men eyebrows raised in surprise. The youngest of them, Umaq and another boy, had already been confronted by Yupanqui, but they hadn't expected this. A threat already upon us? It was far more serious than they first believed. But Yupanqui was an impressive speaker, and they didn't doubt the truth of his words.

Sonco Amaru, however, was not convinced. He stood, matching Yupanqui's glare. "What evidence do you have about these claims, other than an ancient prophecy no one believes anymore? Except... except your Q'ero elders?" He said the word Q'ero almost as a dismissal. The Q'ero were a mysterious people, and though true they were the closest living descendants of the Inca, there were so few left that no one paid them any attention.

Yupanqui was expecting resistance from the oldest

Quechuan among them, and he'd prepared. He needed patience, but just a little, for the time for action was upon them. He was done waiting, and according to the prophecy, one that he believed with every atom of his being, Yupanqui the chosen one had been waiting five hundred years.

"I know that not everyone believes in the ancient prophecies the way we Q'ero do," he said. "I understand that. My people held tight to their beliefs that a new Pachacuti would come. I know it isn't a widely believed legend, but that's the problem. For hundreds of years, Inca blood weakened after assimilation of the Europeans, diluted so much that the vast majority of descendants are linked by nothing more than a textbook.

"Most Incan descendants have long forgotten our proud history and do not understand who we were and where we came from. It is up to me, the chosen Pachacuti, the living proof of the ancient prophecy who will begin our new dawn, a new and glorious era. It is from among the living stones of Vilcabamba that I will begin our rebirth, and from where the mighty condor will once more spread its wings and cast a shadow over the cathedrals of the false god as they burn to the ground.

"The history and traditions that made us who we once were are all but gone, and like our beloved and sacred condor, a belief in the old ways is on the edge of extinction. There is little pride among our indigenous people anymore, except for a few brave warriors, and if we do not act now then we will lose the Inca bloodline forever. Everything that our ancestors fought so bravely to defend five centuries ago against the Spanish invaders will be for nothing, lost to history, and dead for all time.

"But you, and I mean you sitting around this fire, your

brothers and sisters, your friends and relatives… we all have a chance to act. Yet it is not a choice. We face annihilation once more if we wait, for the adversary we face is strong. We need to rise up and arm ourselves for the battle to come. But like I said, the first of the gringo enemy is already close."

Yupanqui flicked his head toward the expedition camp with undisguised hatred, and the eyes that watched him from around the flickering fire widened even further.

"You all know why we are out here, so far from our warm beds, carrying heavy loads as if we're nothing more than animals to the lazy tourists. Do you not? Of course you do. But do you realise that by helping them in this way, almost as slaves like our conquered forefathers, we are actually helping them to steal what is ours.

"Do you think that when they find our revered ancestor Atahualpa's lost treasure, that its rightful owners will ever receive any of it? They won't. They will steal it, just like they stole everything from us before. They stole our treasure, they stole our land, they subjugated us as slaves, and crushed the empire through their disgusting diseases and immoral ways of living. They know we are rising up, but we can stop them. And not only can we, but we must. It is our duty, our moral obligation to our people and our heritage.

"But there is more. Five hundred years ago it was prophecied that the age of the new Pachacuti would arrive, and with it a new era of peace and prosperity for our people. How many of you want to remain as you are in life, living in crumbling homes, deep in poverty, lacking education and carrying the load of wealthy thieves for a pitiful living?"

There was an excited grumbling of ascent from the group surrounding Yupanqui, and he didn't fail to notice the nodding head of Sonco Amaru. He was getting through, evidence and justification that he was their rightful leader.

"But we have no wealth or means with which to rise," suggested Sonco. "How will we arm ourselves, as you say?"

It was an obvious question, but the answer was simple. Yupanqui nodded with confidence.

"The answer to that, my wise friend, is easy. We let these ignorant foreigners, led by the man they call Kane and his alleged map, lead us to the treasure. When they find it, we will take what is rightly ours."

"But how will we take it? By fighting?" asked one of the younger men.

"My young friend," replied Yupanqui, his eyes wide with burning passion. "We will kill the Catholics. Our voices will be heard again, and this time…" He paused, and looked up to the dark skies.

"This time, all the world will hear."

Soldier of God

T he last of the day's sun filtered away to nothing, and darkness fell over camp. A general feeling of exhaustion settled over the group after a long day of many uphill miles, and most had eaten a quick dinner and retired to their tents. It was the opportunity Angelo De La Cruz had been waiting for. He motioned to Edgewood and Hooper to follow him to the far end of the camp, and they duly obliged. In his calm but strong voice, with perfect English and the merest trace of a Spanish accent, he addressed the two of them.

"Let me take a moment to remind you why you're here. You may think it's because your... friend... Ferdinand Benedix, encouraged you to join our mission. That's only half correct. You're here because I wanted you here. But then again, even that is only a half-truth. God is my master, and I answer only to him, and when it became clear we'd need a dedicated team to once more conquer those uneducated heathens, then that is what I've put together.

"You are Catholics. Which means you have a duty to your God to act upon his will. His will demands your action when needed, and He needs it now. There is an uprising of a people that are the very antithesis of our beliefs, an antithesis of what is true. The Incas, nothing more than pagan peasants, have some notion of importance, and the soft utterance of some long forgotten fairy tale has given a few of their number a belief that they should rise against us. They are poor villagers, little more than a nation of discarded slaves. Yet, it is true they once held great power in these lands, and along with that power they had unimaginable wealth. Our forefathers, the conquistadors, took only a matter of days and weeks to bring that empire to its knees, and plundered that wealth and took it home to Spain to serve a more worthy master. But some of that wealth eluded us and now eludes even the heathens that buried it somewhere in this God forsaken jungle in these Godless mountains. They want to rise up, though there is no chance of their success. However, if the lost treasure did somehow find its way into the hands of the heathens again, then the Catholic church would face an unprecedented threat. It has fallen upon me to stop that. And I must stop it at any cost.

"Together with the two of you, we have the necessary skills to accomplish our mission, and we will succeed. But, I need to be sure—are you prepared to do whatever is necessary for that success? I have to know. God demands to know."

He stared at Edgewood, saw a coldness in her eyes, and had no doubt she was capable of anything. She nodded, and held his gaze without emotion. His partner Ferdinand Benedix believed in her, and he believed in her too.

Looking at Hooper, he wasn't so sure. Yes, he was a devout Catholic, but he was also a mercenary, and might be swayed from their holy mission by the lure of riches. De La Cruz was sure that, given half a chance, Hooper would sell his soul to the highest bidder.

"I'm ready," said Hooper. "Haven't I already showed my

willing?"

"You have showed you would try, yes." There was a trace of sarcasm in the Spaniard's voice.

"I won't fail again." Hooper meant it, angry there was any doubt.

"I know you will not. God knows you will not." For now he would trust the American, but if needed, De La Cruz would sacrifice Hooper himself.

What Angelo couldn't know at that moment, despite what he believed was God-given knowledge, was that Kate Edgewood had her own agenda, and working together as part of this team until its mission had concluded wasn't part of it. The sacrifice part was true.

But that Angelo himself was in line to be part of it was something God had elected not to tell him.

VII

Day 7

Murderous Intent

John Haines was having a fabulous time. Despite his age, the professor was as healthy as anyone on the expedition, but even he seemed surprised with his endless supply of energy. He didn't want to waste the moment.

Many of the others were still in their tents, some sleeping, others relishing the slow start to the day. However, John felt compelled to explore, and ventured off a little way by himself on a narrow trail that wound in and out of some unusual rock formations. He had with him his notebook and a pencil, and the old professor was ever ready to take down some obscure note or observation he could share with his beloved grandchildren once home.

He strolled at an easy pace, basking in the quiet and solitude among the rocks that were, in some cases, as large as houses. The wind from the valley couldn't penetrate the natural fortress, and the birds had fallen silent after their animated dawn chorus. He took a seat on a rather comfy rock, enjoying its natural incline and revelling in the peaceful surroundings. Closing his eyes, John tried to put all the previous drama out of his mind, and instead imagined what Vilcabamba might look like.

Professor Haines had a reputation among his students for falling asleep at will, even in the middle of a student's important presentation, though he always amazed them when it was finished, making points and observations as if he'd heard every word.

He was just dropping off then when the strangest of faint noises drifted his way from further along the small gorge. It sounded like a woman's voice, which surprised him because nobody else was around. He listened, more intent now, and this time heard the unmistakable sound of a man's voice, followed by the woman's again. It was his student Kate Edgewood and the Spanish Professor De La Cruz, and knowing it was them, and though it was a little odd, he relaxed back into his snooze. But then he heard a third voice and knew it was Howie Hooper.

He wasn't sure why, but his instincts niggled him. Why were they speaking together, and so far away from the camp? Like Kane, Haines had never been that comfortable with the American, a man who'd been aloof the entire time. He had shown compassion when A. J. Waters was forced to return to Cuzco, but aside from that he seemed to have no other redeeming features. In simple terms, nobody seemed to like him.

From where John was sitting he felt sure the group couldn't see him. His interest piqued he continued to listen. The voices came to him louder now, as if more animated. It sounded as if there was some anger among them, maybe resentment, and his mild curiosity grew to suspicious scrutiny. *What on earth could that unlikely trio be arguing about?*

Haines strained his ears, and what he heard next shocked John to his core. It was the voice of Howie Hooper, and this is what he said. "I *will* take care of it. He'll be dead by morning."

Dead! Who would be dead? Professor Haines was a calm

man by nature, but in that moment his instincts screamed at him that things were about to go very, very bad. He had to get back to tell Kane what he'd heard, and was about to dash back to camp when he saw a flash of colour, and he knew that the conspirators were coming his way. If they saw him, they would guess John had heard them and he would find himself in mortal danger. With no time to make it out of the gorge before they did, and knowing they were imminent, the old professor threw himself into a crevice between two large rocks, and holding his breath, he hoped beyond hope they'd miss him as they passed.

Their conversation over, the three colluding people made their way along the narrow gorge. John didn't dare risk a look, and lay as still and silent as possible. Only one person was on his mind: Kate Edgewood. He just could not bring himself to believe she would get involved in anything so heinous as murder. But his ears hadn't deceived him. It was her, and there had been talk of killing. *What has happened to her? Has she been corrupted by the lure of treasure?* John had no idea yet that it was De La Cruz orchestrating things, and that their mission was in the name of Catholicism. His best guess was that the three of them were using Kane to locate Vilcabamba and claim the treasure and the glory for themselves. It was a terrible notion, and John was disgusted with them all. Especially his own student Kate. He could not know, but the truth was many times worse than he imagined.

But what he knew was this: sometime before tomorrow's dawn one of their contingent would be murdered. He had to tell Kane, and quick. The old professor didn't know where to begin. What he had to tell Kane was both shocking and unbelievable. Despite his ongoing reservations about Hooper,

Kane was known as a pragmatic man, a realist, and tried only to see the good in the world and the very best in people. To learn some gang of criminals might be using him and his skills for a heinous cause would be heartbreaking.

However, a life was at stake, maybe more, and Hiram had to know. John knew he had to approach Hiram in such a way so as not to arouse suspicions among the three criminals. On top of that, he could not risk creating a situation where Kane would confront the group in a rage. There was no time to waste, and it would be difficult. It had to be now, and now was not the time for mistakes.

Walking back into camp, he soon saw Kane sitting by the fire, sipping pensively at a cup of tea. He was alone. Good. "Hiram, how do you feel this morning? It was a tough day yesterday." Haines oozed calm. It was an act.

"Morning. Tell you the truth, I feel out of sorts. Didn't sleep well. Something's niggling me, but I can't put my finger on what. Middle age, I suspect," and he grinned. "How about you? How are those joints of yours holding out?" The pair enjoyed their ageist banter.

"You know," John replied, "same as always, plenty of life in this old frame yet." John smiled momentarily, but then his face hardened. "We need to talk. Now. Follow me."

Hiram couldn't ignore the rare seriousness in the professor's face. Something was up, and he followed John without a word. Clear of the camp, Haines turned to face a worried Hiram.

"Hiram, what I'm about to tell you will be difficult to understand, but I need you to promise me you won't react. We need to be careful." John said it with such quiet authority it snared Kane's full attention.

126

Hiram nodded. "Go on."

"Your map is the only known map to Vilcabamba in the world. Few people even know it exists. Whether it's accurate only time will tell, but as you can probably guess there are people out there who'd do anything to have it. But even if someone else had the map, chances are high they wouldn't possess the skills to use it. So, what I'm…"

"What are you getting at, John?" Kane cut in.

John Haines paused. He had to select his words with care.

"I think there are people on this expedition with nefarious motives. I can't be one hundred percent certain, but I think they plan to use you to get to Vilcabamba, and take the treasure by force." The professor watched Hiram's reaction, waiting for shock to appear. But Kane sat there stony faced, almost as if he had considered this already.

"Go on, John," he said again.

"I overheard a conversation between Kate, Howie and the Spaniard, Angelo. They were beyond the camp, I guess for secrecy, and Howie said… well, said 'he'll be dead by morning.'" John held Hiram's gaze to let him know he was serious. "I guess their plan is to kill you and use the map themselves."

Kane stared back into the pale blue eyes of his friend and knew he'd spoken with honesty. He believed John, and what John had heard made sense. Kane did have the only map, and he knew there were criminals around who'd do whatever it took to get their hands on the treasure. But now? On this expedition? And right then, everything he had thought about Howie Hooper came roaring into focus.

Without another word, Kane strode with ominous intent towards camp.

127

Haines was an old man. He was fit, no question, but he was closing in on seventy and speed was a distant memory. He couldn't know what Kane had in mind, but one look in Hiram's eyes and John knew it wouldn't be good.

He had to stop him before he got to camp, and the way he moved after the much younger man belied his age. He tore after Kane as if his life, and the lives of the others nearby, depended on it. For all John Haines knew, they did. He didn't want to shout and raise any suspicions among the criminals, so with his last ounce of energy and with his aged knees protesting, John was at last close enough to grab Hiram by the shirt and stop him in his tracks. The way he next gripped onto Kane's arms, his strength a surprise to them both, meant he was serious. But Kane's rage was bursting for an outlet, and he shook free of the old man's grip.

"Get off…"

"Wait, Hiram. You must wait."

Kane stood still, muscles taut and breathing hard. He stared over John's sagging shoulders, trying to see into the camp beyond. There was murder in his eyes.

"Listen. I don't know exactly what's happening," cautioned Haines. "But I do know this. There're some sinister characters down there, and they're probably armed. We must act with caution."

When Kane was younger, in the aftermath of his brother Danny going missing, he got into too many fights. He wasn't violent by nature, but that event had unleashed in him a fury not seen before. He wouldn't exactly look for trouble, but at the slightest provocation, whether intended or not, Hiram would take out his sadness and guilt on anyone who crossed him. And right now, that dormant rage was about to explode in the direction of Hooper, whether armed or not. But John placed his hands once more on Kane's forearms, pleading for a moment of calm.

"Hiram, we have to make a plan. Who knows how organised this gang is. They may be carrying guns for all we know. Rushing in there now to confront them is dangerous, both for you and for the others. Think of Evan. Think of Alex."

Kane took some deep breaths, and despite his rage he knew John was right. He clenched and unclenched his fists, furling them in and out of tight balls, the skin on his knuckles strained white. But after a few moments, Kane nodded.

John spoke next, and it was decisive. "The next decisions we make will be the most important of our lives."

He couldn't know how prophetic his words would be.

True Colours

The majority of the camp awoke late, and since sunlight arrives slowly between the peaks and cols of the Andes, it was a chilly start. The porters had the campfire roused and all the expedition members except Kane and Haines had huddled close.

Holding centre stage, and oblivious to the nefarious plans scheming around her, Alexandria Ridley shared a story about Kane. The audience sat in rapt attention, and even Yupanqui the cook listened in.

"He was like a kid with a new bike," she said, her affection for Kane clear. "The map was meant to remain secret, but he just had to tell someone, and he trusted me. You're here, so of course you already know." The fire illuminated Ridley's pretty face, and her own excitement was palpable. She went on. "Hiram always felt it was his destiny to find Vilcabamba, and as you know his family has a long and interesting connection to the mystery. But–" Ridley paused, careful with her words. "But he always worried somebody else would unravel the secret first, and not because he wants glory for himself. You all know that. Hiram is the most conscientious person I've ever met, and he cares for the Peruvians and feels great kinship among them. The main reason he's so keen to locate Vilcabamba first is to safeguard whatever treasures he finds for its legitimate heirs. Considering the estimated value of Atahualpa's hoard, that's a lot of pressure."

"What is it worth?" The sharpness with which Edgewood blurted her question surprised them all, including herself, and she scrambled to hide the greed from her voice. "What I mean is, it's one of the greatest unsolved mysteries of the last century." She looked around at the others, and in a quieter voice, said, "Aren't you all curious?" They all were.

"Well, the world's experts all have opinions about the treasure's current market value." Ridley looked about with mock concern in case Hiram was listening, before saying, with a conspiratorial wink, "The purist Hiram would never divulge such things, but in his absence, I'll say that recent estimates–figures he actually agrees with–value the lost Inca gold at over two billion dollars." Edgewood gasped aloud, but the others sat in astonished silence, lost in their thoughts about such a staggering sum of money. Only Yupanqui stirred, and with a strange expression on his face, walked away from the fire.

As they sat there, each thinking about Kane and the map and what it meant for them as individuals, their inner thoughts could not have been more diverse. Evan was just excited he was involved, but moreover, he was pleased for his friend, who would finally locate what'd driven him all these years. As designated photographer, he'd get to share in the moment, and if this was work, Craft thought, then this is as good as it gets. I might even get a tiny slice of the pie, he mused with a bashful smile.

Hooper was on a holy mission, in that stinking jungle doing the work of God. And yet... all that money. I could take just a little and disappear forever. So tempting. Hooper wasn't the most devout of Catholics but had sufficient faith to dismiss the idea rather than face the wrath of God. And if not God, he didn't want to face the wrath of Angelo De La Cruz, either. The man scared him with his intense fundamentalist beliefs, and if he crossed him, Hooper knew his fate would be worse than if he'd sinned before God.

Kate Edgewood had heard those estimates before, though she thought them fanciful and exaggerated. But now the same wild figures came almost literally from the horse's mouth. It was Ridley who'd told them, but she said Kane agreed, and the Kane family were considered experts on the subject. Edgewood also knew that the map allegedly came from Hiram Bingham himself.

Before the expedition, Edgewood believed that without the map Kane had no more chance of discovering Vilcabamba than anyone before him, just another tainted yet whimsical explorer. But now she'd met him and seen his skill and passion first hand, she wasn't so sure. The map alone would be useless without his abilities. But with the map in Kane's hands, you not only had the world's only known map to Vilcabamba, but the world's most equipped person to use it. It had to mean success.

What Edgewood now knew, Angelo de La Cruz had always known. As was his habit, he sat adrift from the group, and what might have appeared as rude aloofness was instead a calculated tactic to remain outside the collective and analyse everyone with discretion. He wasn't only keeping an eye on Ridley and Craft, and the old man Haines, whom he didn't trust at all, but also Ferdinand's choice of accomplices. Edgewood had let herself down earlier, and now everyone knew how much she craved the gold. Nevertheless, he trusted her.

Hooper was another matter. He was Catholic, but that wasn't enough to be a loyal servant of God and not just one of the flock. You had to carry out orders, one of which he'd already failed, and have the courage to put yourself on the line. If required, you would sacrifice yourself for the greater good. De La Cruz was capable, and had almost died several times serving his Master. Despite her selfish desires, the Spaniard believed Kate was also capable. But Hooper worried him, and he had a distinct notion that one way or another the American wouldn't be leaving those godforsaken mountains alive.

That was okay. If his death was necessary to complete the mission, so be it, even if it was at the professor's own hands.

"He'll be dead by morning," said John. "That's what Hooper said. He must mean you, Hiram."

Kane and Haines were trying to figure out a plan. With the map, Kane was the obvious target of the group, but it still made little sense. Without Kane, they'd have no chance of success.

"Let's think about them for a minute," continued John. "It's an un unlikely trio, isn't it? A Spanish professor, an English student, and an American writer? What's the link, and how did they come together? What do they have in common, other than criminal intent?" It was a good question with no obvious answer.

Kane thought hard but was so angry that clear thought eluded him. "I don't know John, I only know I want to strangle Hooper and throw him off a cliff."

With a look into Kane's eyes, John knew he'd do it. "Look, we need to work out their plan and stop them before anyone gets hurt. What's the common factor between them?"

They didn't speak for many minutes. Unseen birds chirped, and the swaying of jungle trees broke the silence as a thought materialised in John's mind. He didn't like it. "They're all Catholics."

"Catholics? So what?" Kane didn't get it.

"They are all Catholics. Now I think about it, I've seen them all make the sign of the cross on multiple occasions." Haines nodded as he spoke, as if it made perfect sense.

"But what does that mean? So what if they're Catholics, doesn't make them criminals."

But as the moments passed, John became more and more sure of himself. "Have you ever heard of the Eagle Alliance?"

Kane hadn't.

"The Eagle Alliance is a little known Catholic group based in Europe. Nobody knows who leads it, but it's believed they're responsible for several low-level terrorist acts across the continent. They've never claimed responsibility, but the rumours won't go away. I wonder if…"

"Are you suggesting they're Catholic terrorists? Those clowns? You're joking, right?" said a bemused Kane, but John wasn't smiling.

"Think about it, and bear with me. Take Angelo, a professor with Spanish heritage. A Catholic. Probably the leader. And I agree it sounds far fetched, but Kate's a determined woman with financial influence. Also Catholic. And Howie Hooper. Strong, dedicated and Catholic. Those factors alone mean nothing, and doesn't explain why they want the gold. Unless…"

Kane couldn't believe it, and if he wasn't so angry it would've seemed comical. To learn there was even such a thing as Catholic terrorists, let alone on his expedition, was beyond his imagination, but when he looked at his friend he saw a man with total faith in his convictions. He'd never seen John more sincere.

"Hiram, listen to me. In recent years there's been a swell of national pride among the native Peruvians, leading to attacks on churches, like we saw in Cuzco. Plus, numerous incidents of vandalism against conquistador monuments, including Pizarro's statue in Lima. What if… What if the Eagle Alliance, who aren't directly affiliated with mainstream Catholicism, are after Atahualpa's treasure, and plan to use that wealth to crush the Inca Uprising? It makes some sense. With your map, they'll find Vilcabamba, and who knows what contacts they have in Peru to trade the gold for weapons? With international terrorism these days, anything's possible, especially if theories about the treasure's worth are true."

If anyone other than his former Professor John Haines had said those words it would have sounded to Kane like some ridiculous conspiracy theory. But he trusted and respected John unconditionally and knew he wasn't one for fairy tales.

"Let's just assume you're right for a minute. What do you think they'll do? They can't just shoot me. They'd never find Vilcabamba, even with the map. They need me and Sonco to lead them." An unnerving thought then struck him. "What about if it's not me they mean to kill. What if it's… what if it's you, or Evan? They know I'd do anything to protect you both."

"You mean, they kill one of us and threaten the others so they can control you?" John nodded, considering Kane's words. "Actually, that makes sense. They know you'd never put anyone at risk, and if they threatened us they know you'd help them find what they want." John fell silent for a long moment, ruminating all they'd discussed before his eyes narrowed with intent.

"Listen, Hiram, and listen well. We must *never* allow the treasure to fall into terrorist hands. Never. Let's assume we're right. It seems very likely, given the knowledge we have. We have to take responsibility to stop them. First, no one gets hurt. And then we have a choice. We can subdue the criminals. I'm not sure how, but they are only three, and including Sonco's men we're ten. That's asking a lot of the others, I know. But the other choice, and it breaks my heart to say, we... we never find Vilcabamba."

The suggestion hit Kane like a punch to the sternum. For so long he'd dreamed of laying his eyes on the lost city, perhaps the first person to do so in almost five hundred years, at least the first foreigner. But something in the sadness in John's eyes and the slump of his shoulders let Kane know he was serious, and he had to consider what the wisened professor had said.

That was the thing about history. Sometimes it was best left alone.

How many people had died searching for legendary arte-facts such as the Holy Grail or the crown jewels of King John, and how much blood had already been spilled in the search for Vilcabamba and Atahualpa's gold? Too much. Perhaps Haines was right? Perhaps the lost city should never be found.

Kane was no fool. He knew that with his map and unique skills, combined with his own experiences and vast knowl-edge of the area, he was more likely than most to find the lost city. So, if Vilcabamba wasn't located on this expedition, it would probably remain hidden for years, maybe decades more. His thoughts turned to Sonco and his family, and all impoverished Quechuan families throughout not just Peru, but the other former Incan nations, like Ecuador to the north and Bolivia to the east. They were some of the world's poorest people, and the discovery of their lost gold, if used well, would go a long, long way to ease their poverty for many years to come.

Kane now accepted the odious idea that a killer might be among them and chastised himself for not acting on his instincts about Hooper. But now they were near certain about what was happening, they had to act. What should they do? What could they do? They weren't armed, they did not understand who they were dealing with, and they didn't want to involve the innocent people with them. There was no easy answer.

At least they had one thing in their favour; the Catholics didn't know they knew. That's what they believed, anyway, and if true it bought them some time. But killers obviously didn't abide by common sense, so they assumed time was short. Kane and John as yet didn't know which of the men the Catholics targeted. It was either one of them or Evan, and letting Evan know could cause panic. But that was the dilemma they now faced and if these people were capable of killing one person, then why wouldn't they kill others if necessary? Of course, they would, and Kane's mind turned to Ridley. Their bond was strong, and in his deepest of hearts, he knew there existed unspoken love between them. He had to make sure that not only Ridley, but Evan, Haines, Sonco and all his team were safe from what Kane now believed were

Catholic terrorists.

Falling Apart

It was all just so crazy. This was supposed to be an exciting and momentous expedition, those involved making history, and present when one of the world's greatest and most endearing mysteries might at last get solved. Yet, and Kane just couldn't understand how it had happened, everything was going wrong. Not only was their expedition in danger, but the lives of some of the people he cared most about in the world were threatened. Kane didn't see any alternative than to speak to Sonco and his most trusted men, then confront and overpower the terrorists.

Kane knew they could overpower Hooper, De La Cruz, and Edgewood if they weren't armed, and he'd seen no sign of any weapons. Of course, if they'd concealed guns in their backpacks he wouldn't know it. Confronting them was risky. Although one middle-aged professor, a skinny writer, and an outwardly frail female academic hardly inspired fear, for all Kane and Haines knew they could be trained fighters.

They deliberated for a while before a frustrated silence settled over them. There seemed no obvious course of action, and the situation was so out of their usual comfort zones that both men were at a loss. And the clock was ticking.

Kane's grandfather's three simple words drifted into his mind, and for the first time he really appreciated their meaning. *A heavy burden. So this is it,* thought Kane, *this is my burden.* But he also remembered the other words his grandfather said as he handed over the map all those years ago. *It couldn't be in better hands.* That's what he'd said, and Hiram had always doubted it. *Am I really that special, that trustworthy?* But now was his chance to prove it, both to his grandfather, and more importantly, to himself.

A plan formulated, and as Kane thought it over, and as the components aligned, he knew it was their only realistic option. It wasn't a great plan, but if they pulled it off it would bring a satisfactory end to the mounting drama. Satisfactory, that was, except to the terrorists.

But for Kane's plan to work, an age-old friendship would be tested to its limits.

Sonco Amaru was on edge, an honourable man torn between two honourable choices. Yupanqui had a point. They were all descendants of the Inca, which by default meant they all had ancestors who'd been subjugated, enslaved or killed, whether by the bloody hands of the conquistadors, or by diseases the Europeans disseminated to the so-called New World. In principle he agreed with Yupanqui; Atahualpa's treasure was theirs, and should be used to help their own people, especially if the Catholics were planning an attack. Sonco didn't like violence, but even less he liked the idea of violence against his own people... his family.

On the other hand, he knew anybody planning something against his people were a minority, and not all visitors to Inca lands were bad. He thought of his great friends, Hiram Kane and his grandfather, kind and noble men who only did good for the people of Peru. But…

Searching his heart, Sonco despaired at his choices. The Kanes weren't Catholics, but if he sided with Yupanqui's uprising he would have to betray his friend Hiram. The tough old Quechuan sat on his haunches and grabbed a handful of earth, kneading it in his strong, thick fingers. He knew it was provided by the great goddess Pachamama to sustain his people. Thus, it was to both Pachamama and the Sun God Inti that all Inca people and their descendants owed their allegiance and loyalty.

Now Yupanqui was fulfilling an ancient prophecy, one that Sonco himself had always known about but never thought would come true. The time of the great change was upon them, the Pachacuti, and whether he liked it or not, Sonco Amaru was in the middle of it. He was Inca, and by that decree alone he had a responsibility to defend his people against any threat. The Inca of half a millennium ago were weak, too easily betrayed and defeated by Pizarro's Spanish invaders. They could not let it happen again.

Sonco knew that if it did, it might erase their entire culture forever.

He stood up and closed his eyes. He thought of his family, his wife and children, and his small house just outside Cuzco. They were everything he had, everything he held dear.

They were worth fighting for.

Haines agreed with Kane's plan, and in essence it seemed simple. In private, they would explain the dire situation to Sonco, who knew the map as well as Kane and knew their precise intended route. But their plan would not follow the map to Vilcabamba. Instead, they'd lead the team to a different collection of ruins, a recently discovered Inca settlement, that while impressive was historically insignificant. Few foreigners had even heard of it.

Lying within a couple of hour's hike, they would arrive later that day and claim it was an outer perimeter wall of the lost city, evidence they were on the right path to Vilcabamba. Once there, and with Sonco's pre-warned team, they would swarm, overcome, and restrain the terrorists, surprise their biggest ally. Once they had them contained, Sonco would rush to Cuzco and bring the authorities.

Kane and Haines returned to camp, and it took a determined strong arm from John to prevent Hiram veering straight towards Hooper. "Not now," he whispered through clenched teeth, and with great force of will Kane allowed himself to be led to a seat by the fire.

Hiram soon sensed many eyes on him, and glanced at Ridley, who opened her hands out and flashed a guilty smile as if to say, *what did I do?* Kane relaxed and let it slide, then scanned the camp for Sonco. He spotted his friend at the edge of the clearing, busy dismantling a tent. Kane stood and approached him, but soon noticed how distracted he looked. Sonco's face, usually so jolly, was more worn than Kane had ever seen, as if carrying the burden of an ancient tragedy alone. *What was it?* Sonco wasn't himself, that was certain. He'd known Sonco since his own childhood, and as a family friend, he trusted no one more than the noble Quechuan. But Sonco's eyes were filled with a sorrow so alien to Kane it unnerved him.

But he didn't have time to worry about that now. He needed his old friend more than ever, and grabbing him by the forearms Kane said, "We have a serious situation, Sonco.

142

There are bad people in our group, and they're about to do something terrible."

Sonco looked at Kane in utter disbelief, not comprehending how Hiram knew about Yupanqui's dire plans. But when Kane mentioned the Europeans and not the Inca Uprising, Sonco was perplexed. It was only for a second. Now he was in shock. First, the Incans, led by Yupanqui. And now the Catholics, led by De La Cruz. Enemies all around, and he in the middle.

His mind was clear about his decision regarding Yupanqui, and that wouldn't change. But he knew he had to help his friend Hiram. Banishing thoughts of Yupanqui, the uprising, and his family he listened with intent to his friend's plan. Under the circumstances, it was their only real chance of securing the safety of the others. Sonco was to push on ahead of the group under the pretence of locating a camp area, but in reality, it was to find a spot to make an ambush. He would then locate a secure place where they could detain the Catholics and wait out in an arched stone entrance he and Hiram knew of. With a quick hug and a wish of *buena suerte*, good luck, Sonco collected his things from camp and sought out three of his trusted porters. Out of sight of Yupanqui, he briefed them on the plan. He only hoped they trusted him enough to help. Satisfied they did, Sonco set off toward the ruins.

Kane trusted Sonco to do anything necessary when the time came, and felt their plan might actually work. The fact something was troubling his old friend worried him, but he put it to the back of his mind, took a deep breath, and walked to the centre of the camp.

"I have good news," he said with feigned optimism. "So far our expedition has gone well, other than the unfortunate injury and departure of Muddy. We're making excellent

143

progress. In fact, tonight we'll arrive at the very outer walls to Vilcabamba, and that's where we'll make camp."

A brief but unmistakable look of acknowledgement passed between Edgewood and Hooper. Neither Kane nor Haines missed it.

"I've sent Sonco ahead to check the trail is clear for the rest of us, and unless he returns we'll meet him at the ruined walls later this afternoon. As soon as everyone's ready, we'll be off."

Hooper was indeed ready. He knew what he had to do, and his plan was in place. Tonight, Haines would die, the next step on their path to glory.

Edgewood was ready too. Kate was there as part of the Catholic contingent, but she had her own agenda. A Catholic in name only, she followed the Catholic doctrine for show only when De La Cruz and Hooper were about. She was only using those who were using Kane's expedition, and she would help herself to the treasure. Beneath the greed and odious objective was a young woman genuinely fascinated by history, and if it wasn't for her end goal she would be revelling in the adventure. The dichotomy left her conflicted, but Kate was confident she'd overcome that at crunch time.

Angelo De La Cruz was as calm as ever. His mission was from God, and nothing would stand in his way.

Yupanqui didn't know where Vilcabamba was, though he believed beyond doubt it existed, and was completely at the mercy of Kane and his map. And the fact Sonco had gone ahead concerned him, and confirmed his doubts about the man's loyalty. He knew of Sonco's skill as a guide and his friendship to the Kane family, and he hoped to use both to his advantage. Once they had disposed of all the foreigners,

Yupanqui thought, Sonco could lead them to the lost city and claim its riches for their just cause.

Yupanqui pondered Sonco's move. Either Kane was honest about the reason Sonco had surged ahead, or Sonco had deserted them all, turned his back on his Incan heritage, thus turning his back on the Inca Uprising. *No matter*, Yupanqui thought. If, like Kane had said, the guide was ahead, then all well and good. If not, then by whatever means necessary, he, the new Pachacuti, would succeed in his mission.

Nothing could stop him, he knew that. He had on his side five hundred years of history, a group of like-minded young Quechuans who would do anything he asked. More importantly, he had the support of their Inca Gods, Pachamama and Inti.

No mere Catholic mortal could prevent him becoming the modern day Inca King.

Renewed Hope

To an onlooker the atmosphere within the group might have been attributed to the excitement of the coming momentous moment in history. Few words passed between them, each with a lot on their individual minds. But Kane knew the truth. His friends Ridley and Evan were focused, oblivious to the deadly game around them, and Haines of course knew the plan, keeping his distance so as not to risk any uncomfortable questions.

Hooper, as he always did, kept himself to himself. As a killer he was an immoral man, though he didn't see it that way. His was the work of God, though he answered to De La Cruz, which sometimes felt like the same thing. He had failed the first time, and then had a lucky reprieve, and Hooper knew he couldn't afford another failure. He was feeling the pressure, and it showed.

Edgewood was quiet too, cloistered by her own focus because she knew they were getting close. As she walked, she imagined what the hoard would look like. Was the gold hidden in a natural cave, stacked from earth floor to rock ceiling? Was it even gold, and if so, did it glimmer in the dark? Was it buried, and were there booby traps? Her imagination was getting the better of her, but she didn't mind. It only added to the allure of the treasure. In reality, she believed the treasure was somehow hidden inside the precision stone walls the Inca were famous for.

Once they found Vilcabamba–and she was certain now that they would–how long until they found the treasure? Days? Hours? Surely they couldn't just move a few stones and find it waiting for them? If, beyond all hope, it was, could she execute her daring plan?

Execute. The word made her throat dry. People were going to die, and she would be responsible. Not directly, however. For that, she had disposable help. Edgewood believed the dumb native kid Umaq was onside, and Craft was wrapped far enough around her finger that manipulating him as an asset was within reach. As for the rest of that so-called team, well they were mere pawns in a game that they didn't understand. It was her game, and it was a game she would do anything to win.

Kane fought hard to stay calm. He'd been in difficult, often dangerous situations before, but this was on a whole new level. In a matter of hours he would attempt to overcome three people who could have weapons, and although not afraid for his own safety, he was afraid for the safety of his friends. He would have to tell them his plan soon. Ridley would be a valuable asset; he'd never met a tougher, more courageous woman. But he worried for Evan. His friend was a conscientious objector to violence at all costs, and though brave he would rather talk things out. Kane doubted if they'd get that chance.

As the distance to their target location shrunk, so Kane's anxiety levels rose. He simply could not wait any longer and had to talk with Ridley and Craft before it was too late. He called for a lunch break in the shade of some large boulders, and most of the group sat and stretched out their weary limbs. Whispering to Haines, he tasked his old professor to occupy the Catholics in discussion any way he could. Taking two handwritten notes from his pocket and acting as casual as possible, he walked past Craft first, followed by Ridley, and dropped a note in each of their laps. On the folded papers was the simple message: *Open. Don't speak!* He just hoped it went unnoticed by the Catholics, and that his friends didn't give the game away. Looking up, both seemed to sense the urgency in his stride as he walked off in silence, and with a glance around, they opened and read their notes. Ridley's note said: *Trust me. In two minutes, take north trail five minutes. Don't talk to anyone.* Evan's note said: *Trust me. Five minutes after Ridley returns, take south trail three minutes. Don't speak to anyone.*

Both Ridley and Craft were bemused by their notes, but it was so unlike Kane that both felt an innate sense something was wrong. They followed their orders to the letter.

Kane ducked into a thicket of trees and waited, unsure how to tell his friends they might be in danger. Right on cue, Alex came into view along the trail, and without uttering a sound he grabbed her wrist and pulled her behind the trees.

"What the…" she started to say, but seeing Kane, and noticing the severe look of concern etched on his face, she fell silent.

"Listen to me. There's a… we have a serious problem." And in as succinct a way as possible, he explained to Ridley that in their midst were three terrorists.

Of course, it sounded unbelievable to Alex. She'd formed a nice bond with Kate Edgewood, and in no way had she

148

observed in her a criminal intent. But she believed Kane and had no doubt he was sincere in his belief.

"Are you prepared to help when the time comes? I'd understand if you'd rather…"

"No way. I'm in this with you… as you knew I would be. In fact, why wait, why not…"

"No. Sonco is with us, and it's the way it has to be. Got it?" He didn't like to talk to Alex in such a harsh way, but he had no choice. He knew she'd understand, and she did, nodding her assent. "Go back to camp as if nothing has happened. You have to. Evan knows what to do." Kane looked into Ridley's eyes and saw no fear there. What he saw were anger and courage. He had a sudden urge to lean over and kiss her, but thought better of it and instead said simply and with an encouraging nod, "Go."

Kane waited thirty seconds, then followed Ridley back to camp, ignoring her as he passed and continuing along the trail south for a few hundred yards. Just as he had before, he found a hidden spot and waited for Evan. Three minutes later and his old friend came into view, apprehension evident on his face. Kane emitted a low whistle and caught Evan's attention, and like he had with Ridley, explained the situation to his uncomprehending friend.

"It must be a joke, right? Right? Hiram?" He saw no humour in his friend's eyes. "I mean, you can't be serious. Terrorists? For what organisation?"

"They're a splinter group of hard right fundamentalist Catholics. There are rumours of an upsurge in Inca power, and we believe they will do what it takes to stop them. I've never heard of an Inca Uprising before, but John Haines has and he's certain this is what it is. And now I'm certain too.

149

We need to stop them, and we need to do it tonight."

Evan shook his head, dumbstruck, and Kane appraised his friend. Evan was in shock. "Listen, I know you're having trouble believing me, and I agree it sounds too crazy to be true. But we have to assume John is right. If we don't, and something bad happens to Alex, or you or John, I'd never forgive myself. And I know you'd rather take the diplomatic route, try and avoid violence, but we can't risk it, we…"

"But Kate… Kate seems so nice, I can't believe…"

"I know, I know. It doesn't seem possible, does it? But if even a quarter of what we see and read in the news is true, the world of terrorism is changing fast. We have to fear the worst, but if we stick together and don't panic, we'll be okay. It'll be dusk when we get to the ruins, and there's a stone archway that leads into the complex, perhaps twenty feet long. If two of us are ahead, and two behind, and with Sonco's porters alongside us, we can overpower them in the tunnel."

Evan was not convinced. "We're not soldiers, and if they're terrorists then they must have weapons. It's too dangerous. Why don't we just sneak off in the night and get as far away from them as possible? That's the smart thing to do."

Kane agreed with Evan. They should try and escape, get his people out of harm's way, away from danger. But… that wasn't his nature, not anymore. He had underestimated danger once before in his life, and he wasn't about to make that mistake again.

"You're right. They probably have guns. But we will be ready. If we maintain ignorance to their scheme we'll surprise them, and with a little luck it will all be over before it starts." Kane's eyes took on a distant look, as if lost in thought. But his gaze soon focused back on his mate, and he spoke with authority. "There's something else. I have a responsibility to everyone on this trip. I'm in charge of this expedition, and despite the danger I will not abandon it. However, I don't expect you or anyone else to stay, and I'd understand if you made a run for it… in fact, I encourage it."

He meant it. This wasn't Evan's fight. In reality, it had nothing to do with any of them. The terrorists simply wanted the map and the treasure. The other players in this escalating narrative were an unfortunate obstacle, and though innocent, they were in the way. But as Kane looked at his old friend, a familiar look came across his face. A narrowing of the eyes, a crinkled brow and a clench of the jaw. It wasn't a look of fear, as he might have expected, nor was it the look of a man who wasn't scared. It was a look of defiance, and it gave Kane renewed hope.

"I've known you a long time, pal," Evan said, "and I've never known you to let anyone down. Ever. And I won't let you down now. Just tell me what to do."

Timing

The sun was lower in the western arc of the sky, which meant mid-afternoon and about three more hours of daylight left. Kane figured at their current rate they'd arrive at the ruins by four-thirty. Too early. He needed to slow them down a little in order to reach the archway entrance during the darkening skies of dusk. Any earlier and they'd arrive in daylight, and that would make an already dangerous surprise attack way more difficult.

Kane had encouraged Ridley, Craft and Haines to act as if everything was normal, and suggested that Evan try and engage Kate, a person who, for all they knew, was planning to kill one of them. But despite his unease, Evan gamely fell into stride alongside the pretty graduate student.

"Just another beautiful day in the Andes," he said in the most cheery voice he could muster, "but is it me, or does everything seem uphill?" He chuckled, keeping his eyes on the path. It seemed to work.

"You know what, Evan, I think you're right. Always up and never down." She smiled at him, and he relaxed. He still couldn't believe it.

"I never see you taking photos though," she said. "Aren't you documenting the expedition?"

"I am, but once you've seen an Andean mountain peak,

you've seen them all, right?"

Kate chuckled, no suspicion evident, and they chatted more as they hiked.

Ridley wanted to mingle among the Quechuans in an effort to keep her anger hidden from the Catholics. She was still in shock about Kane's revelation. Other than Hooper, who'd acted weird since they set out, they seemed normal, and not dangerous terrorists. The Spanish professor was quiet, a little aloof perhaps, but that just seemed his natural character. De La Cruz kept himself on the periphery of the group, and Ridley herself appreciated that. She hated false people, those who needed to fill quiet voids, needed their voices heard. She liked quiet men. The girl too seemed harmless. Calm and considerate, Ridley's only moment of doubt about her was the over-eager question regarding the value of the treasure. That was understandable. She was young–early twenties, Ridley guessed–and why wouldn't she be excited? They were on the verge of making history.

They had all seemed okay, at least until Kane's shocking revelation. Now she knew the truth about them, she saw them differently. As unbelievable as it was they were dangerous criminals.

So Ridley walked among the few Quechuan porters out ahead of the main group. If she could garner some affinity between them, then it could only help Kane later. The young men were always busy with their camp duties and hauling the equipment, and until then she hadn't had a lot to do with them, not wanting to hinder what was a difficult and demanding job. Alex knew that Kane had long admired their toughness and fortitude, and he'd told her more than once that Westerners could learn a lot from the humble and underprivileged native Andean cultures. She could see why. Shy and unassuming, they were diligent in their duties while always ready with a smile and a helping hand.

One among them though seemed more distant than the others. Sure, he smiled when she said *hola*, and he worked as hard as the others. But there was sadness in his eyes and his face wore a lost and vulnerable expression. Amidst all their other concerns and excitements, nobody paid the young porter any notice. Except for Ridley. She'd taken a shine to the modest kid over their days on the trail, and he always returned her smiles when they were close. Today though he seemed in a daze, as if dealing with some unseen inner turmoil.

Ridley looked at the boy named Umaq. The mestizo porter was short and lean, wiry strong, and his eyes dark and melancholy. He looked no more than eighteen, but those eyes seemed to carry in them generations of sorrow. His worn skin was the colour of raw sienna, an exotic fusion of Caucasian and Indian. But unlike the other natives Umaq didn't seem proud. How could he, Ridley thought, with no pure and defining identity of his own, neither Andean nor European, neither Inca nor Catholic? Ridley wondered if all mixed race and cross-cultured people felt the same, especially if mixed as a result of conquest. She would never really know, but in the eyes of the harried boy before her, she thought she understood.

With a glance up Kane saw only blue skies, but he knew the light would soon fade. They were getting close to the ruins.

If all had gone well for Sonco, he would already be there in hiding, waiting ready to strike. Kane still didn't believe it. This expedition was meant to be the discovery of a lifetime, and yet because of the twisted beliefs of a few religious fanatics, it was fast unravelling into a nightmare.

Kane had always been an independent man, preferring to rely on and trust himself over anyone else, except for perhaps Sonco, and he was truly relying on Sonco Amaru now. Despite his friend's distractedness earlier in the day, he knew the tough Quechuan would not let him down.

Timing was crucial. Too early, and Sonco might be unprepared. Too late, and darkness would hinder their plans. One more hour. That's how long the last stretch had to take. Kane was not a spiritual man, and certainly not religious, but right now he needed some luck. Looking out into the hazy distance of the trail, casting his eye over the always majestic and powerful vistas of the sacred valley of the Incas, Kane came as close as he ever had to saying a prayer. It wasn't a prayer in the Christian sense, rather a few words of encouragement to the Earth Goddess Pachamama, asking her to look out for a man who'd done nothing to damage her lands or its creatures, and who'd always respected the earth beneath his feet and the rocks and trees around him.

He'd been a good subject for the Earth Goddess; Kane only hoped she felt the same way.

Turmoil

Turmoil clouded Sonco Amaru's mind. A peaceful, proud, and hard-working man, nothing made Sonco prouder than his Quechuan roots and his home and family. That was until Yupanqui gave his speech asking them to search their souls and join his Inca Uprising. All Quechuans descended from the Incas, but Sonco was content to live in the present, working hard to support his family and send his kids to school. He'd always enjoyed the traditional annual festivals and parades in Cuzco that honoured their Incan Gods, but for Sonco that was as far as it ever went.

But after hearing Yupanqui's eloquent and engaging speech, his Quechuan pride had arisen. Yupanqui reminded him of his Inca heritage, and despite himself, Sonco felt more emotion than he believed possible. He knew about the atrocities inflicted upon his ancestors by the Spanish, all Quechuans did, and he knew the conquistadors had almost wiped the Incas from the earth.

But that was five hundred years ago, and it scarcely affected him and his life in any way. But Yupanqui had told them about the prophecies, that five hundred years after the conquistadors killed Atahualpa a new Pachacuti would emerge and make the world right again.

Whether Sonco liked it or not, Yupanqui fully believed in

the prophecy, and more important than that, the man believed he himself was the chosen leader. He was a big man, and highly intelligent, and his erudite speech was full of authority. Just days ago, Sonco would have never believed an uprising was possible, but he'd heard the evidence first hand, and much as he tried to quell it, his heart soared with passion when he heard Yupanqui's rousing words.

And Yupanqui was right. Sonco was Inca, and he had a duty, not only to honour his ancestors but to protect his family, and to quash any threat to his people. And that threat, once more, was the Catholics. Kane had asked for his help. He wasn't sure how much Kane knew about the Inca uprising, but right now that was irrelevant. Kane and his friends were in danger from the Catholics, and he, Sonco, had to help.

Sonco found the stone archway he'd discussed with Kane, and although significantly reclaimed by nature, with thick tree roots warping the walls and stretching like writhing snakes across the trail, he knew it was the perfect spot for an ambush.

Using that burgeoning nature to his advantage, Sonco's first task was to attach ropes to the roots and then disguise them. That would make it easier to restrain the Catholics once overpowered, though he didn't think that would be too difficult. An old man, a skinny woman, and a weak writer were hardly an elite fighting force. But Sonco prepared himself anyway. He had his trusty machete tucked into his belt, he'd secured the ropes, and hidden them, and he'd arranged a stash of fist-sized rocks to use as weapons if needed. And above all else, and thinking back to what Yupanqui had said and what he himself already knew, the Gods were on their side.

And with Pachamama and Inti watching over them, they couldn't lose.

"Are you ready?" asked De La Cruz, his tone stern.

"Yes. It will be done," replied Hooper, surprised he'd been addressed directly by the Spaniard. Edgewood was the usual mouthpiece, and Howie knew it meant things were getting serious. He met eyes with his leader. "I won't fail again."

"We don't have time for failure. Once he is out of the way, and then the others, nothing will stop us achieving our goal." The professor gazed out across the horizon, a vacant look on his face as if seeing far beyond the rugged line of the mountains and further still, right into the many cities of Tawantinsuyu, the four corners of the Inca Empire. "These lands… they will be ours again. The land is too good and too rich for these pagan heathens. We will again control it all, and from here we'll rule an entire continent."

Hooper knew he was expendable, and if he didn't succeed in his next task he probably wouldn't leave the Andes alive. The Spaniard was not a physical specimen, but he had about him a presence, some inner power that De La Cruz himself believed was God given. Hooper's friend Ferdinand Benedix was the only other person he knew who carried such a presence, and the two of them, Benedix alongside De La Cruz, made a formidable partnership.

The Eagle Alliance was a relatively unknown organisation on the world stage, and Howie himself knew little of its reach. But one thing Hooper did know was that with those two passionate and loyal fundamentalists in charge, they would stop at nothing to achieve their targets. He didn't even know what their ultimate goals were and only knew his minor part in it. Ferdinand had tasked him to help De La Cruz secure the Inca's lost treasure in whatever way the Spaniard asked of him, and after that, quash the Inca uprising. With the arrogance of Benedix and the unflinching belief of De La Cruz in the Catholic's moral right to rule, Hooper wouldn't be surprised if they were planning to take over the world. The thought made him smile inwardly. At least he thought it was inwards.

"Is this funny to you?" questioned the Spaniard. "A joke? If I were you," he said in flawless English, "I'd wipe that amateur smile off your face and focus on your job. This mission is far greater than either you or me." The professor stared so long and with such intent at Hooper that the American's throat went dry, and the smile slipped away. De La Cruz had just five more words. "Failure is not an option."

Hooper didn't miss the undisguised threat.

Other than his harsh words with Hooper, Angelo De La Cruz looked as if he were on a leisurely walk in the woods. He appeared so calm, in fact, that anyone who didn't know better could never have guessed his odious intentions. He was that calm because he had total faith that the mission didn't rely on the work of men, or in this case, of two men and a woman. They had their part to play, but the true destiny was in God's hands. However, if they played their parts well, not only would God be grateful, but He would grant them even more Earthly power to carry out *His* will.

And His will, De La Cruz knew, was to destroy all infidels.

They would start with the Inca.

Danger at Dusk

Sonco sat silent and motionless, the only sounds the slight whispering of leaves and a few chirping birds, readying their mates for the evening roost.

And then a voice.

With a tilt of his head towards the sound, he strained his ears, and Sonco was in no doubt he'd heard Kane's deep voice. And it wasn't far away. *This is it*, he thought. He estimated that Kane was still a ten-minute walk away, but he was ready. Halfway into the arched entrance to the city was a deep set niche, in which for a long time had once sat an Inca idol, guarding the city's entrance. Now though, it was a perfect place for Sonco to hide, and ready himself to ambush the Catholics. He edged his robust body far back into that dark niche, and knew he couldn't be seen until it was too late. He expected that if possible Kane would lead the Catholics through the narrow passageway together, and if he did so, Sonco felt sure that with a couple of quick commands to his team of porters, they could overpower them with ease.

Kane was close. Just a few more minutes and they'd be within site of the ancient stone ruins he knew were ahead. There weren't any insignificant Inca ruins, Kane believed, and all were important in their own way. But these were not, as he had told them, related to Vilcabamba, and the others had no reason to disbelieve him. To let the group know they were close, he called out aloud. "Almost there," he shouted, "Just five more minutes," but the volume was for Sonco's benefit more than for theirs. He also clung onto just a little hope that, misguided as it was, despite their heinous plans the Catholics may actually get caught up in the excitement at being at the outskirts of the lost city, and delay their murderous schemes for a while. Using surprise to his advantage, Kane would capitalise on their awe.

A dusky gloom descended fast, and any residual natural light barely filtered through the trees above. Kane had timed their arrival to perfection. Leading the single file procession on, he focused his eyes ahead, and just as he knew it would be, the stone structure appeared out of the falling darkness.

Regardless of everything else going on Kane was excited. But he allowed himself only a few seconds to bask in the moment and refocused his attention on the task ahead. He stopped and faced the group. "Welcome to the outskirts of Vilcabamba." For Sonco's benefit he said it loud, and for himself he said it with forced confidence.

Forced, because in less than a minute all hell would break loose.

He appraised the group. As he knew he would, he saw a mixture of expressions. The barely disguised scowling face of Hooper fixed eyes on his, and behind him the wide-eyed look of appreciation on the face of Edgewood. The impassive neutral gaze of the Spanish professor De La Cruz appeared behind them, followed by an acute nervousness in the eyes of his friend Evan. It was only a fleeting glance, but Kane saw everything he needed. The Catholics didn't expect an ambush, that was clear, and the undeniable look of steel in Ridley's eyes filled him with more confidence than he felt.

She was ready. He trusted Sonco, and knew he was ready. Now Kane took a deep breath, went eye ball to eye ball with Evan, and as he turned his back on them all he asked himself if he too was ready. With a few slow yet deliberate strides towards the ruins, Kane knew that he was.

He entered the passageway first and peered into the gloom for any sign of Sonco. Nothing. *He's here somewhere.* It seemed the perfect place for an ambush, with almost no light and visibility no more than eight feet. Kane could see no hint of what was to come, but he sensed it and felt it within the still and cloying air.

And then out of the darkness came a couple of deep, harsh words barked in Quechuan, and storming from the shadows, Sonco was upon them. A blind struggle ensued, clashes between bodies, the thud and smack of fist upon flesh, and the grunts and groans of both pain and confusion. Kane was slammed into the cold solidity of an ancient Inca wall, cracking his head on the unforgiving stone. Two young porters bundled forward to help, and Kane heard Ridley say with uncensored rage, "No you don't, bitch," as she overpowered the girl Edgewood.

Next Kane heard an angry, "Get the fuck off me," and recognised the voice as Hooper, but what followed was a sound that chilled Kane to his core.

A gunshot, loud and unmistakable, swiftly followed by another.

Kane wasn't hit. He called out, "Evan, Alex, are you hurt?" to which Ridley just nodded. However, no response from Evan. "John, Sonco?" Kane groped in his pack for his torch and pointed it at where he thought the gunshots had sounded. More torches flashed on, and he soon understood the carnage.

On his knees, with his face in the dirt and hands trussed behind him, was the Spaniard, De La Cruz. Sonco stood over him, machete drawn but unused. *Good*, Kane thought. Ahead of him he saw the blonde-haired Edgewood restrained by Ridley, who had her right boot wedged dangerously into the young woman's neck. Ridley had her pinned against the stone wall, and she looked terrified. The young Quechuans stood over the two of them, as per instruction from Sonco. Bringing up the rear, and blocking any way out of the passage, was Yupanqui the cook, looking fierce and powerful, as if he had murder on his mind. Unbeknown to most of them present, he did, but the hatred in his eyes was missed in the darkness. To Kane's great dismay he spotted Evan slumped against a wall, blood spreading out from a wound in his shoulder, like a concentric red ripple on a pond. Evan looked up at him, and between winces managed a smile, injured but not serious.

Kane breathed deep, relief washing over him, yet something was still wrong. He looked again and saw to his absolute horror that Hooper was gone. In the darkness he had obviously pulled a gun and shot his way through the melee, hitting Evan in the shoulder. He could only have gone forwards into the ruinous complex, and into what was now the swallowing darkness of an Andean night. The fact Hooper had a gun and was prepared to use it meant Kane knew it was both stupid and dangerous to follow.

He checked on his friends and the porters for further injury, and once satisfied he checked on the Spaniard and the girl. When they were fully restrained, a machete-wielding Sonco led them with caution into the ruins.

After ten minutes of forward movement, made difficult because of the darkness and the tangle of roots and fallen stones, they came to an open area, where Kane helped Sonco secure the prisoners to more roots that snaked over and around the ancient Inca structure. With Sonco stationed to keep them under strict guard, Kane turned his attention to Craft and was relieved to learn his injury was more a graze than an actual bullet wound. It would need treating, and they would have to guard against infection. But Evan was lucky, and they both knew it.

Now the issue was how to stay safe themselves, and keep the terrorists separated and secure, knowing there was another out there with a gun. It was time to speak with De La Cruz and Edgewood, and Kane wanted answers.

By torchlight, Kane and Ridley first searched the Catholic's backpacks, and soon learned that the girl was unarmed. Although she admitted being a part of the Catholic organisation, she asked in a frantic, almost hysterical voice to speak with Kane in private. "Soon enough," he told her. In De La Cruz's pack, he found two small handguns but little else, which didn't seem much weaponry for people with such violent intentions. Hooper, though, had left with a backpack that could be loaded with weapons, and Kane had to assume the worst.

With Sonco's help Kane dragged the Spaniard to his feet and escorted him deeper into the ruins. They sat him on a low wall, and Kane shone the powerful torch beam into the professor's face.

"Are you in charge, Professor De La Cruz?" Kane thought that if he treated him with at least a little respect then he might be more forthcoming with answers.

The Spaniard looked impassively into Kane's eyes for a long

moment, before answering with measured words. "Well, Mr Kane, I suppose I am a leader of sorts, but I do not command these people. Their orders merely come through me, from God. But of course you knew that." The Spaniard was the epitome of calm and seemed in no way concerned about the failure of their mission. In fact, it was his calmness that had Kane most worried.

"And Hooper? Is he armed?" This time there was no response, just a look of complete indifference. Hiram pushed on. "I understand that you–your Eagle Alliance–is using me to get to Atahualpa's treasure? Is that true?"

De La Cruz considered for a moment. "Yes, it is true we intend to take the gold. But we are only taking what belongs to us."

"And what do you intend to do with the gold? If it's even there."

Again there was no verbal response, but the look in the professor's eyes betrayed his odious intentions.

"Angelo, I understand your plan. But my friends and these young Quechuans have nothing to do with that. John overheard Hooper saying something about killing somebody, which is why we overpowered you."

De La Cruz cast his eyes over the torch beam and strained them into the darkness. He couldn't see much, and he certainly couldn't see the Quechuans, who were not close by. But De La Cruz knew they were there. "Mr Kane, I did not want your friends to get hurt, and I am sorry for the young man. That was just an accident, and I am sure Mr Hooper didn't mean it." But then he surprised them by spitting with vehemence onto the dusty ground, and in an icy, measured voice said, "However, I cannot say the same about these heathen natives. It is because of these uncivilised pigs that our mission was born." He now stared with intensity into first Kane's eyes, and then Sonco's. "Mr Kane, listen to me, and listen with diligence. If any of these heathen pigs stand in the way of this mission, they will perish."

Kane didn't think the Spaniard was in any physical position to be making threats, but the steel in his tone unnerved him, and the unwavering belief that he would succeed, despite his current predicament, only furthered that feeling of uncertainty. Kane assumed the confidence of De La Cruz rested on Hooper's shoulders, and that the American would likely come at them by force using the darkness as an ally. It meant they faced a long and dangerous night.

Confession

Leaving Sonco to guard the professor, Kane returned to Edgewood. He aimed his torch at her face and saw only a young woman way out of her depth. He sat beside her and waited for her to speak. He didn't wait long.

"I want to tell you things, but not if anyone else can hear us." She glanced about, apprehension and fear evident.

"It's okay. We're alone." He turned to face her, moving the torch beam away from her face. "So, what's your role in all of this?" His tone was passive, almost friendly, as if to encourage her to open up. According to John Haines, she was part of the terrorist cell, but she looked far from that right now.

"It's true," she said in a voice so quiet it was barely a whisper, "I'm not who you thought I was. I am here with the terrorists, but I am not one of them. I am using them, and we are using you. In other words, I'm guilty of a grave deception, but I'm not a terrorist." Kate looked down at her boots, her apparent shame evident. But Kane wasn't convinced.

"How are you using them? It can't be for anything good."

"You are right. It's not. They're using you to get to the treasure, and by being part of their plan, I... I would be safe."

"Safe? Safe from what?"

"Whatever De La Cruz tells you it's probably a lie. You're meant to help them get what they want, and once they have it, you're all expendable."

"Expendable? You mean, they plan to kill us all?" Kane was incredulous.

"I'm sorry, but yes. I wanted no part of that, and I planned to help you once I…"

"Once you what?"

"All I wanted was a small part of the treasure for myself. Not much, just enough to get me started out in life."

"You were just going to steal it?" If it wasn't such a serious situation, Kane might have laughed. Then he remembered the guns. "How, and how would you get away with that?"

"I don't know. But please believe I'm not like them. I'd never have hurt anyone, and I would've warned you when the time was right."

Kane finished speaking to the girl. He didn't know who or what to believe anymore, but he didn't think it was Edgewood. However, he couldn't believe she was a terrorist. Nevertheless, her intentions were bad, and she was a fool if she thought she could steal the treasure and simply walk away.

He pulled her from her seated position and ushered her back to where Sonco was guarding De La Cruz, and together they hustled them to where the others waited. After securing them once more with the ropes, Kane led Sonco away to talk in private. However the moment they turned their backs the two captives looked at each other, and without a word, shared a knowing nod. Satisfied, De La Cruz relaxed against his bindings and closed his eyes.

Unless he was mistaken, in just a matter of hours Hooper would return with all guns blazing, and they would be close to victory.

Somewhere across camp Yupanqui paced like a crazed rhino. He had not expected the incident, and thus he was ill prepared to help against the Catholics. He had no loyalty to Kane, but he was a sworn enemy of all Catholics and would have stepped in had he have known. *No matter*, he thought. He gathered the young Quechuans around, and in the secrecy of the far end of the camp he told them his plan.

"It seems the Inca Gods are smiling upon their sons tonight. Smiling upon us. Part of our job is done. We have two of the enemy tied to trees like the dogs they are, but the other dog has run off like a coward. We know he has guns, so we will need to be careful, because he will return during the night to free his fellow Catholic dogs."

Yupanqui looked about the group, five including Umaq Huamani, and all listened with intent. They were young and nervous, excited looks in their eyes. They were with Yupanqui, and they would follow him to the end.

Only Umaq wavered. He didn't want to fight, though he believed in Yupanqui's cause. But he'd already made an agreement with the woman, and all he cared about was to get paid and go home and support his family. That was his duty, and thus, that's where his true loyalties lay. But the big man scared him, and he had to keep up appearances and appear on Yupanqui's side.

He focused his gaze and listened as Yupanqui explained what he expected of them, both from him–and, more importantly–from their Incan Gods.

Deserter

With De La Cruz and Edgewood detained and Craft out of immediate danger, Kane called a meeting of those left; Ridley, Craft, Haines, and Sonco. The good guys. He led them to the centre of camp where a fire sent crazy shadows dancing across the timeworn and venerable Inca stones. The scene would have been beautiful, were they not in the midst of a deadly terrorist plot.

Though Kane was shaken by everything that had happened, and although an armed and dangerous man was loose somewhere in the surrounding jungle darkness, Kane believed they had dealt with the drama well. He thanked his friends for their bravery. But now he turned to Sonco, the man who he believed their very survival might depend upon.

"My friend," he said, "I have needed you so often and for so many years out here in Peru." He paused, staring at the Quechuan. Sonco was shaken too, and the troubled look he had worn for days remained. Troubled, with a hint of rage. Kane continued. "But now I need you more than ever."

But Sonco couldn't hold his friend's gaze, and Kane didn't understand. He had never seen Sonco look so... so... what was that look? Kane appraised the man. His head hung low on wide shoulders now slumped, and the perpetual smile was absent.

Defeated. That was it. Sonco looked like a man defeated. Kane was about to ask his friend what was wrong, when the defeated look of sorrow evaporated, replaced by hardened eyes that bore into Kane's with an intensity he'd never seen. The gaze lasted several seconds, and in little more than a whisper, Sonco said, *"Lo siento.* I am sorry."

Before Kane asked *for what?* Sonco turned and disappeared into the darkness. By the time Kane reacted Sonco was gone. Kane bolted after his friend, but he'd only gone a few yards before he knew it was futile. He would never catch a man born in the Andes, and sadness and concern heavied his heart and clenched his gut. It was yet another surreal moment on an expedition that had rapidly descended into chaos.

Haines knew Kane himself was greatly troubled. He had witnessed it evolve in his eyes over the last days, but now it was apparent in his sagging shoulders. Hiram and Sonco were close, almost like brothers, and John knew it made little sense.

But what Kane didn't know, couldn't have known, was that Sonco believed they would never see each other again.

"Hiram," John said to no avail. And then, louder. "Hiram!"

Kane snapped to attention.

"I don't know what just happened," said John, "but you have to let it go." He lowered his voice. "Maybe he's gone for help? Maybe he'll be back with support from a nearby village. I don't know, but we have to focus our attention on the prisoners, and keep a vigilant lookout for Hooper."

Haines was right. Sonco's sudden departure was a big blow, but going after him would leave them more exposed when Hooper returned. Another question now became a concern. In Sonco's absence, Kane wondered if he could still count on the Quechuan porters. They had obeyed him when overpowering two of the terrorists, but now he was gone, and Hiram assumed the eldest and most experienced of the remaining Quechuans, Yupanqui, would take control in his place. He needed to speak with him, and given Sonco's affinity and affection for Kane and his family, he hoped for the same allegiance from the cook.

But that conversation never happened.

A Coup

"Are you ready?" asked Yupanqui. It wasn't a question. He knew they were. He eyeballed them one by one, and watched as their eyes all became hard as flint. Their blood surged.

"Vamonos." *Let's go.*

Led by Yupanqui the porters emerged from their hidden meeting and circled the camp. They came fast at the terrorists from behind, and in less than twenty seconds had taken control of their enemy and were marching them at gunpoint across the clearing. In the light of the fire, Yupanqui seemed to have grown and had the appearance of a fearsome Inca warrior from another age.

Kane was dumbstruck. Not only did the young Quechuan porters each carry a gun, but now their youthful features were replaced by a hard-edged patriotism to their new leader. It was a shocking turn of events, and with half a dozen guns trained on them they had little choice but to stand there, unmoved, and listen to what the man had to say. "It is both fortunate and unfortunate you are involved in this, Mr Kane. Of course, you have the most important role to play in this drama, because it is your map and your skills we need. The Incan people have been waiting a long time for this moment. We thought we were close when Mr Bingham was here in Peru all those years ago, and your grandfather after that.

173

But unfortunately for your grandfather, he didn't come into possession of the map until he was too old to use it."

Kane was surprised at Yupanqui's knowledge, and Yupanqui didn't miss it. "Oh yes, Mr Kane. I know that the Bingham estate did not release the map to your grandfather until 1991 because they did not believe it was accurate. You received it on your eighteenth birthday, is it not so?" He didn't wait for an answer. "We even thought you yourself would be the man to lead us to glory the last time you were here, but, as I recall, Pachamama had other ideas for you then." He smiled, but behind that smile hid fierce determination.

Kane recalled with alarm the last time he was here, when only a landslide had prevented a successful mission to Vilcabamba. Yupanqui continued.

"But never mind. That is history. You are here now, and this time we will succeed." Yupanqui looked around at his team with pride, boys that had evolved into men overnight. "I said you were the most important person, but maybe not. That honour goes to him." He pointed at De La Cruz and did not hide the look of hatred mixed with an animalistic anticipation in his fire-lit eyes. Few of those listening understood quite how the Spaniard was so important to Yupanqui, but Professor Haines had a good idea, and it sickened him. John kept his thoughts internal as the big man pressed on.

"As you can see, Mr Kane, I am now in command of this mission, as is my duty."

"What duty?" spat Ridley. "The Quechuans are peaceful people... why do you have guns?"

"I suppose that is a fair question to an ignorant European, so allow me to enlighten you. I was once known as Yupanqui

Atoc, descendent of the Q'ero people, and living member of a bloodline of Inca Kings. I'm directly descended from Cápac Yupanqui, fifth Sapa Inca of the Kingdom of Cuzco. It is true I was once a cook. But no longer. I am the Inca Yupanqui. I am the chosen one, the chosen Pachacuti, which to you ignorant heathens means…"

"I know what it means," said Haines, cutting off Yupanqui in a quiet yet authoritative voice. "Or, at least, I know what *you* think it means." Haines raised his voice so the others could hear. "The Q'ero Indians have, for five hundred years, clung to an ancient prophecy that a new Pachacuti will come, meaning 'a turning over of time and space.' It also means 'earth-shaker,' or an event that signals the end of one cycle of history and the beginning of a new one. By giving yourself that name, you're declaring the start of a new period in history."

Yupanqui looked surprised by Haines knowledge. "Very impressive, professor. You know your history. But does that mean you accept and understand our mission?"

"I understand how the ancients could hold onto such beliefs. But you're a young man, a man who's grown up in a modern world, a world with radio and television and internet. You're educated, which means you should know it's just tradition, folk stories passed between generations, and not to be taken in a literal sense. Of course, that could also be said about the Catholics," he said, pointing to the prisoners. "I mean no offence, however, at its best religion is just a collection of stories. You need not do this. Nobody else needs to get hurt." John looked over at Evan, lucky he hadn't been killed. "We can keep these two detained, lead them back to Cuzco and hand them over to the proper authorities."

Yupanqui just glared at the professor, who gamely tried to

buy some time. In reality, Haines had a lot more sympathy for the Incas than he let on. There would be bloodshed, almost guaranteed, and he couldn't risk appealing to the man's vanity. He also believed in his heart that anything any of them said now would be futile. He saw nothing but victory in Yupanqui's eyes, and it frightened him.

"At first I thought you understood," replied the Inca leader, "but it is clear you do not. We are just a little group in these mountains. But a wide-scale uprising has been growing for one hundred years. We are a small part of it, though we are on the front lines, so to speak. The mission to locate Atahualpa's treasure is more important than ever. It seems you have learned their plans, but these... these Catholics... they are the terrorists. Not us. They are here to steal the gold and use it against us. It is my duty and my honour to make sure it can not and will not happen." He stepped closer to the detained Catholics, and while De La Cruz remained defiant and unmoved, Edgewood visibly shrank away from the big Incan. "As I said," Yupanqui continued, "I have been chosen, and anyone who tries to stop me will pay the ultimate price."

And all those who saw the look of steel in Yupanqui's eyes knew he was deadly serious.

"So what now?" asked Kane, trying to keep the rising anger from his voice.

"What now? Well, Mr Kane, we sleep here for a few hours and continue to Vilcabamba in the morning. You know the way, and you will lead us there. And once we are among the hallowed stones of the lost city, we will have our glorious victory. First the glory, and then you will all witness the worthy revenge against the Catholics for which the Inca people have waited almost five hundred years."

Kane thought on his feet. Yupanqui was right, he knew the way to Vilcabamba, now almost certain he could get there with or without the map. But Kane saw a chance to stall. "The thing is, I don't know the way to the lost city. The map is fake," he lied, "created as a way to make money by leading people into the jungle. The lost city has never been found, which you have to agree is good for business." Kane hung his head in apparent shame, but Yupanqui didn't buy it.

"Mr Kane, I admire your attempt to mislead me. But you and your family have a fine reputation in the field of exploration, and you especially are known for your great conscience and admirable dignity. You would not lie to these people, and you would not lie to the Quechuans. Sadly for you, or perhaps not, depending on how you see your role in this now, you and your map will lead us to our destiny, and you *will* be remembered as the man who found Vilcabamba. That *is* your destiny, isn't it, Mr Kane? Fulfil your destiny and help the Inca fulfil theirs. The glory will be ours to share."

Kane took a second to appraise their dire situation. Outnumbered and out-gunned, he saw little chance of escape. For now, he had no choice but to push ahead, go along with the expedition and let the drama unfold, at least until an opportunity presented itself to either escape or apprehend all the terrorists.

His one regret was that his most trusted ally Sonco was no longer by his side.

A Fading Alliance

Howie Hooper sat as still as the immovable stones around him, invisible to human eyes and just fifty yards from where Yupanqui conducted his sinister speech. Hooper heard everything, and it was all he could do to restrain himself going into the camp and shooting dead the oafish native right there and then. But by sheer effort of will he refrained, knowing that the Quechuans now controlled almost all the weapons, and being tied up, Edgewood and De La Cruz could do nothing to help.

Hooper would bide his time. It was dark and risky. But when the moment came, and using his military training, he would ghost into camp and neutralise the enemy, one heathen obstacle at a time.

Howie had heard enough of the speech and the following discussion to know that come first light the group, still led by Kane, would head further into the mountains, and all the way to Vilcabamba. He would flank them, and when chances arose he would take out the natives. And more important to the mission, sometime between now and their arrival at the lost city he would kill the Inca leader Yupanqui.

Edgewood couldn't believe her plans–and those of the Eagle Alliance–had unravelled before her eyes. It was a devastating blow, and her anger raged just below the surface. But what was strange to her was how calm Angelo De La Cruz seemed. He hadn't uttered a word since they'd been apprehended by the Quechuans, and hadn't even struggled. His composure unnerved her. She herself felt genuine fear for her life, and now cursed herself for being in that stinking jungle in the first place. She looked at De La Cruz, his eyes passive in the gentle flicker of the nearby fire. He seemed relaxed while she was a seething, nervous wreck.

"What will they do to us?" Her voice wavered, the tears imminent. "They will kill us, I know it."

The Spaniard looked in her direction without emotion. His face took on a ponderous attitude, as if considering that, yes, they might just kill them. "It is true, they might, though I don't think they will get the chance. Even if they kill us, have no fear. As I have always said, we are only pawns in a much greater game than just us. If it is what God needs of us, to die for His cause, then that is what we will do. There can be no greater glory than becoming a martyr in His name." De La Cruz appeared enraptured to some unseen deity, his eyes reverent. "But, like I said, it will not come to that. Hooper is out there, and he will come. Have faith, Kate, have faith." He smiled and looked away.

But in that moment faith was the last thing Kate Edgewood possessed. If they needed to rely on that useless Hooper to survive then they were as good as dead already.

Edgewood was raised Catholic, but rather than practice the faith she had neglected it for more than a decade. Instead she had a new religion, and it didn't involve supernatural beings and worn out old fairy tales. Edgewood's new religion was gold, and Kate worshipped it. She was only on this expedition to acquire some of her own, and not just any gold; Inca gold.

The stuff of legend. The stuff dreams were made of. But her dream was slipping away.

She had just one more chance to turn this to her advantage, and she knew just the person to help.

Captives

Kane and the others were held under close guard, the Catholics guarded even more closely in another area of the ruins. All any of them could do was get a little rest. As sleep eluded Kane and his friends, they tried communicating in whispers, confident the porters only understood their native Quechuan and a little Spanish.

"Well, this is another fine mess you've got me into," whispered Evan in his best Oliver Hardy voice. Despite his injury, at least he wasn't panicked. "On a serious note, do we have a plan?"

Kane remained quiet for a moment. It was almost pitch black, the only light the distant flicker of a dying fire. But there was enough of an ambient glow for Craft, Ridley and Haines to see that Kane was not happy. With something playing out in his mind he stayed silent for several minutes. But at last he spoke, and though his tone was quiet, the determination could not be missed.

"We cannot underestimate what we're dealing with here. Make no mistake, we're in a deadly situation. Out there we've got that loose cannon Hooper, and I know we haven't seen the last of him. He's armed and unhinged..." Kane stopped, his disappointment clear. "I should have known... I... since the first day I..."

"You did notice, Hiram," said Ridley, "It's the rest of us who didn't respond. We're to blame, not you."

Kane ignored his friend. "It's my mission Alex, and I'm responsible. My hunch was that Hooper caused Muddy's accident, and I should've stopped him. Anyway, he *will* be back, and this time I'll be ready. On the other hand is Yupanqui, who's no fool. He's convinced the others to join his mission, and although we can handle them individually, we now know they have guns.

"But more importantly they have a charismatic leader who's invoked their Inca heritage and his role in the prophecy. They will follow him to the end of his mission, which makes them dangerous. I say we go along with Yupanqui's commands, and I'll lead us to the real Vilcabamba. Though no one knows for sure my grandfather and I believe the lost city is vast. With a little luck and teamwork, we can use the ruins to escape."

They settled down as best they could, each processing the dire situation in their own way. Calmest among them was the old professor, John Haines. Belying his advanced years, his mind was as sharp as a man a quarter his age, and despite the actual danger they faced, he remained composed. He knew whatever the outcome they will have done the best they could to resolve the situation in the safest way possible. Moreover, he had unshakable belief in Hiram Kane.

Haines had known Kane for almost two decades, since the young Hiram had first attended his popular lectures at the University of East Anglia, and they'd become close friends. Over the years John had seen how dedicated and resourceful the man could be, and knew anyone foolish enough to cross Hiram Kane had better be prepared to lose.

Though his injury was painful, Evan knew with a little

more rest he'd be ready to do whatever Hiram needed. Like Haines, Craft had an almost reverential faith in his oldest friend to get them out of their predicament alive. There was just something special about Hiram, always was. He was brave. Resilient. Confident. Kane had all those attributes and more, and had displayed them over many years of adventures and by faultlessly leading his expeditions. Though Craft himself hadn't always been there in person to witness it, he had heard and seen enough to know that under these terrible, dire circumstances, they were in the best possible hands.

And sat beside them, knees clutched to her chest and the hint of a smile on her face, was Alexandria Ridley. She would rather not have found herself caught in the middle of a double-edged terrorist incident. But there was nothing Ridley liked more than an adventure, and nobody she'd rather be alongside on an adventure than Kane. She knew Kane was at his best with the odds stacked against him, because she'd seen the man in action and knew the depth of his will and instincts. And like the others, she knew with zero doubt there was no one better on Earth to get them through this than Kane.

They would get through this. Ridley knew it. They all knew it. Kane knew it. But what none of them knew, what they couldn't know, was just what horrors they would all face before the denouement of this extraordinary saga.

VIII

Day 8

A Power Shift

Just before the following dawn, Kane emerged from a poor sleep into a changed world. Power had shifted, and he was no longer in charge. Kane didn't seek power, but when your position is the leader of a dangerous expedition in the Andes, retaining control was essential. It was his job. But not any longer, that position now held by the man they thought a cook. Yupanqui was clearly a dangerous man, though his apparent intentions were good in terms of helping the Quechuan people. But good intentions did not justify violence. Kane had to assume he was capable of anything.

Likewise, Kane had no doubt the Eagle Alliance possessed murderous intentions. Evan was shot, and they were lucky there hadn't been more injuries, even deaths, when they tried to overpower the Catholics.

But the most pressing issue now, their frightening reality, was that Kane and his friends were caught between two deadly and ancient rivals, and their very lives were at stake.

Both sides were driven by religion, a notion that had always troubled Kane. For two decades–longer, if he counted his childhood adventures–the world's religions had fascinated him, not for their philosophies and flawed systems of blind faith, but for the products of those faiths. The magnificent temples, mosques, and cathedrals, and within their paintings and sculptures inspired by religion left him in awe. In fact, religion has inspired ninety percent of all art throughout history, but not, Kane knew, because of divine intervention. Cultures from all over the world, each claiming their God was the one true God, had somehow created beautiful structures, monuments, and works of art in the name of their God. They couldn't all be right. In fact, Kane knew, they were all wrong.

In simple terms, the human race has been remarkable at expressing its feelings, and has evolved so far that it could develop those expressions into mind blowing megalithic buildings that have stood for hundreds and thousands, if not tens of thousands of years, all the result of humanity's limitless imaginations and technical brilliance.

And yet here they were on the verge of a disaster at the hands of religious zealots, and that thought angered Kane more than he believed possible. It had, he realised, become personal. People he loved and cared about were in direct danger because of religion. It sickened him.

He did not want to die, but he was not afraid to. Hiram Kane had already lived an extraordinary life, and if he was to die in this drama, he would die a fulfilled man. But the fact John and Evan and Alex, not to mention Sonco's young team, might be killed by the hands of terrorist cowards instilled in him a feeling rarely felt.

Rage.

Blinding rage. And yet it was more than that. If the Catholics prevailed, they would no doubt kill all those they considered heathens, including Sonco and his family, and countless other thousands and eventually millions of their people. If Yupanqui triumphed, then the opposite would be true. He mentioned a foretelling, a five hundred year prophecy that stated when the sacred condor rose, as he claimed it had, then the new Pachacuti would begin, and he would be its leader.

What Kane knew about Inca mythology suggested Yupanqui had assumed the role of the Incan 'earth shaker,' or destroyer of worlds, and that could only mean bad news for non-Incans. It was a fact; the Incan people had suffered unimaginable horrors at the hands of the Spanish conquistadors, all but wiping them and the memory of them from the planet. And it was clear Yupanqui wanted revenge. Well, Kane understood the principle, but killing people was never the right way to do it, even if they would kill you first, something he was sure the Eagle Alliance intended. Kane recalled what Gandhi once said; *an eye for an eye makes the whole world blind*. The way the world was shaping up, with war and death and destruction an epidemic on every continent, those prophetic words were more relevant now than ever.

Kane's thoughts turned to Edgewood. The young scholar confused him. Why was she really here? What were her true intentions? He did not believe her capable of murder, or could even be complicit in someone's death, and assumed she was only there for more personal reasons. Like gold. She was using the Catholics, the way they were all using him. He vowed to get to the bottom of that side issue before this was over. But for now he had to focus on what was best for his friends.

Destiny

Dawn as always was cold, but not only physically; the mood in camp was icy, as if they all knew death hung in the air. Kane had an ominous hunch. One way or another, he believed many of those in the collective group of fourteen would die before nightfall.

However, to Kane's surprise the Quechuan porters greeted Kane and his friends with breakfast and tea.

"There is no reason we should not be civilised, is there?" said Yupanqui as he approached. "In truth, my people have nothing against you and your friends."

Kane noticed the privilege of food was not extended to the Catholics. They had a little water, but that was all. Whatever Kane thought of that, he at least understood. They were the hated enemy.

Once the nefarious darkness had given way to a clear yet no less ominous morning, all prisoners assembled in the centre of camp under the armed scrutiny of the Quechuans. They waited. Tension charged the frigid air with static-like electricity, and as the morning's earliest lukewarm rays crept through the ruins, it did little to enhance hope of a day any better than the last.

Yupanqui looked them all over, and once sure he had their attention he addressed them with disdainful authority.

"Listen with care. You are our prisoners, some our enemy, others because I need you. I need not explain who is who, and I need not explain that your situation is precarious. Very precarious. But there is good news. If you do as I tell you, not all of you will die." As he said those last words, he directed his gaze at Kane.

Haines didn't miss a trick. He felt Yupanqui's subtle glance at Hiram was evidence to back up what he already thought. That, before laying his hands on Atahualpa's treasure, in order to please the Gods the Inca leader planned an offering to Pachamama and Inti. And John Haines did not need to be a world renowned professor to know what that offering would be.

Yupanqui would offer the blood of the enemy. Catholic blood. A grisly sacrifice to the God and Goddess of sun and earth. Yupanqui would drain the lifeblood of their ancient foe at the scene of the Inca's last stand. As well as retrieving their long-lost gold the act of revenge would strike a blow for the uprising, and solidify his belief he was indeed Pachacuti, new and chosen leader of the Inca people.

It was Yupanqui's destiny, and he would soar with the newly risen condor.

It seemed it wasn't just Haines who'd understood Yupanqui's intimated threat. Craft and Ridley shared an anxious glance, while Kane stared at the big Incan, trying but failing to keep his rage in check. *How dare you threaten members of my expedition,* he thought, not grasping it was only aimed at the Catholics. Blood hammered in his temples as he thought of what the Incans would do to his friends if he couldn't lead them to safety. He was about to make a move for Yupanqui, but Haines wisely placed a restraining hand on his chest.

"Not now, Hiram. We wait."

Seething, Hiram paused.

Angelo De La Cruz also glared at Yupanqui, his passive smile now replaced with a look of barely concealed amusement. He knew it was only a matter of time until the disgusting heathen would get his comeuppance.

Edgewood though was far from amused. During the long, cold, and sleepless night, any remnants of anger and disappointment were usurped by the frightening reality of her situation. Her eyes wide, she stood quivering in fear. Kate knew enough about ancient cultures and what had happened to the Incans at the murderous hands of the conquistadors to know not only was her life in danger, but in all likelihood her death was decided. As her imagination ran wild, just how they'd commute that sentence chilled her to her core. Dark thoughts of sacrificial rituals under a high moon with glinting blades and solemn words and not a moment of hesitation with those blades and blood… lots of blood. Her blood. Edgewood wobbled on thin legs now drained of strength. Seeing her falter, Yupanqui smiled. *I have you now,* he thought, *but not for long. Soon you will belong to Inti and Pachamama.*

Yupanqui motioned for Kane to approach him. Breathing deeply to control his rising anger, Hiram stepped forward. Kane was a tall man, with wide, strong shoulders. Yet he was smaller than Yupanqui, and it crossed his mind the man had grown. It was true he'd barely noticed him before the drama unfolded. *Grown in stature, feeding on his own perceived power,* Kane mused. He was strong looking, an oak of a man who looked capable of destruction. With hard, steely eyes to match the physique, he was physically impressive.

But Kane wasn't impressed. For many years he and his grandfather before him had served the native Andean people with their generosity and philanthropic ventures, and hundreds of employment opportunities. Yet, here he was, held against his will with the threat of violence hanging over them all. Again, Kane had to focus hard not to lash out at the man before him.

He would act soon. For now, he would listen.

"Mr Kane, I see you are uncomfortable with our arrangement. I understand. But listen to me now. You have a map, and you will give it to me. There is no point denying me, because if you do, your precious friends…" He nodded over at the huddled trio, guns raised at their backs. "Hand over the map, or I will kill someone and take it anyway." Yupanqui smiled and held Kane's gaze. But in three seconds the smiling eyes were replaced by ovals of flint. "Now."

It was a precarious, tense moment. Kane did not know just how volatile Yupanqui was, and now was not the moment to find out. He slid his backpack to the floor, and on his haunches reached into the waterproofed compartment inside. Then he paused. *I could launch myself at this coward now,* he thought, *and take him down in seconds... but the guns... my friends... Alex.* Kane gritted his teeth, retrieved the map, and with just a moment's more hesitation handed it to Yupanqui.

"Gracias," he said, "Thank you. That was the wise thing to do. Keep making wise choices and your friends will not be harmed. However, if not…"

The threat was clear, and Kane's rage grew just that little bit more.

Kane had memorised the details on the map two decades ago, and he didn't think he would actually need it to find

Vilcabamba. He'd brought it with him as inspiration more than anything else. But that wasn't the problem. He didn't have it, which meant someone else did. And that someone was a man driven with murderous intent. And perhaps worse, if the map was somehow claimed by the Catholics, then–

That didn't bear thinking about. He would not allow that to happen.

He could not allow that to happen.

With the map now in the hands of the Inca leader, the unlikely procession of prisoners and their captors filed out of the ruins and back onto the trail. It remained almost dark due to a low sun still concealed by the magnificent but unseen mountains all around.

Kane still led the group, but only in a physical sense after the power shift, and close behind him was a gun toting Quechuan. The boy looked only eighteen years old and thin enough that a decent breeze could topple him. But the gun in his hand empowered him, and with his leader Yupanqui looking on he was keen to impress.

Next in the sombre convoy were Haines, Craft, and Ridley, with two more Quechuans close behind them. Further back were De La Cruz and Edgewood. Yupanqui was right on their heels and watched the Catholics with narrow-eyed suspicious for the slightest hint of aggression. The Quechuans were also on the lookout for Hooper in what they expected would be an imminent attack by the rogue American. He had guns, and wielded the element of surprise in his armoury. He could fire upon them from any angle and at any moment, and there was nothing Yupanqui could do other than stay vigilant.

The Inca leader muttered private prayers to Inti and Pachamama to keep their protective watch over them, but in truth he wanted the man to attack. It would give him the perfect excuse to carry out his plan of revenge, and sooner rather than later.

There would be some poetic justice if he performed his acts at Vilcabamba. But if it was to take place somewhere before they reached the fabled Inca city, so be it. The result would be the same.

Revenge would be theirs, and it would be final.

Escape

Kane focused on their situation as he walked. At some point during the next couple of hours Hooper was sure to make an unwelcome appearance, and he needed to do something before then. Once Hooper was back in the picture he'd lose any last semblance of control. Also, it was just two days more hiking until they reached the real Vilcabamba, and once there Kane knew all hell would break loose.

Kane had to act soon. Thinking hard, a plan took shape in his mind. What he needed first was a chance to confer with Ridley and the others, easier said than achieved under their current circumstances. He slowed his pace, not enough to impact further back along the line, but enough that those nearest would inadvertently close the gap to him. Despite the time pressures, Kane needed to show patience.

It was another ten minutes of slower walking until he believed Ridley was close enough to hear him, and he chanced a quick glance behind, a flash of anger rising when he saw her. With relief, Kane caught her eye at the first attempt, and looked at her with intent and just the hint of a smile. In her hard eyes he saw defiance, anger to match his own. Alex Ridley did not scare easily, and she wasn't afraid now. Kane had her attention, and with a deft raise of the arm he pointed to his ear.

Listen, Ridley realised, *he's is telling me to listen.* She edged a couple of feet closer to the young porter in front of her and strained hard to block out the natural sounds of the forest. Yupanqui had told them not to speak to each other, but Kane had no choice. In a voice so quiet that only the porter and Ridley could hear, Kane told a story.

"Once upon a time a man and woman were hiking through a forest when a noise spooked them. Probably nothing, maybe a wild pig? An alien? The friends sprinted, understanding there was no danger but running anyway and relishing their freedom. *Go,* the man cried to the woman, and don't stop until we're there. *Where?* the woman cried back. But it didn't matter. She would have followed him anywhere."

A tight smile formed on Ridley's lips, because she knew exactly what Kane was referring to. Many years ago, maybe ten, they'd hiked the Pacific Crest Trail together, starting in Mexico and heading first through southern California and onwards into the north. They were on the trail just outside Santa Cruz, in the woods of the Big Basin Redwoods State Park, when they were startled by something in the trees. They were experienced hikers, and knew it was probably just a pig, perhaps a bear, maybe even another hiker. But Kane just laughed aloud and shouted *Go,* and set off at a sprint to leave Ridley in no doubt she had to follow him or be left alone with whatever monster had made them jump. So she did, and they sprinted hard for an age until they came upon a clearing at the crest of a rise to be greeted by a stunning view of Monterey Bay.

"We're safe now," Kane said, hands on his waist and breathing deeply of the crisp autumn air, and he turned to hug Ridley. It was a fond memory for her, and one she treasured. She hadn't known Kane had clung onto that memory too.

Hearing Kane's tale, it was obvious he was planning an escape, and his message was clear. She'd be ready, and when he said *Go*, they would go. But a doubt formed. Should I warn Evan and John, or does he mean just us? But Ridley knew Kane, and knew his plan must only include them, or she would have known otherwise. Ridley focused her eyes on Kane, tuning out all else other than listening for his deep voice. She walked on, adrenalin flowing and blood pounding trough her temples. She was ready.

Kane's plan was simple. He and Ridley would burst away at such a pace that the Quechuans could not react. They were both supremely fit and fast across the ground, and they would be out of sight in seconds. Kane didn't believe this group of porters knew the area, and although amazingly adept in the terrain, the confusion alone would give them time to escape. It meant leaving John and Evan behind, but Kane believed they would come to no harm. He had handed over the map, and Yupanqui could now locate Vilcabamba without him. He also knew the old professor wouldn't panic, and would assume Kane had thought it through with care. If it went as Kane expected, the commotion would prompt the Quechuans to snare the nearest prisoners to them, and by the time the dust settled and Yupanqui learned of their escape, they would be long gone.

Once they were a safe distance, he and Ridley would deviate from that trail and source an alternative route to the lost city, and Kane had confidence he could make it there before the others. If they were very lucky, Hooper wouldn't know of their escape. However, if they did run into the armed terrorist Kane would do anything necessary to subdue him.

Considering what the rogue American Catholic had done to his friend Evan, taking down Hooper would be a pleasure.

His plan to bolt was just a matter of timing. Too soon, and they would have too far to travel. Too late, and it gave Hooper more chance of showing up and ruining their chances. Kane considered hard, and decided.

His plan made, Kane lengthened his stride in slow and steady increments. The line of hikers would extend, and in doing so edge him further away from the rear of the convoy. Further away from Yupanqui.

"Han shi-gan," he said aloud, then *"Han shi-gan, gwa ga-ja."* Kane assumed correctly only Ridley knew the Korean language like he did, a skill they'd picked up during their years of Tae-kwon-do training.

"One hour," he had said, "One hour, and go."

Less than fifty yards away Howie Hooper crept alongside the convoy in silence. His military training kept him not only out of earshot of the group, but also invisible. However, his patience was at tipping point. Every step creeping along the trail had pushed him closer to his limits, and his mind was made up.

He would go in hard and fast, his primary focus to shoot dead the Quechuan leader. There were six Quechuans in total, and Hooper figured he could bring them all down without reloading his automatic pistol. He may not have been the most decorated of American soldiers, but he was an excellent marksman. However, if one or more of the others got shot in the process, like Craft, or the girl Ridley, that was too bad. Nothing more than collateral damage. And if he was honest, he wouldn't mind if that bitch Edgewood got hit by a stray bullet. In fact, he might even consider her *accidental* death a small bonus for his troubles. That would teach her to talk down to him.

Hooper had only two goals now that things had gone so badly off target; secure the map, and rescue De La Cruz. If he could achieve those objectives, then he would surely gain God's graces. However, if he could just lay his hands on the map and walk away as the only survivor, he could live with that too. He alone could then lay claim to the greatest treasure on Earth and disappear to some anonymous beach town in Central America and live out the rest of his sinful days living like a king.

And why don't I deserve that? he asked himself. On numerous occasions he had been willing to put his life on the line, first for a government that had easily discarded and forgotten him, and now for a God to whom he felt unworthy and unknown. No. He would make one last attempt to win God's favour, and if not he would, for the first time, favour himself.

Shaking off his selfish thoughts of greed and self-pity, Hooper knew he had to get his timing perfect or be out-gunned. He wondered whether the younger Quechuans would be as brave if he eliminated their leader. *Maybe?* But maybe not. Hooper decided it was too risky. He could not just pick off Yupanqui like a sniper, because in the unlikely event he missed, the others would then have a momentary chance to take cover. He had to hit them fast, and take them out with deadly, single shots. Surprise was his ally, but quick-fire successes were his only chance.

Bang. Bang. Bang.

Hooper turned his attention to Kane, and assumed the expedition leader would have a plan too. He considered Kane a tough adversary and guessed correctly he would not go down without a fight.

So the timing was critical. "An hour," he whispered with a wistful look to the sky, as if for a last chance of some divine assistance. Then his eyes turned hard.

"Strike in one hour."

The minutes dwindled towards the hour, and just as the sun sets fast in the shadows of the Andes so it rose fast now, already penetrating the forest canopy with intense heat, the hottest they'd witnessed since setting out from Cuzco. Sweat poured down Kane's face and stung his eyes, reminding him their escape on the difficult trail would be tougher than it should have been.

But Kane felt sure Ridley understood the plan and knew she would follow without question.

Not long now.

A few yards behind him, Ridley prepared herself for the escape. She tuned her senses and made her breaths deep. *Soon.* She noticed Kane up his speed a little. *Clever boy*, she thought, and adjusted her own stride to keep up. There was only the young Quechuan between them, a brainwashed kid with a gun. But she believed in Kane and knew he could deal with it.

Just minutes…

The Condor Uprising: Earthshaker

Yupanqui's eyes scanned the trees with vigilance, surprised Hooper had not yet shown himself. *Soon*, he thought, and strained his eyes into the forest. Nothing. He was satisfied. The young Quechuans were proving dedicated to his cause, and he knew barring some terrible luck he would soon become a legendary figure in the Inca's turbulent history. Moreover, he would lead them into a new and more powerful era than his ancestors could ever have imagined.

Pachacuti. Earthshaker.

Yes, I am, mused Yupanqui, his pride and vanity for a moment getting the better of his genuine beliefs. But seconds later he felt real shame, and as he raised his arms wide in a beseeching show of humility to Pachamama and Inti, the deafening sound of a gunshot echoed throughout the valley, quickly followed by another, and then a third.

The young porter in front dropped silent to the ground, blood pulsing from a hole in his temple. Up ahead another of the Quechuans fell to his knees, clutching his side as if shot.

And then Yupanqui felt it.

He raised his hand to his neck, and as he pulled it away a torrent of dark red blood streamed through his fingers. The Inca leader was shot.

At the sudden retort of the gun Kane reacted in a flash. He

202

turned, smashed the Quechuan kid in the jaw, and without waiting to see him crumple to the ground in an unconscious heap, yelled, "Go." And before two seconds passed he and Ridley were tearing up the trail and gone before anyone noticed.

Craft and Haines threw themselves to the ground, unsure where the shots had come from but sure who'd fired them. But they weren't hit, and stayed down while all around them descended into chaos.

As he charged through the convoy of captors and captives, Hooper knew with a sinking feeling he had once more failed. Yupanqui had not gone down, and though he was bleeding from the wound in his neck, he stood his ground and fixed his rage filled eyes on the American. In desperation Hooper fired off more shots at the Incans, changing his clip as he ran, but time and again he missed and as he sprinted directly at Yupanqui, in one final effort to take him down, his own leg crumpled, his left kneecap shattered by a bullet. Intense pain consumed him, and he screamed out in fury, both from the searing pain and the sickening knowledge he was now at the mercy of the Inca leader, who he failed to kill but who would not fail to kill him.

Yupanqui survived the assassination attempt and ordered his young charges to cease their own shooting. As he fell, Hooper had dropped his weapon, the retrieved gun now trained back on him by the ice-cold steadiness of Yupanqui himself. Hooper looked him in the eye. He saw only hatred, and expected the big heathen to shoot him right there and then. But the bullet did not come. Hooper craved death, wished it to arrive, for in that moment he had never felt so low. He had failed again, the latest in a long line of failures, and he could not take it anymore. "Do it," he screamed, spittle flying as the blood drained from his destroyed leg. "Do it," he said again, quieter now as a realisation dawned that Yupanqui would not shoot him.

Hooper closed his eyes, the pain forgotten, now certain the hated leader of the enemy had in store for him a much worse fate than death by gunshot.

Yupanqui assessed the scene and soon gathered Kane and Ridley had gone. That was okay. Nobody said this would be easy. Victory had waited five hundred years. It could wait a few more hours.

Haines and Craft had also noticed their friend's absence, and before Craft could panic and wonder why Kane abandoned them, Haines placed a restraining hand on his shoulder and said in a quiet yet authoritative tone, "It's alright, Evan, they'll be back for us."

And Craft knew it was true.

Amidst all the mayhem, Edgewood had dived to the floor and buried her head in her hands, sure she was about to die. After what had felt like hours but was just a dozen seconds, she at last raised herself from the dirt, amazed to find herself unhurt. Looking about, she was surprised to see Hooper beside her, prone, inert and obviously bleeding to death. Her survival instincts kicked in. *What does this mean for me? It can't be good,* she thought, and closed her eyes. *And yet?*

And for the first time since the entire narrative had unfolded, the implacable face of Angelo De La Cruz wore a worried look. The disposable help had failed, and he looked toward a sky that broiled with dark intent. For a long minute he searched the brooding sky for a sign, and though he saw nothing other than the constant swirling of ominous clouds, his concern was momentary.

His fate–and the fate of the mission–was now in God's hands, and De La Cruz smiled.

Just as it should be, he thought, *just as it should be.*

They sprinted flat out for sixty seconds, paused for a moment to look behind them and catch a breath, then sprinted flat out for ten more. At the giddying altitude of 4,550 metres, just hiking was a challenge, but to run at real speed left them exhausted. They were not, however, short of motivation, and knew being caught could prove fatal.

Kane and Ridley struck lucky that the trail was more or less flat, the gentle undulations and twisting turns not too precarious along that particular stretch. Kane believed they were clear, but he kept them moving anyway. Putting distance between themselves and the armed Quechuans was of course prudent, but so was taking a break, and after a further thirty minutes of hard graft Kane allowed them time to rest. Ridley sat beside him on a fallen log, and with a sideways glance she shot him a mischievous grin. "You do love an adventure, don't you Kane."

Unable to deny that truth, but unwilling to find what had happened fun, Kane didn't speak. But after a gentle nudge from Ridley, a half smile cracked across his jaw. "If we all get out of this alive, and if Atahualpa's gold ends up in the rightful hands, only then will I consider this adventure fun." He kept his face almost straight. "But…" He looked at his old friend, amazed at how beautiful she still looked despite all they had been through. He couldn't help himself. "But you're right… I do love an adventure."

On they walked, mindful of their voices in case Hooper was nearby. They didn't know exactly what had transpired back among the group, which meant they could not know the American was badly injured and detained. They just hoped their friends were unharmed and had survived the attack.

Andean weather was a series of extremes between hot and very hot, and cold to freezing, and by late morning the jungle heat had risen to ferocious. Their clothes clung to them and sweat stung their eyes, and though both Kane and Ridley were excellent athletes in great shape they were feeling the strain. But as each mile passed Kane felt more secure, certain they were not being pursued. *Small mercies*, Kane mused, a trademark wry grin out of place in that moment.

But the reality of it was that he and Ridley now faced a race against time. They simply had to arrive at the real lost city first, because Kane knew what would happen if either terrorist group laid their hands on the riches.

If Yupanqui and his men found and seized the gold ahead of them, the only good thing that could be said about that was that they were the rightful heirs. But that was stretching the truth. Yes, they were genuine descendants, but they were descendants with a dangerous agenda, and would not be honouring their Incan ancestors in a justified, honourable manner. Revenge was for the weak, an ancient notion. If they did retrieve the lost hoards, and distributed that wealth among the millions of poor Quechuans across all the former Inca nations, then that would be a fitting way to honour their people, their ancient traditions and their Gods. But that was not their aim, and Kane knew they would spill blood to take revenge against the Spanish conquistadors who'd so brutally destroyed the Inca civilisation half a millennium ago.

If the Catholics regained control of their situation, however, then Kane believed things would plummet to even worse depths, in lieu of what had happened on this expedition so far. He didn't believe this small band of Catholics were on a direct mission ordained by the Vatican. But Kane thought if the Vatican did discover some of their subjects possessed the lost Inca riches, then they would surely stake their claim. If that happened, then the gold's rightful heirs would never see a single penny's worth of the value, and would continue to suffer harsh and relentless poverty. If the Vatican did not involve themselves, De La Cruz and his Eagle Alliance would be free to wage an internal war against the uprising, crushing the Incans to death as their forefathers had five centuries previous.

Either way, the result would devastate the modern day Quechuans.

Kane knew there were limits to what he could do. He was just one man, with an able sidekick in Ridley, and for all he knew, Evan and Haines were out of commission and unable to help. And Sonco was missing in action. Kane though was not a quitter and would do all he could to prevent either side claiming the treasure.

So it came down to doing what he had always planned to do. Kane would make it to Vilcabamba, the first westerner to lay eyes on the site for hundreds of years.

And once he was there, he would do everything in his power to prevent a war.

Realisations

The blow was brutal. Already weak from severe blood loss Hooper collapsed to the ground. He couldn't raise his head, though his eyes remained clear, and anyone who saw those eyes in that moment knew that behind them lurked murder.

If he could just get up he would slit the throat of Yupanqui and smile as he did it. Frustration ruled his world in that moment, and it hurt as much as his injuries. He had failed, and now he was being punished, not only by Yupanqui but by his own leader. De La Cruz refused to acknowledge him, and Hooper knew he'd been forsaken by the man whom he had followed into the jungle and tried to save. And if there were ever any last doubts, he knew he was once and for all forsaken by God.

It was now obvious that he would die there in those mountains, but it would not be the glorious death he always imagined. They would string him up like a pig, and gut him while everyone looked on. Except he would not be a martyr. What had he achieved? Nothing. All his life had been one disappointment after another. Hooper agreed to join this mission after his old associate Ferdinand Benedix convinced him it was his path to atonement, a way to make up for all of his failures, and a way to ensure a spot in God's heaven.

Despite his pain, Hooper managed to smile at the irony of

it all. He was there in that Godforsaken place, on a mission for God himself, and rather than be hailed for his valiance, instead he was being forgotten and left to rot.

Well, he thought, *I'm not finished yet. I'll show them. I'll show them all.*

Twenty miles away

Sonco Amaru sunk to his knees. Quietness surrounded him, other than the windswept rustle of the nearby trees and distant hum of the rampaging Urubamba River far below.

He had left his old friend Kane at the Inca ruins, and in despair at the internal conflict he faced, he had fled. His dilemma was twofold. Although he agreed in principal with Yupanqui, that it was time all descendants of the Incas regained power in their countries rather than remain marginalised under their European colonial governments, Sonco did not believe violence was the answer. There had been enough bloodshed in the history of the Incas. Sonco was not a political man, far from it, but in some way he believed there was the need for an uprising.

Also, Yupanqui had insinuated that all foreigners were the enemy, Catholic or not, and that had bothered Sonco. He knew that Hiram and the Kane family had only ever the best intentions for his people. They were his friends, and the decision to leave them had been the most difficult of his life. And right then, on his knees in front of an ancient rock carved altar to Pachamama, the tough Quechuan guide shed rare tears of frustration.

Sonco had been well on the way to his home in Cuzco. He wanted nothing more than to see his wife and kids and make sense of all that had happened. He had heard stories of isolated acts of vandalism by the uprising, but didn't know how big the movement was, whether it was a nationwide underground organisation or the aspirations of one man, albeit a man who believed he was the chosen leader of the Pachacuti.

Yupanqui frightened Sonco. Not in a physical sense, but of the power he wielded, at least in the eyes of his subjects. But Sonco also knew bravery wasn't the absence of fear. Bravery was being terrified and still doing what needed to be done.

Sonco sat up and faced out into the Sacred Valley. No matter how many years he had lived and worked in those mountains they never failed to move him, stir his heart and regenerate his soul. The mountains were a part of him, his heritage, and he was a part of theirs. He didn't know the truth about the uprising and wasn't sure he wanted to. But there in the dirt, high in the Andes and far from home, Sonco understood what it was he had to do.

With a silent prayer to his family, and another begging the support of both Inti and Pachamama, Sonco Amaru made up his mind.

He hoped he wasn't too late.

With their hands bound Professor Haines and Evan Craft felt like goats being herded along a lonely mountain path. But both men were lucky. Neither was injured, and although Craft's shoulder still ached the wound escaped infection and the pain was minimal. Also, being so close together meant they could at least communicate, though they were careful not to antagonise their captor, Yupanqui.

The Inca leader had no personal issue with them, but

it was clear they might be important as insurance if Kane tried anything stupid. They were unhurt and treated with indifference, but were far from happy at being prisoners. They both expected that Kane was already plotting their escape, and agreed not to attempt anything themselves. Until Kane revealed his hand they would go along with whatever Yupanqui decided.

Craft had known his friend for more than two decades, and if there was one thing he knew about his old sparring partner, it was that he would not panic. Despite their banter Evan knew Kane was a good and decent man, and diplomacy would always be his first tactic to diffuse any situation. But it hadn't always been that way.

In their younger years, with Kane still reeling in the aftermath of his brother Danny's disappearance, it was Evan who'd often had to use diplomacy to prevent fights, Hiram unable to control his pent up rage after a few beers. But Hiram had grown, and though he still retained vast amounts of guilt and anger over his brother's probable death, he was more at peace with himself than ever before. Evan was sure Kane would again try the diplomatic approach first. But if diplomacy failed, Craft knew Kane would do anything to save them from the violent terrorists.

Something else troubled Craft. Over their long days on the trail, before any of the drama unfolded he had spent a lot of time chatting to Kate Edgewood, the young English scholar. He understood she was somehow involved with the Catholic group, but he was far from convinced she was a terrorist. Something was not right about her, but he could not accept that. Throughout their chats he had grown fond of the pretty masters student, and felt that they had a lot in common, and there was even talk of a trip together once the expedition in Peru was over. But Evan had endured a long history of bad luck with women, and Kane delighted in teasing him over his dubious choices. Evan liked Kate, though, and he felt sure the feeling was mutual.

Now, though, the entire expedition had gone to shit, and Evan no longer knew what to believe. Sure, Kate was a little floored, but who wasn't, and despite what he'd seen he believed she had a good and moral heart. There was no doubt life would never be the same again for all those involved, whether their intentions were noble or otherwise, and in those minutes of quiet walking side by side with Haines, and under the armed scrutiny of the guards, Craft vowed not to give up on Kate Edgewood.

Fifty yards behind Evan Kate struggled along, feet scraping dirt and shoulders sagged under the weight of fear and pain. Her face and body were bloodied and bruised due to a beating by the guards, and every step was a mammoth effort. She had never felt so vulnerable and low.

Everything Kate had ever believed about herself and the world was now in question. She knew she wasn't a good or moral person, though those failures she attributed to a tough father who had stepped on many toes and ruined many lives to achieve his successes in life. Kate had believed in God once, and was technically raised a Catholic, though she knew her father was a cynical man, and as corrupt as the Catholic church itself. But she was not there in the Andes for any spiritual or religious reasons, and cared nothing for the Catholic cause so important to her professor and pseudo-lover Ferdinand Benedix.

Benedix thought he had convinced Edgewood to join their

fight for righteous reasons and in the name of God. But it was she who had used him all along, seeking favour to secure a place on the expedition. She was selfish. She was corrupt. And she wanted Atahualpa's gold more than anything else in her life. But she knew now that greed would cost her that life.

Was there any way out of this? She liked Evan, and though she had lied to him she clung onto a shred of hope that he'd seen through her bravado and witnessed the younger, purer version of herself she hoped was not yet dead.

Maybe Craft was her only hope of survival. And maybe, if she did make it out of these mountains alive, just maybe he'd become the catalyst to turn her wretched life around.

She would not pray for intervention to a God she no longer believed in. Instead, she would hope for some grounded, more Earthly intervention. Ultimately, she hoped the good deeds of a few good men and one woman would prevail.

That's what she hoped for, because hope was all Kate Edgewood had left.

Yupanqui felt good about things. Kane and his girl Ridley had escaped, and if he was honest he could not blame them. It is what he would have done in their situation. But their escape was of little concern. He had the map. He had detained Hooper. True, he had lost two young Quechuans, which both saddened and angered him, but in the bigger scheme of things they were warriors and they were on the brink of war. Warriors died. They were Inca, or at least descended from Inca, and Yupanqui believed it should be a privilege to die in service to the Pachacuti. In service to him. And soon he would serve their vengeance.

Their passage to Vilcabamba was slower than Yupanqui wanted, but in detaining the captives they had sustained injuries, and in Hooper's case, life threatening. *Good*, he thought.

In reality, the Incans had been awaiting this moment for five centuries, and he knew they could wait another two days. The result would be the same. Yupanqui was certain it would be well worth the wait. The Inca would once more rise to where they belonged among the world's great empires, and he, Yupanqui Atoc, would be crowned Sapa Inca, supreme ruler of that empire.

But Yupanqui's ambition did not stop there. He dreamed bigger than that, and if things went as planned not only would he control the ancient lands of the old Inca empire, but he would gain rule over the entire continent of South America. There was a long hard journey ahead, and many, many sacrifices to make before that moment. But it had to start somewhere, and it would start at Vilcabamba.

And, Yupanqui had his first sacrificial offerings to Inti and Pachamama under his control.

Yupanqui by nature was not a violent man, and he knew he was merely fulfilling the role chosen for him. But he could not deny that he would enjoy spilling Catholic blood. The man had changed since his calling, but it was a change he thrived on. Yupanqui would live up to his duty and the sacred honour of Pachacuti bestowed upon him, and to show that pride and honour to his duty he would relish smearing himself in heathen Catholic blood to worship and acknowledge his ancestors.

And when he did, he would unleash the condor to soar to its former heights.

Descent into Chaos

Light spilled between the branches onto the uneven path in playful patterns, dancing on the earth and rocks as if to signify the day's light performance was ending. It would have been a beautiful scene were it not for the horrific circumstances that had sent them careening through it.

Despite the debilitating heat Kane believed they had made significant progress and felt confident of making it to Vilcabamba before Yupanqui and his crew. But they needed to rest. Due to their hasty escape they had no camping supplies, and with the cold night coming soon they would have to find shelter.

The path itself was the worn out remnants of an old Inca trail, which Kane surmised no foreigner had used in decades, if ever. The area was uninhabited, not even frequented by Quechuan villagers, and it was likely the path was only still a path because of the wild pigs and deer that used it.

They needed to locate shelter before darkness, and with one torch between them time was running out, but Ridley soon spotted what turned out to be the narrow entrance to a small cave, little more than a crack between two gigantic boulders. As long as they weren't hit by a deluge through the night, it would provide them with sufficient protection from the elements for a few hours until dawn.

It was only a little after five in the afternoon, but with the fading light there was nothing for it but to hunker down and rest. It was lucky they still had their backpacks, and though they only carried basic hiking essentials, such as water and snacks, and a little extra clothing, it was enough to survive. In any other situation, each thought privately–it might have been romantic. They would make the best of it.

"What will we do, Hiram?" Ridley rarely used Kane's first name. It meant she felt the tension. "I mean, all those guns, and our friends being held? What can we do?"

Kane paused. He wanted to sound confident, show Alex he thought things would be okay. He needed her to feel confident in him at least, even if he didn't feel it himself. "At this moment I honestly don't know. I'm certain we'll get to Vilcabamba before them, and that has to be our immediate focus. But somehow, once we're there we have to stop them from finding the gold, or..." Kane paused again, this time for a moment too long.

"Or what, Hiram?" Ridley probed.

"Or... Or the world will suffer. We have no choice. We must stop them."

Ridley fell silent, her back wedged against the rocks and her legs folded out in front as if in deep meditation. She closed her eyes, and Kane knew she was thinking hard. She was one of the smartest women Kane had ever met, just one of the many reasons he had fallen for her over and over again, despite his subconscious efforts at self-preservation. Evan once told him a theory he had heard about love, something about each person on Earth probably loving three times in their life, and that only one of them was that person's true love. You might not know who 'the one' is at the time, but in the course of your life you would find out. Kane rarely believed Evan's nonsense theories about life, love, and the world in general, but he knew this: if it was true then Ridley was 'the one' for him, because he had loved her first, and despite the perpetual knock backs, he loved her still.

There had been no one else for Kane, not even close. They had shared and been through a lot together, both incredible adventures and painful losses, all of which had given them memories, both good and not so, that would last a lifetime. She was a tough and independent woman, and Kane knew it wasn't just him who'd failed to break through her emotional barriers. He also knew he had come closer than most. She trusted him and cared for him, that much was certain. Kane just had to settle for that.

He also believed it would take something special, some shift in mentality, for Ridley to fully lower her emotional walls. Sitting there in that dark and inhospitable cave, in the middle of the wild mountains of Peru, Kane wondered if this disastrous, dangerous, and life-threatening expedition could be the event, the unwanted catalyst, that would at last bring them together in the way he had so long craved. A wry smile curled his lips up to the left. Kane hoped that if nothing else came of this terrible series of events then maybe, at last, he would finally get the girl.

"We will have to kill someone."

The abrupt and decisive way in which Ridley spoke from the darkness startled Kane and snapped him back from his reverie. He could not make out the expression on Ridley's face in what was now the stygian black of their shelter, but in his mind's eye he saw her jaw set firm and focused, the eyes clear and strong. And when Ridley spoke she spoke with efficiency.

217

Never one to waste words on small talk, she believed people should speak literally and to the point, a philosophy to match her forthright attitude to life. Given what he knew of Alex Ridley, Kane knew she was serious.

But more than that, he knew, Ridley herself was prepared to kill. From what he had learned about his unattainable love over the years, he knew she had endured a torrid childhood. Her parents died young in a fatal car crash, and Alex was shuffled between multiple foster parents, some unsavoury at the least, and at their worst downright disgusting. She had defended herself more than once from the wandering hands of alleged guardians, and had even fallen foul of the juvenile courts for an attack that put one such man in hospital. At eighteen, Alex finally emancipated herself from a system that had ultimately failed her, and with her new found freedom, she set out alone in the world as a tough yet street smart young woman who could hold her own in any situation.

There was money. After a decade of world travels her parents both become successful in their fields as specialist doctors, and had in place a considerable life insurance policy for their only child. After going off the rails for a while, Alex saw the proverbial light and got herself the education she craved. She spent the next decade both improving her life and the lives of others. She ran self-defence classes for young women on campus, and many other charity projects aimed at helping underprivileged children and vulnerable girls and women. She was an inspiration for many, and she was an inspiration to Hiram Kane.

But what she had just said both shocked him and yet was not that shocking. It wasn't shocking because Kane knew it was probably true. They weren't dealing with simple treasure hunters. They were up against two groups who had both shown they would kill religious fanatics who believed they were rightful claimants to the treasure.

Kill.

It seemed so easy when you just thought about the word. But Kane had always held an open hatred for guns, and could not respect anyone that hunted animals for fun. Humanely killing an animal for food he understood, and even that notion was becoming a struggle. But the senseless killing of animals for so-called sport left him questioning what had happened to humanity. Evolution was fact, no longer doubted in scientific communities, yet had humans evolved so much they now transcended nature, earning the right to kill another creature? No, was Kane's simple answer.

But that old phrase came to mind; *sacrifice the few for the good of the many*. Could it be that elementary? Was life that simple? Did it justify taking one life, or a few, in the hope of saving many more, perhaps thousands? Hundreds of thousands? Kane was just a normal man, born and raised in England into what he believed qualified as a normal family. How was he in a position to judge such things?

"I'm just a fucking tour guide," he blurted into that same darkness, surprising Ridley as much as she had surprised him before. "Why is this happening? Why me? I can't kill another person."

Ridley knew Kane was struggling with the implications of what they might have to do. She slid over and squashed in beside him, embraced him and rested her head on his shoulder. She couldn't be sure, but he might have been crying.

"It's okay," she whispered, "we'll work this out. I'm here, and we'll work it out together. For now we need to rest, and at first light we'll head to Vilcabamba. By then things will seem clearer, and we'll know what we have to do."

Kane didn't respond at first, and sat in quiet, relishing the closeness of the woman he loved as his thoughts calmed and his breathing slowed to its normal pace. He was okay. Made of stern stuff. He thought of his grandfather would do in their situation. He thought of his great-grandfather too, and imagined him in the same circumstances. It was obvious. To prevent further death and tragedy they would have do exactly what *he* had to do.

The answer was simple; they'd all do whatever it took.

And if that meant they had to take a life, then he would do the same.

Trying to put aside their stark dilemma and the dangers of the hours and days ahead, Kane and Ridley got to talking about life and love, and as they often did after a few drinks, putting the world to rights. They talked about how they met, about their carefree days back at university, their friendship with Evan and their respect for John Haines, their families, both the good memories and the bad. They loved to chat, and it came so naturally to them, and for a while it took their minds off their situation. But eventually, after a few minutes' reflection, Ridley asked Kane what he thought Sonco was doing at that moment.

"I don't know, but I hope he's safely with his family. I know he left us, but he is a trekking guide, not some kind of hero. He put his family first, as he should have."

They couldn't possibly have known it, but at that very moment Sonco Amaru was on his way back to them, as fast as he could through the darkness.

Sonco could not have known either, but in just thirty-six

hours he would indeed become a hero.

IX

Day 9

Procession

Yupanqui was so anxious to get to Vilcabamba he marched the beleaguered–and in some cases injured–guards and captives right through the night. The sub-zero temperature bit deep after the immense heat of the day, and Haines figured it was better to keep on the move than to freeze without a proper camp. They trudged on.

Andean trails are difficult to navigate under the best of conditions. Combine that with darkness, genuine cold, their weariness, and their fear of the armed escorts, then it was dangerous in the extreme. Ancient roots of gnarly trees tripped them from out of nowhere. Bones almost always collided with unforgiving rocks when they stumbled. Despite the numbing cold, mosquitoes droned with fervour at their ears and eyes, and the unlucky few leading the sombre procession often found themselves shrouded in the unbelievably strong webs of unseen tarantulas.

It was hardly an official phobia, but those webs were still a nightmare come true to Craft, who had always feared spiders of any kind, despite their modest sizes in his homeland. To know that all around him were massive tarantulas the size of his hand sent shudders through his already chilled frame. Walking just steps behind him Haines did well to conceal a chuckle each time he saw Evan twisting out of the webs, and with his arms bound behind him, doing a kind of crazy, straight-jacketed insane asylum dance. John didn't mean to laugh at Evan's discomfort, but he couldn't help it, and blamed it on the heightened tension they must all have felt.

Haines had no idea of the time, and in his disoriented state he could only guess at around 4 a.m. It mattered little, other than the summation that they must be closing in on Vilcabamba. John's thoughts turned to Kane, and it saddened him.

Haines had believed in Kane and the map for a decade, and yet like much of the world these days it seemed terrorists were involved in everything. He still expected Kane to make some sense of the mess, but just as he knew that in a few hours the first rays of Andean light would illuminate their futures–if they had any–he also knew that as the hours wore on, their futures–if they had any–would fade to dust.

Haines just couldn't see how any of this could end well. People would die, he was sure of it, and he just had to cling to the hope that the innocents among them, such as Evan, Kane, and Ridley, the young brainwashed Quechuans, and he himself, would somehow make it out alive.

He wanted no one to die, but there were among them some heinous villains, and if anybody should suffer it should be those who had warped their faith into blinded, misguided terrorism. He would rather see justice served to the likes of Angelo De La Cruz, Howie Hooper, and Yupanqui, or even Edgewood, who he doubted was a terrorist but who definitely had dubious intentions. This whole drama should end up with those nefarious characters in prison. But that is not what the professor expected.

The professor believed that one way or another, perceived

justice would be meted out by one of the terrorist groups, their hands stained by the blood of alleged enemies. It was so barbaric to Haines that five hundred years ago, deep in those very mountains, the conquistadors betrayed an empire and slaughtered hundreds of thousands in the name of an imaginary Catholic God. Evolution? Haines knew it was a fact.

But it seemed man's evolution had somehow taken a backwards step.

Umaq Huamani rarely spoke. He was and had always been a quiet boy, and since his father's friend Sonco had disappeared from the expedition Umaq hadn't spoken a word.

His first experience of working as a guide had turned into a nightmare. People had been injured, and two of his fellow Quechuans were dead. Now the self-proclaimed leader Yupanqui had said things part of him wanted to believe but another side of him abhorred. He hated violence of any kind, and yet he'd believed in the uprising. Believed in it, or at the very least been enamoured by the impassioned way Yupanqui explained its importance to their very futures.

And there was the matter of the English woman Kate, who had given him the opportunity to secure his family's future for many years. He just needed to help her when she asked. Well, it seemed to Umaq that she desperately needed his help now.

But his emotions were being ripped between the pull towards his heritage and Yupanqui, and the innate love of his family. It seemed to the young man that whatever he decided and whichever way he turned, he would betray someone. *How much do I believe in the uprising?* he asked himself. *Do I really believe in Yupanqui?* His answer would ultimately decide his dilemma. He wondered if it would also determine the fate of his life and the lives of his family.

He did not know Sonco Amaru well personally. Sonco and his father were close, and his father trusted him as an old friend would. Since Sonco had left the mountains Umaq hadn't stopped asking himself a pertinent question: *did Sonco leave us because he faces the same moral dilemmas as me? Maybe he too is torn? Maybe he has left it to the fate of the Gods and gone to be with his family?* Umaq could not know.

Yet he knew one thing. He would never betray his family, even if it meant betraying the uprising and his ancestors.

Race Against Time

After enduring a few fitful hours of sleep in their makeshift rocky shelter Ridley and Kane were awake and ready to face the new day and whatever hostile challenges it provided. With just enough light from their one torch to illuminate the way for an hour or two before dawn, they set off at a careful pace, aware of but blind to the unseen dangers in the darkness. Any injury now could prove fatal, and it was not a chance Kane was prepared to take.

Kane figured it should take around three to four hours of hard trekking to arrive at where he would find the outer edges of Vilcabamba. Kane had always believed in the authentic truth of the map, but until he laid his own eyes on the lost city he didn't know what to expect. Kane had explored countless Inca ruins, and few people alive knew more than him about their architectural styles. But if Vilcabamba was anything like other previously undiscovered Inca sites, then its location would not at first be obvious.

First they'd find themselves in tangles of jungle so thick the beautiful Inca walls had remained hidden for centuries, the structures reclaimed by a jungle that cared little for the brilliant craftsmanship of the Andean people. Next there would be the outer walls, built at a clever incline to make it more difficult for intruders to scale. Through those walls via the ornate trapezoidal doorways they'd find the inner sanctums, assuming that the most mysterious of lost cities was built in traditional Inca style. And then...

This was pure speculation on the part of historians and adventurers. Atahualpa's legendary lost gold could have been hidden in a remote cave, simple yet impossible to find. But if the myths and legends of Vilcabamba had any truth in them, which Kane and his predecessors believed they did, it would have taken more than a mere cave to conceal such a vast hoard from the Spanish invaders, and the reams of treasure hunters in the centuries since.

For more than two decades Kane had dreamed about finding at Vilcabamba a site to match the sheer scale and beauty of world famous Machu Picchu. The awe felt by Hiram Bingham upon his first sighting of the magnificent Inca stone walls–that he so eloquently recorded in his diaries and later book, *The Lost City of The Incas*–was the stuff of adventure legend, and like Bingham Kane believed that whoever was the first outsider to discover the real Vilcabamba was in for the same experience.

He hoped it would be him, though technically it would not be a discovery at all. Kane believed with all his heart that, not only did it exist, but he knew exactly where it was.

It was during Bingham's search for Vilcabamba a century previous that he inadvertently 'discovered' Machu Picchu, an accident that bestowed upon him world fame but scarred him with a lifetime of disappointment, a despondency shared by his assistant Patrick, Kane's great-grandfather. That same sense of failure was then handed down through the generations like an unwanted heirloom, a cursed legacy that would never cease to haunt them until the ghost was laid to rest.

The irony he now felt was like a Conquistador's sword through his heart. After all the decades since the fortuitous stumble upon Machu Picchu, it seemed as if one of the Kane family *was* to be the first outsider to step among the legendary and mythical stones of Vilcabamba. A great success, yet unable to enjoy and celebrate the moment.

There were terrorists marching to the hidden walls even then, more desperate than Kane himself, and Hiram knew if things went against them, as they surely would, then there would be more than just metaphorical ghosts haunting those stones in the decades to come.

Sonco's breaths came hard. It wasn't a lack of fitness that tired him, nor was it his age–fifty-two, despite what he told his friends. In modern Andean folklore Sonco was famous for being one of the fastest Andean guides of all time, setting numerous records for the annual Inca Trail race. No, it was the sheer tenacity with which he scaled rocks and scrambled over ledges combined with the emotional dilemmas he had faced in the last twenty-four hours that wore him down. But ignoring his pain, the rugged Quechuan put his own feelings aside, and focused on only one thing; Vilcabamba. If he was fast, Sonco knew, he might just prevent a war and save his friend's life.

Like Kane Sonco believed the ancient map correctly indicated Vilcabamba's location, and also like Kane had it stored deep in his memory. He had never trodden along these trails before… no one had in centuries… but Sonco was so in tune with the landscape and so adept at seeing dangers, despite the dark, that it seemed he was guided by some supernatural force far beyond a mere sixth sense.

Sonco would agree. Sonco felt he was being guided on this mission by a higher force, a spiritual, even physical guide, and that guide was Pachamama. He was not a deeply spiritual man, more a part-time worshipper of the old Incan Gods, yet he had prayed for guidance at Pachamama's altar, and despite his earlier misgivings, he was no longer in doubt that the Earth Goddess herself now guided him along ancient Inca trails to his destiny.

If Sonco had ever doubted in the power of the Gods before, then he never would again, and repeated his silent prayers to Pachamama for her continued guidance to Vilcabamba, and to the aid of his friend Hiram Kane.

Edgewood was desperate, her nerves shredded, and it was all she could do to keep herself from a tearful breakdown. If she became a burden to Yupanqui, she guessed he would kill her there and then, a deadweight on their passage to Vilcabamba.

Yupanqui must assume I'm part of the Eagle Alliance, she thought, and I'm as much the enemy as De La Cruz and Hooper. Why the fuck have I gotten myself into this? She had barely believed in God before this so-called mission, and since the whole thing had gone to shit she was certain anyone who did was morally and emotionally flawed. If there was a God, at least a good and just God, then how and why would he allow people to kill each other?

She was now starting to realise the foolishness of religion, though she reminded herself of the real reason she had come to the Andes. The gold. But even Inca gold was ceremonial, in other words, a religious icon. How could I have been so stupid? Haven't I inherited at least some of mother's good sense, or just the greed, selfishness, and immorality of my father?

Edgewood knew that none of that mattered any more. There was little she could do to get out of the hole she'd created for herself, and she would get her comeuppance: a grisly death at the hands of Yupanqui. She considered appealing to the man, pleading his forgiveness and begging clemency. But she knew it was futile. He would not listen to a Catholic, the enemy. And even if Yupanqui did believe in her sorrow and spared her life, then given even a quarter of a chance the Eagle Alliance would also kill her as a heathen traitor. She was doomed.

Whichever way Kate Edgewood looked at it, she was doomed.

Unless…

Kate remembered her deal with the kid, Umaq. Was that his name? She had made a deal with him to help her in exchange for US $10,000. He had wavered at first. But with Evan out of commission, and her unlikely to get any sympathy from Kane if he showed up, Umaq was her only chance.

She had to talk with him. And time was fast running out.

Vilcabamba: The Lost City

Kane had no idea what would transpire when he and Ridley got to Vilcabamba. He had considered a whole raft of differing scenarios, but without knowing the exact layout of the place, the state of the ruins, the geography, even the weather, and without being able to see into the mind of their adversaries, all they could do was prepare the best they could and see what happened. It was not how Kane liked to operate, but for once in his life, he was not in control.

They were close, within an hour of the famed lost city. At least, that was what he believed. Yet, despite the dangerous, probably life-threatening situation they were actively putting themselves in, Hiram Kane just could not prevent the tremor of adrenaline that surged through his body.

It was cold, barely dawn, but his shivers came not from the frigid mountain air but from an immense and building excitement. Kane was about to do what so many had attempted to do before him, included in their numbers a host of famous explorers. Not to mention, members of his own family.

Kane was soon to step among the fabled stones of Vilcabamba.

History would never know the truth, but there was a very real chance that the last person to do so was of Inca nobility, perhaps even Atahualpa himself. In reality, Kane believed indigenous farmers most likely inhabited the city in the preceding centuries, and maybe still were. But the jungle was so thick and the trails so unused, Kane believed it had been decades or more since any humans had trodden those stones.

It was a moment he had been waiting for all his life, or at least since his grandfather had first given him the Incan sun disc he still wore around his neck. That beloved necklace, and later the map that was now in the hands of a terrorist.

Putting those thoughts aside Kane and Ridley surged on, their strides and breaths quickening with the flow of adrenaline. It was just the two of them on that trail, but Kane sensed a presence with them, more than one. In fact, so strong was the sense that others were with them he felt as if he were leading a procession.

But Kane knew what that presence was, knew who it was. Matching their strides as they trekked were the ghosts of great-grandfather, his grandfather, and none other than Hiram Bingham himself.

It was just his imagination. He knew it, but their presence felt real and it did not perturb him. Rather, it instilled in him a confidence he didn't feel and an energy long sapped by the harsh terrain. It also made him fully appreciate the very real and significant role he was to play if any of them were to survive this ordeal. There were people, bad people, who had proven themselves both willing and capable of murder, and Kane knew they would not stop there. He had seen it in their eyes, both Yupanqui and De La Cruz, and though each other's enemies they were cut from the same warped cloth. They considered themselves leaders, soldiers, in the Andes on disparate missions but each with the same objective: Get the gold, and use it against the enemy.

They had to be stopped.

Powered on by nervous excitement and eager to see Vilcabamba with his own eyes, Kane sped up to a jog. Ridley struggled to keep up, her lungs on fire from both the speed Kane dragged her along and the thin air she so greedily inhaled. She wanted him to slow down, warn him of the unseen dangers ahead, but she knew the man, knew he'd narrowed his focus to things only he understood.

She fought to stay close to him, eyes fixed on the wildly bobbing beam of torchlight now twenty yards ahead. But suddenly Kane slowed his pace then stopped, so sudden Ridley almost careened into the back of him.

The very first flickers of light began to filter through jungle more dense than anything Kane had ever seen. Branches and vines closed in around them, the trail almost impenetrable, the light little more than useless.

Ridley stood still, attempting to catch her breath and letting her eyes adjust to the darkness, then raised her arms out either side until her hands disappeared into the black foliage so close around them. Unnerved, she soon drew her arms back to her sides. Who knew what lurked in there.

The jungle was quiet, as all wooded areas are when humans pass through, and Ridley could not shake the notion they were being watched by someone. Or something. The only movement was the gentle swaying of the canopy far above and out of sight, the branches whispering as if in warning. It was an ominous feeling, and Ridley's body tensed into a fighting stance.

"This is it."

Ridley thought she heard a voice, but it was so faint she wasn't sure if it was just the jungle playing tricks with her mind.

"This is it," she heard again, a little louder this time. It was Kane. "We're here."

"I'm sorry?" she answered.

"Vilcabamba. This is Vilcabamba."

Ridley sidestepped around Hiram to hear better, and in the evolving light made out the unmistakable silvery sparkle of a tear on his cheek, slithering like mercury in the near dark. She stepped into his arms and slipped her own around his waist, her face pressed against his body. She felt his strong heartbeat and the rise and fall of his chest.

She felt power. She felt pride.

And she felt love.

Kane had done it. He had fulfilled his life's dream. Kane had made it to where so many had failed before him, and whatever happened, whatever anyone did to him, no one could deny him his moment.

Kane took a deep breath, took half a step back from Ridley and wiped the tears from his eyes. Embarrassed, he smiled. But it was fleeting. "We need to move on," he said, "but we must be careful and stay quiet. I think we're alone but... well, you know."

And she did know. Sensing Kane didn't want to dwell on his achievement she resisted the urge to congratulate him. Anything was possible. The area could have been booby trapped, though Ridley guessed that was just in the movies. She looked beyond Kane to appraise the jungle ahead. Was this really Vilcabamba? She couldn't make out any obvious sign of a lost city. No ruins. Not one carved stone. Nada.

"Erm, Hiram?" she whispered, "What is it you see, exactly? I can't see anything in this gloom."

Kane looked at her and smiled, the unmistakable glow of adventure in his eyes. "Follow me," he whispered back, and took her hand. Slowly, and with great care, Kane led her forwards into even thicker jungle, and after perhaps thirty yards he stopped. Guiding her hand, he reached down into thick black foliage. Ridley flinched. And then she gasped.

Out of sight, but unmistakable in its texture, was a large stone, the smoothest she had ever felt, like polished mahogany. Kane edged back the stubborn, leafy vines, and with the torch held close revealed the beginnings of an Inca wall.

Unmistakable. Undeniable.

It was an entrance to Vilcabamba.

Two hundred yards away and entering the complex of Inca buildings from the east side, Yupanqui and the Quechuans led their prisoners slowly into Vilcabamba. They walked in near silence, the prisoners too weak and weary to speak, the Quechuans too overwhelmed by the significance of where they were.

The young men were poor villagers with little or no education, just porters when this expedition had started. But Yupanqui had changed all that. Through his eloquent passion and erudite manner, they were no longer mere human burros, instead trusted and worthy members of the Inca Uprising. It must have been an emotional and powerful moment for any descendants of the Inca to be there in the fabled Vilcabamba.

However, for those young men gold was not on their personal agendas. Their only duty was to serve the Pachacuti and do what was right to restore the Inca to power.

Despite the solemnity of the others, Yupanqui smiled, as if what was soon to transpire he had been awaiting a lifetime to happen. He smiled, yet behind that smile was a fierce and lethal determination to see this drama through to its end. The end would not be today, of course, for this was just the beginning. The end would be when all Catholics and Europeans were either expelled from Peru or dead. To him it mattered little which came first.

He now stood in what most scholars believed was the location of the Inca's last stand. The place that concealed the last remnants of Inca wealth. But that was about to change. The gold would no longer be elusive. And in a matter of hours, Yupanqui knew it would no longer be the site of the last stand.

Instead, it would become the place where after five hundred long years of poverty and oppression, the Incas would at last rise again and reclaim their rightful position of power over all Tawantinsuyu, the land of the four corners.

The Inca Empire would once more be mighty, and he, Yupanqui Atoc, Earth Shaker and newly chosen Pachacuti, would shake up that world.

Then, and with the bodies of dead Catholics strewn on the ground around him, he would fulfil the condor prophecy.

Among Ancient Stones

Minute by minute the night melted away as dawn morphed into a bright new day. They could only guess what that day might bring, but Kane knew one thing for certain: dramas and danger were guaranteed.

He led them forwards. The trail no longer justified such a title, more of a natural obstacle course, and the going was slow. *This was how it must have been for Bingham a hundred years ago,* Kane thought, and smiled. But again, it didn't last.

In such rampant, virgin jungle, any wind from the nearby valleys could not penetrate. A heavy stillness clotted the air, and an eerie silence accompanied the calm, almost as if the bird life were alarmed at the existence of strange intruders. It was perhaps more evidence they were the first humans there in a very, very long time. *Good,* thought Kane. It meant they could remain concealed by jungle with ease should they have to hide. He had a feeling they would.

They edged on, clambering over hidden walls and ducking under concealed ruined arches. Ruins? The stones were so well hidden that the structures might not have been ruins at all, perhaps in excellent condition and held together by the relentless strangle of roots and vines. Only years of careful excavation would really reveal what was no doubt a magnificent site, and as they pushed on Kane wondered if that would ever happen: it would all depend upon what transpired in the next few hours. If things went as well as Kane desperately hoped, no one would be hurt and the reclaimed gold would end up in worthy hands, and not in the paws of one dangerous terrorist or another.

And once the ancient dust of Inca stones had settled over the Peruvian Andes, only then might the majesty and mystery of Vilcabamba be shared with the world.

The sun crept higher, enough to make the torch redundant and cast their shadows about them in jittery, darting movements. Little by little, the spaces between the trees and the stones widened, until suddenly they broke through into some kind of courtyard, which took Kane by surprise. In a flash, he ducked down and pulled Ridley behind a large stone. Even if he believed they were the first there, Kane could not take any risks. They sat as still as the stones themselves and listened. Nothing. Not even the hint of a breeze rustled the branches above.

Edging higher still, the sun slowly revealed their surroundings, as if it was the God Inti himself illuminating their surreal world. And at last, after a further half an hour, the fateful day was upon them.

Kane took a quick look over the wall they were hiding beneath, and with a raised thumb signalled to Ridley they were alone. With a strong arm Hiram helped her to her feet and watched for her reaction. It was a rare occasion when Alexandria Ridley struggled for words, but this was one of those moments. Stretched out before them, in a jungle cleared by an army of slave hands, was the most spectacular and unexpected sight she had ever seen. Mouth agape and eyes wide, Ridley stared, unable to process what she was witnessing.

Kane looked at her and smiled. He understood her awe, and he felt it too. "Need a hand with your jaw?" he teased with a whisper.

Only an eighth of the scale of Machu Picchu at most, Vilcabamba more than matched it for beauty. A dozen buildings lie scattered around, their graceful stone walls immaculate and their trapezoidal entrances built with perfection. Such technical brilliance, such refined craftsmanship. But a question needed asking, and it was Ridley who broke the silent spell. Her question was simple: "How has this never been found before?"

Kane nodded in understanding. "My grandfather once told me," he replied, "that in his deepest of hearts he believed Vilcabamba *had* already been discovered. It was kept secret by a cover-up at government level. Including Google, no organisation was ever permitted to shoot satellite images over this portion of the Andes, and no aerial reconnaissance either, with the threat of being shot down by Peruvian fighter places. The government, according to my grandfather, also believed no one could ever find Vilcabamba from the ground. I know it sounds far fetched, and I never really believed him."

Kane cast his eyes over the scene before him and shook his head. "But now we're actually here, I have to ask the same question. Has Vilcabamba been known to the authorities all along, and if so, does that mean Atahualpa's gold is no longer here?" The trace of a smile snuck onto his face, much to Ridley's surprise.

"Can I assume you're smiling because of the immense irony, I mean, in case what you've just said is true?"

"Basically, yes," he answered. "Think about it. Not one,

but two sets of terrorists are here to steal or claim the gold, whichever camp you're in, then use it to wage war against the other... and there is no gold. You couldn't write it. Poetic justice, wouldn't you say?"

"Are you saying we're all here for nothing, and our lives are in danger for nothing?" Ridley was staggered. "Really?"

"I'm saying it's possible. I don't want to believe that, but it's definitely a possibility."

Ridley continued to stare out at the marvel before her. "It's so beautiful, Hiram."

"I know," he said, and with moist eyes Kane smiled as he recalled the opening words of Bingham's legendary book, The Lost City of The Incas. He'd read it so many times over the years he knew it almost by heart. "When Bingham rediscovered Machu Picchu, he wrote these words in his diary. 'Suddenly,'" quoted Kane, "'I found myself confronted with walls built of the finest quality of Inca stonework, carefully cut and exquisitely fitted together. It fairly took my breath away.' Trust me, I know how he felt."

Ridley knew it too. But as she herself stood in awe over the lost city, she just could not believe what Kane had said. Yet it made sense. The fact the real Vilcabamba had never been found didn't add up, what with modern technology and all the other gadgets contemporary explorers had at their disposal. And why wouldn't the Peruvian government not have invested heavily to claim the riches for themselves? Ridley had to admit, the more she thought about it the more plausible it sounded. And before she could help herself, she released a chuckle as she thought of those idiots Yupanqui and De La Cruz, and imagined their faces as they learned the gold was gone.

"What's so funny?" Kane asked, but he guessed what had made Ridley laugh and tried hard to stifle his own. But the humour was soon lost among the ancient stones. Whether there was still gold somewhere nearby didn't matter now. What mattered was the armed and dangerous criminals coming their way who believed there was.

He took Ridley's hands and led her behind the cover of a wall. "Look, Alex, we don't know the truth about the gold, and if it's here or not, or even if it ever was. But for now let's assume that it is. Yupanqui, De La Cruz and the others, they are all coming here with only one thought: to get the gold. For now Yupanqui has control, but we don't know where Hooper is and we have to be cautious. And there's… there is something I haven't mentioned yet." Kane paused, choosing his words with care.

"Well, what is it?" asked Ridley, concern lining her face.

"I believe that not only do the terrorist groups want to claim the gold for themselves, but… but that they're both planning to make an example to their enemy by way of a ceremonial event."

Ridley didn't quite understand Kane's somewhat cryptic words. "I'm sorry. A ceremony?"

"I think there's going to be… well, I believe there'll be sacrifices." Kane's usually stoic face had a look of weariness and concern the likes of which Ridley had never seen on him before. This was heavy stuff. He continued. "And by sacrifices, I mean that if Yupanqui prevails then I'm sure the Catholics will be killed in some barbaric Incan sacrificial ritual. Likewise, if the Catholics somehow succeed we can be sure they won't leave the mountains without their own form of justice. In a nutshell," said Kane, his eyes full of despair, "there will be blood. Some might argue men prepared to kill for their faith deserve to die, but I don't believe that. What they deserve is justice, and that justice should be administered by government, not some mountain court with no witnesses. We simply must stop them."

Selfless

With stealth, Kane and Ridley advanced deeper into the complex, ducking low and crawling alongside walls when possible. They knew that sooner or later Yupanqui and the others would arrive, but Kane also knew there were more entry points into Vilcabamba, so they couldn't know from which direction Yupanqui would enter the old city. Thus, the need to stay vigilant was paramount, and with no real plan Kane had to keep them out of sight until they had one.

He scanned the area for some kind of vantage point. See without being seen, that was the idea, but he soon realised it was almost impossible. He considered climbing a tree just beyond the central plaza, but that would just limit the range of his view to the immediate vicinity. They continued on, mixed emotions tugging at Kane's heart. From a historical and archaeological point of view, to learn that Vilcabamba was more vast than he'd ever imagined was amazing. But with their lives in the balance, it was bad news.

Ridley tugged at Kane's shirt, and on a hunch motioned for them to angle towards the eastern side of the city. That was where the sun was brightest, thus, it was also where the shadows were darkest. If nothing else, they would be out of the more open central area and could stay more or less concealed.

Without warning Ridley's heart rate quickened. She hadn't seen or heard anything, but had felt with cold certainty the pending inevitability of danger. *It's just adrenalin,* she told herself, and that was good. *It'll keep me alert.*

Then a noise, like a snapping twig. *Am I hearing things?* Kane had not flinched. *Probably nothing.*

Sonco's senses piqued at the sharp crunch of a breaking twig, followed by silence. He listened with intent, his sensitive ears finely tuned to the subtle differences of the mountains and jungle, but he heard nothing more. With strong arms Sonco squeezed tight up against a stone wall and sat still and quiet as possible. He closed his eyes and listened. There it was, that crunchy sound again, though this time more muffled, as if it were someone edging away from him. *Who or what is that?*

Sonco decided to follow, to trust in the skills he'd learned as a kid hunting rabbits to remain unheard by whoever was nearby. He stood and moved forward with the skill of a soldier, and despite his solidity and strength, was somehow graceful in his actions. A sudden soft noise made him pause. *A voice?*

Si. Yes, he was certain. A knot of anxiety tightened in his gut. Something was wrong. He moved on now, sure that someone or something was just a little ahead of him. And then he heard the telltale sound of a cough, quiet though, as if deliberately stifled. *Someone.* And then, to his horror, Sonco heard the unmistakable sound of a gun being cocked. He gritted his teeth, blood hammering in his temples, and prepared to make his move.

The brave Quechuan ignored the chance the bullet could be for him, more concerned it was intended for his unseen friends. With a deep breath Sonco surged forward, just in time to see a porter pointing a gun at the oblivious Kane. Sonco didn't hesitate and launched himself at the kid the exact moment he squeezed the trigger.

At the shocking sound of the fired pistol, Kane and Ridley flung themselves behind the nearest wall, slamming into the unforgiving stone with a thud. "Are you hit?" Kane shouted.

Ridley groaned. After a quick once over, she replied, "No… no, I'm good."

"Stay down." Kane checked himself. He wasn't hit, just scratches from the ragged ground. "That was a gunshot, right? Fuck. Fuck!"

"No shit," yelled Ridley. "Came from behind us, I think. Can't be sure."

Crouched low against the wall, they heard the distinctive moan of a man in pain. It wasn't far away. Someone was hit, and with horror Kane thought he recognised the deepness in that voice. *No. It can't be!* After a cautious peek around the stones, he saw neither friend nor foe, and despite the risk of further shots he moved towards the sound. With cold certainty, Kane knew who he would find.

Sonco sat with his back against a wall, legs drawn up and one arm folded against his chest. The pain was intense. At his feet was the crumpled body of the Quechuan boy, breathing but unconscious, a deep gash across his forehead where he'd smashed into the wall after Sonco pummelled him from the side. He was hurt, badly. But the kid would live.

But Sonco was fading, the blood loss from the bullet wound a constant stream. The shot had entered his right arm on the inside of his bicep, passed clean through, and left a gaping exit wound. What seemed like minutes was only thirty seconds, but Sonco knew that if he didn't get help soon he would be in trouble. He tried to call out, but only managed a dry moan because of the pain. He had somehow broken at least two ribs in the collision.

Kane was close, the sounds coming from just behind the wall. He moved quicker now, the fear of being shot cast aside in a desperate bid to see if his worst fears were true.

He turned the last corner, and those fears slammed home. "Sonco! What the—?"

Sonco's eyes cracked open, just enough to see his old friend, and he forced a smile. But the smile faded, and his face scrunched beneath a wave of pain. He tried to speak, but only managed a croaky "*Hiram.*"

"Don't speak," whispered Kane, then looked down at the kid at his feet. He appeared to be no more than eighteen years old though his dirty face was worn of all innocence. He had been persuaded by Yupanqui, corrupted even, to carry out his violent orders, and now he himself was hurt. Kane unclamped the gun from the kid's hands and placed it in Sonco's. Glancing about it seemed they weren't in further immediate danger, and Kane called out to Ridley. "Alex, come over here. It's safe. It's… Sonco's shot. Bring the packs."

Kane hoped that the simple first aid kit in his bag would be enough to stem the profusion of blood streaming from his friend's arm, as a shaken Ridley arrived and sprang into action. She ripped out the kit and found a bottle of iodine, then tore off Sonco's sleeve and doused a generous splash over the wound. Sonco winced, but the brave Quechuan didn't cry out. *Too brave for your own good,* thought Kane.

Within a minute Ridley had cleaned the wound and tied a tight tourniquet just above the elbow. "I think you'll live," she said with a smile, though she wasn't a nurse and feared that without professional treatment, Sonco was in serious trouble.

Kane cursed. He had a professional medical kit with the main baggage, but in their haste to escape he had left it behind. It contained pain medication and shots of antibiotics, just what Sonco needed now. He kept his annoyance and concern to himself. "Looking good, old friend."

After a few gulps of water Sonco seemed to relax, the worst of the pain eased to an uncomfortable ache. "Gracias, Alex," he said, "Thanks." He looked at Kane for long seconds, his emotion clear, and a single tear slipped down his ochre brown cheek. With obvious shame, he whispered, "Lo siento, Hiram. I am sorry."

Kane placed his hand on his friend's shoulder. "Sorry for what?" he said, his brow furrowed in confusion. "Sonco, you just saved our lives. You shouldn't be sorry for anything, you hear me?"

"No. You are wrong. I am sorry for leaving, and I am sorry for my weakness. I should not have deserted you."

"You didn't desert us. You left to protect your family. And it was the right thing to do. But you came back, and you saved our lives. We should thank you, Sonco. From the bottom of our hearts, we thank you."

At Sonco's feet the young kid stirred, and sat up, unsure of where or even who he was. He had suffered significant concussion and looked weak and vulnerable. Feeling better himself, Sonco saw his chance.

"¿Iman sutiyki?" he asked in their native Quechuan. What is your name?

The boy looked at Sonco, confused and scared. *"Julio-n sutiy?"* My name is Julio.

"Why do you have a gun? Who do you want to hurt?" Now

250

the boy looked bewildered, shocked to see the gun in Sonco's hands. "This was yours."

"I do not want to hurt anyone." His lip trembled, distraught to learn he might have hurt or killed someone. "Did I… Is anyone hurt?" It was clear he remembered nothing of what he had done.

In reality, one of Yupanqui's scouts had spotted Kane and Ridley from afar, and this boy–Julio–was ordered to sneak up and hold them at gunpoint. He wasn't supposed to shoot them unless he had to, but when Sonco charged him the gun fired by accident and almost killed Sonco. Lucky for both of them the bullet only struck his arm.

Sonco wasn't angry with the boy and seized the moment to bring him back on side. "Julio, you hurt no one. It was an accident. You are a good boy, and you will help us now. Can you do that? Can you help us? I will tell your family what a brave man you are."

The boy's face brightened. He nodded, and the flicker of a smile widened his eyes.

Kane took over and spoke to the boy in broken Quechuan. "Where is Yupanqui now? Where did they go?" he asked.

The boy tried to explain with Sonco's help, but still rattled and confused he couldn't tell them much.

They needed to act fast, but Sonco was weakened by injury, and though his life was not in immediate danger his wounds restricted his movement.

"I think you should stay here with the kid," urged Kane. "Stay hidden, and we will get you when this is all over."

The resilient Quechuan smiled and struggled to his feet. "No. Do not even think about it, Hiram. This is my fight too, maybe more than yours. Yupanqui is my countryman, and though I believe in some of his words, I will not allow him to kill people in the name of the Incas. He must be stopped. I *will* stop him."

Kane had known Sonco long enough to know any objection was futile. If he had decided, it would be done, no matter what anyone else thought. He also knew Sonco was hurting from more than just his injury. He suffered emotional torment for what he thought was a betrayal of his friend's trust. Kane himself thought it was ridiculous, but Sonco was a proud man and if he felt that way, then nothing Kane could say would change his mind. Besides, a determined Sonco Amaru was a formidable ally, and Kane was one hundred times more confident about the outcome of this drama with his old friend by his side.

Scanning the surrounding area, they set off for a better location, but had only taken a few steps when a wild scream reverberated around the old stone walls of Vilcabamba, stopping them in their tracks.

Several hundred yards away, Yupanqui was appeasing the Gods.

Sacrifice

Yupanqui Atoc stood tall and proud as the young Quechuans dragged the broken body of Howie Hooper to the centre of the clearing. They forced Hooper to his knees and shoved him forward onto all fours. Yupanqui nodded. It was time.

Yupanqui motioned to one boy, who hustled out of sight. He was gone no more than a minute, and when he returned he was carrying a large sack. The boy was struggling beneath the weight of it as he placed it at Yupanqui's feet and backed away.

If Haines wasn't mistaken, something was moving inside it. *What the hell?*

Yupanqui crouched down beside the sack and withdrew a knife from his pocket, carefully cutting through the twine that held the sack closed. He slowly reached inside, then stood up, his hand still inside the sack. With caution, he slid the sack away to reveal something so surprising it left everyone stunned.

Perched on Yupanqui's arm was a condor. An actual, living, breathing condor. And it was massive. Like Hooper, it too was bound, its enormous wings strapped to its body and its jaw clamped shut. And it looked neither happy nor healthy, as if captured against its will and suffering for many days. It struggled on Yupanqui's arm, but because of its bonds it was futile, and eventually it settled down and fell still. Yupanqui addressed the small, shocked crowd.

"You may or may not know that the condor has always played an important role in Inca customs and traditions. Professor Haines, I'm sure you know of the Yawar Fiesta?" Haines just stared back at Yupanqui, expressionless. Inside, he feared the worst.

"Well, that festival dates back to the time when those heathen Spanish criminals decimated our lands and lifestyle. You are probably wondering what I will do with this magnificent bird, an iconic symbol of our empire, known as Tawantinsuyu, the four corners of the Inca empire. Let me show you."

He walked over to Hooper, whose eyes were wide with alarm. Yupanqui swung a vicious kick into his ribs, and through his gag Hooper growled in agony and slumped to the ground, his strength to resist depleted. Yupanqui pointed down at Hooper.

"This animal here is the bull, and represents the disgusting Spaniards. The mighty condor, he represents the indigenous population, the Incan people. During the celebration we tie the condor to the bull's back and watch as it attacks with its beak while the bull tries to escape. It is a wonderful moment when the condor triumphs over the bull. Shall we see?"

Yupanqui placed the enormous bird on Hooper's back, forcing its claws around a rope that encircled his body. With a couple of deft knots, the condor was attached. Next, Yupanqui grabbed the bird by its neck and yanked off the bond from its lethal looking beak. With his free hand he cut through the strapping that pinned its wings. Then Yupanqui leapt back, and what happened next was gruesome.

The enormous bird, its wingspan close to eight feet, flapped those wings in a desperate attempt to flee, but with each flap became more and more enraged. His claws ripped into Hooper's flesh and Hooper thrashed about, trying frantically to shake free of the bird. That only maddened the condor further and knowing it couldn't escape it attacked Hooper's body with its razor sharp beak. It jabbed and pecked and tore, and within seconds Hooper's back was shredded.

Yupanqui moved around to Hooper's head and pulled off the gag, and his screams could be heard for miles across the valley. He tried to stand, and with the immense power of the mighty condor's wings adding to his momentum, he made it upright, his body staggering and stumbling all over the place in a grisly, macabre kind of dance.

Then he made a terrible mistake. Hooper turned his face to see his attacker, and the condor struck. He rammed his beak into Hooper's eye, the eyeball bursting in a gooey pulp, and again he screamed, further enraging the wild bird who pecked and jabbed at Hooper's face until he was unrecognisable beneath the torn flesh and blood. A few more frenzied, relentless seconds, and Hooper collapsed, his death close.

Yupanqui rushed over and ensnared the bird once more in the sack, and once subdued, he freed the claws from the rope and edged away from Hooper's shredded body.

Yupanqui turned to the horrified group, standing helpless nearby. He smiled. "The condor won. That means the Inca won. It is in the prophecy. It was always in the prophecy."

Yupanqui then opened the sack and released the condor, which immediately flapped its magnificent wings and flew away, blood dripping from its beak and claws, its huge body soon a silhouette against the sun. Five more seconds and it was gone.

255

Hooper was almost dead. Almost, but not quite.

He'd soon wish he was.

Two of the Quechuans hauled his destroyed body upright and tied him to a stone pillar.

Not long now, thought Yupanqui, *until we replace five hundred years of shame and defeat with vengeance and a new power.* Yupanqui addressed the horrified onlookers.

"In a few moments," he said, his voice strong and sure, "we will make the first sacrifice, and undo a lifetime of shameful weakness. We will turn the world on its head. We, the Incan people, will regain our rightful position as rulers, first of the Andes, and then the so-called New World. My reign will mark the start of a new and bloody period in our history. And we will start with him." He slowly raised his arm, his eyes wild with hatred, and pointed a finger at Hooper.

Traditionally, the Incans offered their children as sacrifices to their gods. But in this time of need, when all the world was about to change, Yupanqui would have to make do with these heathen adults. So uncivilised were these Catholics, however, they were child-like anyway, and Yupanqui was sure the Gods Pachamama and Inti would approve.

One thing that bothered Yupanqui was that they offered children because they considered them pure, an untainted offering, but there was nothing pure about Catholics. That was okay though. The Gods would understand. They would accept these offerings, thus accept him as the one Sapa Inca.

Yupanqui would be free to rule the world.

Historically, for as long as two years before the day of sacrifice the Inca would over-feed their children, because a healthy, plump child was a sign of wealth and thus a more respectful sacrificial offering. But Yupanqui did not have two years. He did, however have a rotting corn husk, and promptly stuffed the rancid object into Hooper's mouth. It wasn't quite what tradition demanded, but the symbolism was important and he would not risk the wrath of the Gods so close to his final victory. He waited more than a minute before yanking the husk out of the gagging mouth, smashing out two teeth in the process as the American choked for air. But it wasn't over. Far from it.

Hooper knew what was coming and tried to remain upright and defiant. He tried to appear unafraid. He tried, but he knew he was failing. If there was one thing Howie Hooper knew about his life, looking back now as it neared its end, it was that he wasn't a good person. There were a few moments he looked back on with pride: his years served with diligence in the U.S. Army, the people he had killed in the duty of protecting his country. But that was about it if he was honest. Not much. A short, unfulfilling life.

Hooper had a head full of reasons, but in his last moments all he felt was shame.

Yupanqui approached, and Hooper shrunk away from the Inca leader. Yupanqui loomed just a couple of feet from the desperate American, and their gaze locked. Hooper tried hard to match the Incan's icy glare, but with his nerves were shot and one eyeball missing, to his ultimate shame he whimpered like a baby, a broken down wreck of his former self.

Yupanqui relished the first minor victory. He wanted the man to fear him, wanted him to feel dread, and he did. Yupanqui had won. Satisfied, the self-proclaimed Pachacuti turned to the group.

"It is time." With his back straight and chest puffed out, Yupanqui's voice carried authority. It was his moment, where he was meant to be. "This man is a criminal. He has come to our lands to steal what is ours. Not only that, but he has killed two of our Incan brothers, and the death of our Incan family by this Catholic terrorist has only one just punishment. Death. He will pay for his crimes with his life." He turned back to Hooper. "However, you do have a choice. It is our tradition to offer you a choice of deaths. As it stands, I will burn you alive. But if you admit your guilt, and renounce your Catholic faith, then I will simply shoot you."

Hooper's head dropped. Yupanqui had given him an ultimatum, and neither option was good. He looked over at De La Cruz, pleading with his remaining eye for some guidance, and in the Spaniard's eyes he saw only defiance. No sympathy. No remorse. Nothing. De La Cruz wanted him to resist, demanded with his eyes for Hooper to cling tight to his Catholic beliefs. Howie looked to the sky, searching for a sign from a God who had apparently forsaken him, and the void was vast.

Yupanqui scanned the eyes of the watching people and saw a wide range of emotions. He admired the Spaniard's stoicism, not that it would do him any good. He would soon be given the same choice. The woman, Edgewood, was mortified, all colour drained from her face. But among his young Quechuan recruits he saw only pride. This was all so new to them, and he knew they'd seen nothing like this before. But they did not flinch, and his pride was an echo of theirs.

Just yards away Professor Haines watched on, anger in his eyes, while Evan refused to look. They were powerless to do anything, and even though the American had shot Evan, he didn't want to witness his murder.

Yupanqui looked back to the ailing Hooper. "What will it

be?"

Hooper wanted to be strong, wanted to defy the man before him and hold onto his dwindling faith. But the time for bravery had passed, and he could not face being burned to an agonising death. He looked up at the giant man stood before him, the last of his dignity drained away. With tears in his eyes, he whispered, "No fire."

"What? Say again," said Yupanqui.

"Please, no fire. I am not a Catholic."

"Say it again. Louder," demanded the Incan.

"I am not a Catholic," pleaded Hooper, "I beg you, I am not Catholic."

De La Cruz seethed, and spat on the floor in Hooper's direction. "You will go to hell for your betrayal."

Yupanqui once again turned to the others, the slightest hint of a smile on his face. "This man has proven he is a coward, and he has chosen the coward's option because he is weak." He looked over his shoulder at Hooper, slumped against his ropes with heavy sobs racking his body. "It was the last mistake you will ever make." Facing the crowd again, he bellowed, "There is only one fitting death for a heathen dog such as this, and it will be a death to honour our gods."

Yupanqui nodded to one of the porters, who approached his leader and handed him a large plastic tub. He unscrewed the lid and took a step toward Hooper.

"No," the American begged, "Please, no."

Edgewood closed her eyes, numbed by what she was seeing. She'd never liked Hooper, but this was too much.

"Stop!" demanded Haines, "Nobody deserves this. Please, use your reason." He stepped forward, straining against his ropes, but was shoved back by a gun toting porter.

"On the contrary," replied Yupanqui. "This is just what he deserves," and he poured the petrol over Hooper, soaking him from head to toe.

He took a lighter from his pocket and lit a cloth wound around a stick. He looked at the assembled group, eying them one by one before he looked to the sky. "My Lord God, Inti. My Goddess, Pachamama. Please accept our humble offering. A criminal. A murderer. The enemy. Permit me to exact upon him a revenge in your blessed name. Take his heathen bones from us, and look upon me with your highest favour."

Yupanqui stepped back and appraised his victim for the last time. Hooper thrashed against his ropes, shouting a senseless jumble of words, desperate for intervention. But it was futile, and in those last moments the broken man's bowels emptied, his ultimate humiliation complete.

And Yupanqui dropped the torch, as he shouted, "Ruphay, Katuliku!" *Burn, Catholic!*

Flames erupted in an instant and consumed the screaming American in a glowing fireball, brilliant against the backdrop of grey stone and jungle green. The body thrashed, and the agonised cries continued for a few seconds before falling still and silent, the only sound the thump and crackle of the fire.

The speed of it all was shocking, and the sheer horror caused Edgewood to unleash a scream so loud it reverberated across the ancient city.

The awful, piercing howl was shocking enough, but the following unearthly silence rose the hairs on the back of their necks.

"What the hell just happened?" whispered a panicked Ridley.

"That was Kate Edgewood, no doubt about it," said Kane,

as Ridley clutched her arms around her chest.

Sonco looked Kane hard in the eyes with a fierce determination narrowing his own. "I am sorry I left you, Hiram. I promise it will not happen again."

Kane was about to protest again but Sonco's raised hand silenced him. "Two things must happen. First we find Yupanqui and take him out. He is a disgrace to the Inca. We must stop him spilling blood in the name of the Gods. After that we control the Catholics and take them to the city. There they will face their justice."

With that, they traversed the ruined city as fast as they could towards the provenance of the scream.

Haines turned away, unable to watch the macabre spectacle, as did Umaq Huamani. De La Cruz was angry with Hooper for renouncing his faith, but more angry with Yupanqui for his brutality towards the Catholics. For the first time the usually unflappable Spaniard bared his emotion, and raged against his ropes, eyeballs locked on the leader of the uprising. Yupanqui saw the Spaniard's fury and smiled with satisfaction.

The agony Hooper suffered in those first seconds was excruciating, like a thousand razors slashing his flesh. It took just half a minute for the flames to incinerate his clothes, and another thirty seconds for his flesh to start cooking. The stench of seared human skin and burned hair drifted to the others. Edgewood fell to her knees and puked.

Yupanqui stepped closer to Hooper's smouldering remains, adrenaline raging from the enhanced power he felt. He watched as the last of the ropes disintegrated, and the charred corpse crumbled to the scorched earth. It was over.

Howie Hooper was dead, and the first of Yupanqui's sacrificial offerings had been made.

He quickly made ready his next victim, and dragged Edgewood kicking and screaming to a second stone hitching post as Haines looked on. The professor doubted even Yupanqui knew the significance of that post, known as an *Intihuatana*, a 'hitching post of the sun'. Five hundred years ago it was how the Incas metaphorically hitched the sun to keep it with them throughout the day. Haines was horrified to see it being put to a far more deadly and horrific use.

Nothing would stop Yupanqui from his destiny, but he had to move fast. Edgewood was weak, and too in shock to put up much fight, and Yupanqui trussed her tight to the stone post with ease. With all hope lost, and out of her mind with fear, Edgewood shut her eyes and waited to die.

Yupanqui stepped forward and repeated the same words he used before to appeal for good favour from Inti and Pachamama for his next offering. This time though, the method of murder was different, and Yupanqui grabbed a club-like paddle from a porter. The heavy weapon would strike a killer blow, a more humane death at least, and he stared at the woman before him for a few seconds. He stared at her, and he felt nothing. She had cried for forgiveness, begged mercy of the new Inca leader, which he found amusing. He did not care that she was sorry, that she had renounced Catholicism and sworn allegiance to his cause.

He did not care at all.

It was her time to die.

Saviour

Yupanqui loomed large over Kate's slumped body.

At that moment, the big Incan swung the weighty paddle in a graceful arc behind him, as if it were nothing heavier than a baseball bat. But just as the ancient weapon began its arcing descent Yupanqui was slammed from the side. The surprise was so great, and the impact so forceful, that the weapon clattered to the floor. But before he knew who'd attacked him the paddle smashed into his head and all the world went black.

Umaq Huamani was stunned. He didn't know where he had found the courage to attack the giant Inca leader. It was almost like watching someone else, an out-of-body experience. But like some of the others, he had watched on as Yupanqui burned the American to death, and he'd felt nothing, his innate Incan emotions rising with the flames. Hooper was a bad man who deserved to be punished for what he'd done to the others. But the Edgewood woman had offered his family an escape from poverty, a better future, and even if her intentions were immoral, Umaq's family were his priority.

She had shown what looked like genuine sorrow for her actions, and Yupanqui had waved away her pleas. Umaq understood Yupanqui's philosophy, his intentions, and knew the reasons behind it. But Umaq was raised to trust people, give them the benefit of the doubt, and when he saw the fear and terror in the woman's eyes as Hooper suffered his fate, Umaq believed in her shame.

Looking on, he knew that if she died today in those mountains, his family would never see the future she had promised, and powered on by a combination of rage and fear and justice, he charged Yupanqui before anyone could stop him.

Edgewood heard the commotion, and opened her eyes to see her killer in a heap on the floor, the bloodied paddle swinging loose in the hands of the kid, Umaq. And she wasn't dead. Upon that unlikely realisation, hot tears of relief spilled, her body shaken by violent spasms of shock.

Still stunned by his actions, Umaq was slow to react as the other Quechuans attacked him, beating him to the rocky ground with a flurry of punches and kicks, but just at the moment one of the porters looked set to strike a killer blow with the same paddle, a gun shot rang out nearby.

All eyes turned towards the sound, and a second later, Kane and Ridley came bursting into the clearing, Sonco trailing a few seconds behind.

Kane fired into the air again, the surprise making statues of everyone where they stood. The three Quechuans had just one gun between them, and in shaky hands the boy in possession pointed it at Kane.

"Sayachiy!" he shouted in Quechuan. Stop! Though no translation was necessary. The boy was unsure, more panicked, confused kid than lethal killer. And Kane thought he looked scared. But the gun remained pointed in his direction, so he stopped. Slowly, and with great care, Kane

264

edged towards the youth.

"Put it down," Sonco demanded in Quechuan, though his voice was calm. "Put the gun down."

"Mana!" *No!* he shouted back, but his voice faltered. The boy stared at Sonco, wavering, then looked to the others for support. None was forthcoming, as they each hung their heads in shame.

Umaq struggled to his feet, his bloodied face a mess. But he stepped forward, and with great bravery stood directly in front of the boy with the gun.

"Allichu," he said, his voice soft. *Please*. "This is wrong. My brother, this is wrong. We were tricked by Yupanqui. Yes, we are descended from the Incas, but we shame their name if we act this way." He pointed to the Catholics, De La Cruz and Edgewood. "They will get their justice for what they have done, but not this way. This is not the Inca way. Put down the gun, my friend."

The young Quechuan did not move, and for long and tense seconds no one watching could guess the outcome. But, ever so slowly and with a hint of tears in his soft eyes, he placed the gun on the ground. Umaq took a step forward and embraced the boy. "Wawqe." *My brother.*

Moving in Kane grabbed the gun from the floor and handed it to Sonco, an intense look of relief on his wizened face.

Yupanqui stirred. While unconscious they'd secured him with heavy ropes, and once they felt satisfied he and the young Quechuans posed no further threat Kane and Ridley released Evan and Professor Haines from their ties.

Evan shook his head, tears in his eyes. He didn't say a word before grabbing his oldest friend in a tight hug, but immediately regretting it for crushing his injury.

"Let me guess," said Kane, "You're pleased to see us?"

"I... I thought we were finished after he killed Hooper. I felt sure–" He turned to look over at Edgewood, and Kane and the others followed his eyes. Slumped against her bonds, a physical and emotional wreck, tears of relief and shame stained her ashen face. She was a part of all this, Evan knew, and she was right to feel ashamed. Yet somehow he still felt for her, believed her shame. He approached slowly, Kane and the others turning their attention to Yupanqui.

Trussed ingloriously to that cold stone hitching post, and just seconds from death, Kate was having an epiphany. She said to herself a silent vow, promising to change, to become a better person, and to repay the immeasurable debt of gratitude she had to the boy, Umaq. He had saved her life, and although she believed it was in part because of the money she'd promised, she also wanted to believe that he did it because he recognised her sorrow. Kate Edgewood knew she would spend the rest of her life dedicated to helping those less fortunate than her, and she would start with Umaq Huamani and his family.

Looking up she saw Evan, and although she knew he might never trust her again, and with much justification, she welcomed his weak smile and took his offered hand.

Yupanqui stirred in and out of consciousness for an hour before finally regaining his senses. He groaned, severe pain rocking his head, and vomited on the floor. Umaq had given him a tremendous whack with the paddle; it would have killed lesser men. But not only was Yupanqui a giant man, he was also a warrior instilled with the God's favour. At least that's what he believed. He straightened, and looked over at Kane and the others. He had not heard Kane's speech.

Sonco was charged with keeping a close eye on the fallen Inca leader, and motioned to Kane that he'd awoken. There was no doubt he was still a danger. His sheer size and force of will ensured that. If he somehow got free of his restraints, he would try and rally the young Quechuans again, veer them back to his side with fear and the power of his words, and lead them on a final assault on the gold and the Catholics. They had him securely bound, but would continue to watch him with diligence.

De La Cruz glowered at Kane, his mission in the mountains far from over. The Spaniard was around fifty, average height and small in stature. But beneath his filthy, tattered clothes hid a muscular, wiry-strong man. He strained at his ropes, rage growing with every passing minute. It wasn't the gold that the terrorist wanted, but the power the gold would give him. De La Cruz was a zealot, a devout and dedicated servant of God, and knew he could never rest until he'd carried out God's will. The Spaniard believed the rise of the Incans would cause never-ending problems to Catholics across South America, and although Yupanqui–nemesis leader of the uprising–was stifled others would follow.

The traitor Hooper was dead. Edgewood had abandoned the cause out of self-preservation. He himself was bound like a rabid dog, and he had no ally to help him escape. The Spaniard was alone.

There was, of course, God.

Despite his almost hopeless predicament Angelo De La Cruz still believed, his faith stronger than ever. And the Spaniard knew if he did just one more thing in these mountains before he left, whether as a prisoner or as a successful attendant to God, he knew he would kill Yupanqui.

De La Cruz was aware he would need divine intervention. He would not have long to wait.

Decisions

As the afternoon heat rose with the air pressure, a shimmering haze settled across the valleys. Perhaps two more hours of daylight remained before the mountains would once more swallow the sun, and Kane needed time to prepare.

The previous days were the most challenging of his adult life, an exhausting and emotional drain on both Kane's physical and mental strengths. In need of a little space, he took himself away from the others in search of a few moments of reflection, and after just a couple of minutes' walk through the ruins he found an isolated spot on an intact Inca wall. He sat, his long legs dangling across the ancient stones, and with the sun on his face he tried to force all the drama out of his mind and focus on where he was, if just for a few minutes.

Vilcabamba.

For hundreds of years the world believed Vilcabamba had vanished beneath the mists of time, reclaimed by the jungle and gone the way of the Incas. In more recent times, it mattered little that the Peruvian authorities may have rediscovered the site, because the rest of the world didn't know of its true existence, whether fable or fact, whether legend or lies.

But Kane knew.

Many, many people had tried and failed to do what he was

now doing; to sit on an Incan wall at Vilcabamba, deep in the Andean wilderness, and gaze upon the ruins of one of the last truly undiscovered places of the world. Many even paid with their lives.

It was a momentous moment in the history of world exploration.

And yet humans, as they had a long and tragic habit of doing, had somehow tainted the moment forever.

There was just no way Kane could avoid involving the authorities. He had a moral duty to inform them about the Catholic terrorists, the dead and injured porters, and the attacks on Muddy Waters and his friends. And there was also the issue of Kate Edgewood, who had started out with criminal intentions, but who at least showed genuine remorse. Kane would worry about that later.

And then there was Yupanqui, dangerous leader of the Inca Uprising. The man had murdered Hooper in cold blood and was seconds from killing Edgewood. No doubt De La Cruz would have been next. Only because of the bravery of Umaq Huamani was Edgewood still alive. They had to turn Yupanqui, a murderer, over to the authorities.

Peru only issued the death penalty in cases of treason during war time, and Kane knew if either Yupanqui or De La Cruz had prevailed, war would be upon the Peruvian people. The current president of Peru was of mixed descent, a native Quechuan father and an Italian mother, and Kane wondered where his loyalties lie.

Kane did not know, but he knew it didn't matter. There would be others like Yupanqui. If Yupanqui received a death sentence for his crimes, or at least sentenced to life in prison, Kane's fear was the Quechuans would make a martyr of him, rise up in his name to wage war against the Europeans, whether Catholics or not. It was a frightening thought, but Kane wondered if it might be safer for the innocent Peruvians if they did not turn Yupanqui over.

It was a difficult and unfair decision Kane felt unqualified to make. He could not know his decision would soon be made for him.

Sonco sat huddled with the remaining Quechuan young-sters, holding council with boys that not long ago were ready to kill in the name of the Incas. But Sonco was not ashamed of them. Instead, he was proud of their passion for an Incan heritage they had known so little about until Yupanqui had spoken to them. Until he had corrupted them.

Sonco's mission now was to ensure their passion stayed on the right side of the line. His side.

Sonco himself had been swayed by Yupanqui's powerful sermon. Now it was he who felt pressure to be just as persuasive. If not they risked losing them again.

"My sons," he said, "My brave Quechuan brothers. Do not feel ashamed about what has happened here in our mountains. The history of our people should make you proud, just as it should make the Spanish people ashamed of theirs. But what the Spanish did to our Incan ancestors in the sacred lands of Pachamama was so long ago in the dark past, and the world has changed. Since those painful days, when our people got tricked into slavery and death, those of us descended from the mighty Inca now lead peaceful and settled lives. The years have been unkind to us, it is true. We are poor, and our families have suffered in poverty for decades, even hundreds of years. But ask yourself: Are you happy? Are you loved? Do you have homes, and families that love you?"

Murmurs of assent and subtle nods of comprehension from the young porters warmed Sonco's heart, as they listened to their wise elder. "I know it is true. I too am loved. I too am happy. For now, let that knowledge be enough. Banish thoughts of shame from your hearts. Eliminate thoughts of revenge from your souls. The Incas were strong, brave people. Now is the time to be strong and brave again.

"We can rise. We can show our strength. But let us do it in peace, and let it begin with ourselves. Fighting is for the weak. Fighting is for those led by others. It is the time to become our own leaders. Yupanqui claimed he was the new Pachacuti, the new leader of the Incas. Your king. But he was wrong. Become your own king. Become your own Pachacuti, ruler of your own hearts and in control of your own destinies. No one person has power over that. No one..." Sonco paused and took a deep breath. "Except you."

Sonco gazed at the young men before him, and saw looks of astonishment in the eyes gazing back. He had won their hearts and minds by speaking the truth. As their hearts filled with emotion, each of them stepped forward and embraced the man who had made sense of the world, and who, in their eyes, had himself become Pachacuti.

Sonco turned his attention to Umaq, the quietest of all the boys. It had emerged that Edgewood had tried coercing the boy for her own ends, and Sonco could tell the boy struggled with the guilt, could see it in his eyes.

"It was a brave thing you did to save that woman, Umaq. Very brave. It does not matter about the reasons why, and you should feel no shame about the money she offered. I know your family, and I know as the man in that family you have a duty to support your loved ones. But in my heart I know the truth. You reacted to save her life because Yupanqui was wrong. Killing is wrong. She too was wrong to be involved with the terrorists, though it is not wrong to consider herself a Catholic. It is her choice, just the same way it is my choice or your choice to follow Inti and Pachamama. Or to follow nothing. The world in which we live now is a world in which all men, women, and children should be free to choose. Freedom..." said Sonco, as he looked again into the eyes of the men before him, "Freedom is the greatest of all liberties."

Umaq smiled, grateful for Sonco's attempt to wash away his shame. It would take more than a few kind words to absolve himself completely, but it was a start.

Sonco continued. "Humans, no matter where we live or where we are from, and the colour of our skin and the gods we believe in or don't believe in, once we look inside our hearts and minds we are all the same. Yupanqui got corrupted by his ego, holding onto some wayward belief he was the leader of an Inca Uprising. Some might say his intentions were noble, but noble intentions become ignoble when used in the wrong way. Yes, as Q'ero he is an Inca descendent–just like us–and we shall remember that. But Yupanqui committed heinous crimes, his heart tainted by power and greed. He will receive due justice."

Gold?

After the horrific sacrifice of Howie Hooper and the near death of Kate Edgewood, the atmosphere was simmering. Edgewood had been seconds from death, but was now safe, secured and resting. Angelo De La Cruz was also detained, but for the first time they saw a new expression in his eyes. Rage. His plans had unravelled, and the man was powerless to do anything. He had lost control of his mission, and he seethed. Yes, it was still in God's hands, which was always the most important factor, but now it was personal.

There seemed little danger now from the Quechuans. Yupanqui was securely bound, with no chance of escape, and after a decisive lecturing from Sonco, his former converts had realised their mistakes and sworn allegiance to Sonco and Kane. It was a close call for a few of them, but due to the bravery of one of their brethren, Umaq Huamani, and their respect for Sonco, they had crossed back without too much emotional damage.

With unlikely confidence restored among the group that their mission could still be a relative success, an unsaid question hung in the air among them: Where, if at all, is the gold?

After a couple of hours of contemplation and well-needed rest, it was Evan who at last broke the spell. He took a seat next to Hiram as dusk faded to black.

"Look, I know it's no longer important, I mean we are at Vilcabamba, which was the main aim. Right?"

"Right," replied Kane. "But…?" He could tell what was on his friend's mind.

"But. Come on, you guys can't tell me you're not all thinking about the gold." Evan looked at his friends. Ridley wore a kind of lopsided smirk, as if she agreed with him but didn't want to admit it. Professor Haines was a cool customer, and his poker face did not betray what was on his mind. But behind that facade, he was indeed wondering about Atahualpa's gold.

Kane just shook his head in mock annoyance. He wanted to know the truth, and even though he believed the treasure was no longer in the vicinity of Vilcabamba he couldn't know for sure. It was impossible to know. If there was one thing that all the world's great mysteries had in common, it was that they did not give up their secrets easily.

"Well, old mate, considering everything that's happened I guess I should tell you my theory on the gold." He grinned. "But you might not like it."

"What do you mean?" Evan frowned like a child who'd been told Christmas was cancelled. Ridley and Haines looked more captivated by Kane's cryptic words.

"Look, I've been thinking. Something Sonco said, and some of the things my grandfather said over the years has made me question whether the gold even exists."

"What?" exclaimed Evan. "Of course it exists."

"You're right," Kane agreed. "I'm sure it exists. But that's not what I'm saying. The question is whether it's still at Vilcabamba, or has it gone? Think about it. Why has it never been recovered? Why, with all the technology and gadgets used by organisations these days, has its true location never been found? With an estimated value of two billion dollars, of course the Peruvian government would have done anything and everything in their power to find it, not to mention private collectors and those just in it for the adventure. See what I mean? The chances of it being here are slim. Slim to none, probably."

"Okay, but that's not official, is it? It's just your theory, right?" probed Evan, unwilling to accept everything they had gone through without knowing for sure about the gold. "I mean, if it's just a theory, then a theory could be wrong, and the gold could just as easily still be here as not, right? Right?" The words came in a flurry, almost as if the lure of the fame and treasure had Evan under a spell. He surged on. "Ah, come on Hiram, you can't tell me that we're just going to give up? I know for you it was about Vilcabamba, but still… the glory of finding the gold would be the story of the century." He slumped back on his arms, as if he realised he had let himself down. A bashful smirk softened his face. "Sorry, pal… got a little carried away there."

Kane smiled and nodded, then fell silent for a while, a pensive frown betraying his deep thought. He looked at the people around him. Friends. Colleagues. Enemies. All poised, waiting for Kane's words. Even the enraged De La Cruz was listening, trussed nearby but intrigued by Kane's revelation.

But it was true. Unless a person had been directly involved with the discovery and subsequent removal of the infamous horde, nobody could know for sure if the treasure existed, and if so, where it was now.

It could still be there at Vilcabamba, buried deep in a cave or hidden among the ancient citadel stones. But–and Kane knew it was probable–Atahualpa's gold could have been recovered from the mountains at any time in the last five hundred years, and the likes of Hiram Bingham and myriad other explorers and treasure hunters might have been chasing wild geese ever since.

The conquistadors might have found and shipped the gold to Spain after the Conquest, or anywhere in the Spanish empire, like Cuba, the Caribbean, or anywhere in the vast continent of the New World.

But…

Kane was an explorer. An adventurer. As a child he created treasure hunts for his kid brother Danny. His grandfather had done the same for him. Written deep within his genetic code was a desire to look for things and question everything, and right now Hiram felt torn over the question of what to do.

His heart ached to find the elusive treasure and claim it for its rightful heirs. Though he didn't crave fame, it would be bestowed upon him. Not only for locating the real lost city of Vilcabamba, but he and the Kane family would be known forever as those who returned a lost empire's artefacts and culture to its people. That to Kane was worth a million times more than his own fame and fortune.

It had always been the objective, the ultimate challenge. He had succeeded in the first part. He had found Vilcabamba.

On the other hand people had died in the search of the city and its treasure, including on this expedition. And if the terrorists who'd infiltrated his party claimed the gold, many more would die.

Though it broke his heart, and went against his innate, adventurous philosophy, Kane knew what he had to do. He turned to his friend, a mix of sadness and courage in his eyes.

"Evan, you're right. Atahualpa's gold could be here. It might even be within yards of where we're sitting. But I have to ask you mate, as I ask all of you here now; even if it is here and we could still find it, the real question is... should we?"

Kane let the question hang there for a few moments, and watched as the others digested what he'd said. Among them he saw nods of recognition, bewilderment, and disappointment. But overall, at least among his friends, he saw the hint of understanding.

"What I mean is, the things we've witnessed and been through on this expedition have raised a very important question. Is it better that the truth about the gold remains a mystery? Or do we go one step further and solve the mystery with a lie? Declare the gold has vanished? Think about that. As long as there are those people... explorers, and governments... even terrorists... who believe that unimaginable riches exist somewhere in these mountains, then there will always be people dying to find it."

Kane sensed an air of comprehension settling among his friends as they listened.

"I wonder... I wonder whether it's best that we ourselves don't even look for it. We could return to Cuzco and declare Vilcabamba to the world, yet tell them after a comprehensive search of the citadel and the surrounding we found no hint of Atahualpa's horde anywhere. Perhaps add that we'd found the treasure chamber, but also clear evidence the contents were long since removed from the site? It would once and for all stop people killing and dying for the gold."

A weighty silence hung around the group, each of them lost in their own thoughts. They had all been through hell on this expedition, both the good guys and the bad, and the idea of leaving without even a cursory search for the gold was difficult to swallow for everyone.

And yet, as each of Kane's friends searched their hearts, they knew that he was right. How could they live with themselves if they found the gold, and it later fell into the wrong, corrupted hands, resulting in death and the suffering of many more people? Nobody wanted that on their conscience.

X

Day 10

An Angry Goddess

Lying in his sleeping bag, the pre-dawn hours numbingly cold, Kane's mind drifted to Danny. It often happened in times of stress, and it was a habit he had never been able to shake. He clasped his Inca sun disc, and again thought back to the day his grandfather had given it to him. Danny had never received anything like it. He never got the chance.

"One day I'll make up for it," he whispered. "One day." Kane rolled over, and clutching his sun disc drifted off to sleep once more.

The darkest of the night had melted away over the mountains, and a pale dawn infiltrated the magnificent Inca walls of Vilcabamba.

Unable to sleep any longer Alexandria Ridley rolled over in her sleeping bag. Roused from her semi-conscious state by a gentle shaking, she put it down to a realistic dream. Alex unzipped her tent and breathed in the cool, crisp air. From her position she made out the distant silhouettes of jungled mountain slopes, the tops of which glowed orange from the early sun.

"Wow," she whispered out into the valley, "What a view."

And what an adventure. Now things had settled, and the good guys were clearly distinguished from the bad–only

Edgewood lie in limbo between the two–Ridley stretched out and yawned, relaxing for the first time in many days. Perhaps relaxed was too comfortable a word. She felt safer, and for now that was enough.

All they had to do now was negotiate a safe passage back into civilisation, no mean feat under the circumstances, and escort the terrorists to a police station at the first chance.

They had all agreed with Hiram's philosophy and proposal. From now on, their official stance was that, despite their thorough search, there was no sign of any gold. The press would have a field day with the revelation, but Kane had insisted it was the right and only thing to do. Ridley was only human, and thoughts of all that gold left her smiling ruefully in those silent few minutes. But she was not sad for herself, far from it. She was happy for Hiram that he was the man to at last locate Vilcabamba, and knew how much it meant to him and the Kane family. But she was also sad for him, sad that it had all gone so wrong.

At least they were alive. None of Hiram's group had sustained serious injuries. Muddy Waters had a close call, and Evan and Sonco were shot. But she and John Haines remained somehow unscathed, other than the emotional turmoil and a few cuts and bruises. They had all been lucky in different ways, and who knew, once it was all over they might even look back upon the expedition with something like fond memories.

Content and excited to leave the mountains, and in awe of the majestic vista spreading out before her, Ridley listened to the birds welcome in the new day. But after a few more minutes in quiet contemplation she stood to rouse Kane from his nearby tent.

Suddenly, though, the chirping birds fell silent. *Strange*, she

284

thought, then an equally sudden flash of fear clenched her guts. Ridley knew the animal kingdom was a good portent of unease in the landscape, highly tuned to its faults and nuances. She waited a moment, eyes and ears strained for any sign of danger, but heard nothing. Alex half expected some rumbling in the mountains as she ran to shake Kane awake. He woke with a start, and smiled through weary eyes.

But when he saw the look of deep concern on Ridley's face, the smile faded. "What is it?"

"Listen," she replied, her apprehension clear.

A few yards away Sonco emerged from his tent, and as if it was the most natural thing in the world, said, "I have a terrible feeling."

Three seconds later, the world turned upside down.

The ground shook in waves so powerful that anyone standing got thrown to the dirt with violent contempt. The thundering, primitive roar emanating from within the ground intensified, while thick and ancient trees swayed in wild arcs as though they were dainty flower stems. Massive boulders fell, and Inca stones unmoved for centuries spilled as if pebbles thrown by the hands of giants.

For a brief moment the ground stilled long enough for Kane to scrape himself from the floor. Unhurt, he looked about, amazed to see the whole landscape had changed. Where once the horizon was lost beyond the stone walls and trees of Vilcabamba, now a vast clearing had appeared, stretching as far as the eye could see. The mountains that enclosed the city had grown and now loomed above them with menace.

Kane scanned the area and made a swift head count of those still with them. Beside him stood a shocked Ridley, somehow unharmed, and likewise Sonco, shaking his bloody, bruised head in despair. Kane was again relieved to learn Haines and Craft were fine. *How many near misses?* he wondered. Other than a nasty gash on the old professor's forehead and some severe grazing on Evan's legs, they both reassured Kane with a nod.

In the temporary lull, they the heard a shallow groan. Following the dire sound, they found one of the porter's legs trapped beneath a massive stone slab. He was alive, but his legs were crushed and the kid was clearly in agony. Ridley rushed to her tent and grabbed the professional first-aid kit, and with Sonco's help she set to work.

"Help! Someone help." Evan recognised that voice. Kate.

He sprang to his feet and followed a voice laced with desperation.

"Help!"

Craft and Haines soon located a frantic Edgewood, who pulled at a pile of stones and rocks with her bare hands.

"It's Umaq. He's under here. I think he's… I think he's dead. Help me"

They scrambled into action, ignoring their own pain to shift the remains of a collapsed Inca wall that trapped Umaq beneath. The Englishmen reacted to Edgewood's obvious concern for the kid. They knew he'd saved her life, and knew she had a lot to make up for.

Evan was glad. He had a soft spot for Kate, and despite what they had all seen as selfish and dishonourable intentions, he believed he had seen through all that. Instead he saw a vulnerable, confused young woman. There was hope for her yet, which meant there was hope for him.

As sudden and violent as it was, the worst of the earthquake seemed to have passed. But something troubled Kane, gnawed at the edge of his conscience. *What's wrong?*

Then he understood what it was, and the panic set in.

Yupanqui was gone.

On the Brink

Fuck! Where the hell is he?

And then, although it didn't seem possible, things got even worse.

De La Cruz was gone, too.

Kane shouted to Sonco, fear hardening his voice.

"Sonco! Big problem, and I don't mean the earthquake. Yupanqui and De La Cruz have gone!"

Leaving Ridley with the boy Sonco rushed to Kane, knowing if the leaders escaped, a kid's broken leg was the least of their worries, and the pair hustled off in search of the escaped terrorists. But they hadn't gone far when the ground shook again in a second bout of violent waves. Kane laid down to prevent being thrown. With his worm's eye view, he could see the ground rippling, like waves on an ocean. Sonco grabbed his arm.

"It is Pachamama. She is angered by what has happened on her mountains. She is angry, Hiram, and she seeks vengeance."

Kane did not share Sonco's belief in the pagan Gods, but despite his own atheist philosophy, he could not deny the timing of the earthquake was profound. But despite the very real dangers of the earthquake, they could not ignore the escape of Yupanqui and De La Cruz.

"We have to find them," he said, "We *must* find them."

They split up to give themselves a wider search area. Sonco headed to the east of the ruined city, Kane to the west, and both men struggled to keep their balance across the undulating ground. Despite the fierce tremors, Kane made good progress over the fallen stones and rocks and tree trunks, driven by a furious, almost maniacal desire to prevent the criminals escape or find a gun. Kane cursed as he forged on, hoping it wasn't too late.

He stopped, and climbed up onto a fallen tree trunk, the highest vantage point around. He looked in all directions but saw no one, no hint that a person had even passed that way, and was about to leave when, as improbable as it was, he thought he heard the sound of laughter coming from a little way ahead. *It can't be*, he thought. There was so much noise all around… the creaking of broken trees, the grinding of stone on stone… and he couldn't be sure. He shook his head and strained his ears, but the strange sound was gone. Perturbed and annoyed, he pushed on.

Sonco had also made good ground, but he was afraid. Nothing scared the tough Quechuan, but Pachamama seethed, and he knew it was because of Yupanqui. Sonco was disgusted by and ashamed of his fellow countryman, and if he got his hands on the self-proclaimed leader of the Inca Uprising, he would…

A gunshot rang out somewhere to the west, the sound clear even above the rumble of the mountains. *Hiram*! With concern about his friend etched across his face, Sonco changed course and headed as fast as the terrain would allow directly to where the gun was fired.

Kane also heard the shot, and he sped forward, dismissing his own safety to protect the others. He hurdled massive stone lintels and ducked below fallen trees, desperate to locate the shooter, who he assumed was either Yupanqui or De La Cruz. Kane's money was on the Spaniard.

The route to the gunshot became a twisted obstacle course of fallen masonry and broken trees. He saw no obvious way around and was about to turn back when he heard the now distinctive sound of laughter. And it was Yupanqui. It took all Kane's strength to haul a few large rocks to one side, and then shoved against the remaining thicket of branches and vines, forcing his way through the almost impenetrable tangle of branches and foliage blind. And it was almost the last thing he ever did, as he stumbled through onto what was once a stone paved courtyard, but was now a mile high cliff.

His arms swung about wild as he fought to regain his balance, and just a second before plunging to his death, he grabbed one of the vines, and literally clutched onto it for his life. His heart pounded blood through his temples as he tried hard to secure his feet, and after a desperate battle Kane pulled himself to safety.

It was more than a lucky escape, but the earthquake still rattled the ground, and although its ferocity had diminished Kane feared it was just the calm before a storm of aftershocks.

The massive force of the initial earthquake had dislodged a huge section of the mountainside, sending millions of tons of earth and the beautifully crafted stones of Vilcabamba plummeting into the valley. Those few seconds of destruction left both Kane and parts of the city devastated.

But thoughts of the destroyed city were short lived.

Just twenty yards away stood a laughing Yupanqui. He had a gun, and at that exact moment was herding Angelo De La Cruz towards the edge of the cliff.

It took Kane a nanosecond to work out what would happen. Maybe the terrorist Spaniard deserved to die, maybe not? But that was not for Hiram Kane to decide, nor Yupanqui. He was about to shout at the Inca leader to plead with him to stop when something jabbed hard into his spine.

Kane had seen enough movies to know it was a gun in his back. But what bothered him most was the horrific realisation of who was responsible; one of the young Quechuans, swayed back on the side of the Condor Uprising.

"Allichu, sayachiy," said Kane in his best but broken Quechuan. "You need not do this. Put the gun down, and we can all go home."

The boy said nothing and shoved the gun harder into Kane's spine.

"Bring him here," shouted Yupanqui, his eyes hard. "We will make it a double sacrifice."

The boy obeyed, and forced Kane along the precarious edge until he was just a few feet from both terrorists.

"Why are you doing this?" he asked Yupanqui, though he knew the flawed reasons. The big man told him anyway.

"Mr Kane. I know you understand our culture, the culture of the Incans, but let me further your education. This... this pig Catholic will die, a sacrifice to honour our gods." Yupanqui held out his arms, indicating the destruction and the broken ground that still vibrated in heavy tremors. "Is it not clear Pachamama is unhappy? By sacrificing this peasant I can only hope I can satisfy her. Just in case, I will also offer you to the Earth Goddess. The death of two heathen men should sate my gods. Isn't it so?"

"Yupanqui," responded Kane, "Listen to me. You—"

The boy slammed the gun into Kane's back with such force

he almost went over the cliff edge. Yupanqui smiled. It was just a matter of time anyway.

Knowing he was about to die left Kane with nothing to lose. He tried again. Nodding at De La Cruz, he said, "This man is the enemy, I understand that. But I am not. I am a friend of the Quechuans, and my family have always supported the native Andean people. Killing this man will not help your cause. Let me go, and I will help you take him back to Cuzco where he will face proper justice. I plead with you, Yupanqui, make an example of this man, not a martyr. Use the moral victory to inspire more Quechuans to rise with you. I will vouch for your decency. I will inform the authorities how you saved the lives of my friends."

Yupanqui had listened with intent, and for a moment seemed to consider Kane's words. But it did not last, and his thoughtful eyes turned hard.

"A valiant attempt, Mr Kane. But you cannot expect me to spare a man who would kill me in a heartbeat, and then kill hundreds and thousands of our brave Incan descendants. It will be done. The sacrifice will happen."

Yupanqui looked out across the immense valley before them, his eyes focused on an unseen spot in the distance. If Kane was not mistaken, there seemed to be real emotion in the eyes of the self-titled leader.

"Besides, it is not my decision, anyway," he said, his voice low and reverent. "The deaths of the Catholics was foretold, and the return of the Incas was prophesied five hundred years ago. I am merely fulfilling that prophecy. It is my duty."

Martyr

During the entire exchange, the Catholic leader De La Cruz remained silent. His eyes never left those of the Incan, and in his eyes burned the fire of hateful decades. Time was running out for him, but he knew God was watching.

There was no chance he could escape his ties, but another option crept into his mind. Catholic dogma considers suicide sinful. It was something De La Cruz abhorred. But a suicide mission? That was different. He suddenly believed with all his heart God would favour him if dying whilst killing the Inca leader. And all in *His* name.

De La Cruz fantasised about martyrdom, becoming a hero to millions of Catholics the world over. But there was one man whom he hoped would revere him for his selfless act above all others; Ferdinand Benedix. It was Benedix who he had looked up to as a child, Benedix who had formed the Eagle Alliance and planned this mission from the start. De La Cruz doubted there was any man alive who had more zeal and devotion to the Catholic cause than he himself, but if there was such a man, it was the Dutchman Ferdinand Benedix.

In a way they were brothers, and for many years De La Cruz had worshipped the younger boy, almost as if he was a God. It was Benedix who had shown the older Spaniard the true Catholic way in those Godforsaken mountains of Peru, several decades before, so it seemed appropriate that if he had to die for the cause, then he would die there.

He closed his eyes and thought of his old friend and mentor, Ferdinand. Maybe, at last, the boy he had worshipped as a teenager would now revere him as a man.

De La Cruz now opened his eyes and raised his face to the sky. In a voice little more than a whisper and unheard by the others, he said his last prayer:

> *"Even in the midst of this, I know that you are the Lord.*
> *I know the situation is in Your hand, and I trust You.*
> *I beseech you for strength, and that I can endure this*
> *situation and bring glory to Your name.*
> *I will find out in Heaven."*

And with all his strength De La Cruz threw himself at Yupanqui.

Yupanqui though was a big man, and despite his surprise, he easily deflected the weaker Spaniard. The Incan leader roared in rage, and grabbing De La Cruz by the shoulders he hurled him to the floor. De La Cruz was himself resilient and had been awaiting this moment for so many years it infused him with an almost inhuman strength and determination to please God.

He jumped to his feet and charged again, but again the giant Yupanqui brushed him aside. The Quechuan with the gun was about to shoot the Catholic, but his leader stopped him. "*Mana. Manaraq!*" *No. Not yet!*

Confused, the kid lowered the gun. Even so, it was still too dangerous for Kane to intervene. He stood, helpless, and wondered where the hell Sonco was.

It was inexplicable to Kane, but Yupanqui laughed. He fended off the repeated charges by De La Cruz with consummate ease, enjoying his physical superiority. *Of course I'm stronger*, he thought. *I am an Inca warrior. A leader. This scum is mere Catholic, nothing more than a feeble dog.*

Kane looked on in disbelief, and unable to do anything he watched the drama with morbid fascination.

But suddenly his own situation took a dangerous twist as the armed Quechuan took matters into his own hands. He wanted desperately to impress his leader, and snuck behind Kane and once more hammered the gun into his back, shoving him perilously close to the cliff edge and towards Yupanqui. Kane resisted the urge to turn on the boy, certain he'd be shot or shoved over the edge. Instead he complied, allowing the kid to lead him towards the drama.

Time and again De La Cruz charged in what appeared to be a human version of matador and bull, Yupanqui the graceful matador and De La Cruz the enraged bull. *Poetic justice*, thought Kane, who didn't miss the irony.

Below their feet the ground still rumbled, the tremors once more increasing in power and frequency. But despite it all the ugly confrontation continued, the two mortal enemies oblivious to the monster aftershocks.

Just then Sonco appeared, shocked to witness the crazy scene before him, and horrified to see Kane just inches from death. Thinking quickly he knelt to avoid the eye-line of the kid with the gun and grabbed a fistful of the sacred earth. He held it in his hand, swaying with the ground as it buckled and contorted beneath him, the force of the quake growing by the second. "Pachamama," he whispered, "Ruway ama phiñakuy."

Do not be angry. "Achillu, sayachiy kay pacha kuyuy." *Please, stop this earthquake.*

But Sonco knew that nothing he could say would change it. Pachamama was angry with them, angry for the deaths of her children, angry with the will of men. She would have her vengeance.

The ripples grew wild, splitting the ground and tearing up trees unmoved for decades, even centuries. Incan walls that had stood for hundreds of years crumbled like Lego, their massive size and weight irrelevant to Pachamama's wrath.

Sonco feared the worst for Kane, so close to the unstable cliff edge. Unseen, he struggled closer to the boy, edging behind them and ready to grab them if they fell. It was more when than if.

And then it happened.

The enemies faced each other, the big Incan calm, his control of the situation total, and the older, weakened Catholic a spent force. He had tried his best to kill the heathen. He had tried, and he had failed.

Breathing deep, with his body beaten and all energy gone, Angelo De La Cruz glared at his rival. He knew there were only two choices left open to him: allow himself to be sacrificed, or jump to a sinful death. Either way, his mentor Ferdinand would never learn of his valiant attempt to kill the Incan. The world would forget him. History did not remember nobodies. The shame was agonising.

There was only one thing for it…

Yupanqui took a step forward, eyes focused only on the Spaniard. This was his moment. He would sacrifice the leader of the enemy, and the ancient prophecy would be fulfilled. He, Yupanqui Atoc, would become Sapa Inca, and all the world would come to know it.

Yupanqui grabbed a nearby paddle and raised it above his head. Eyes closed, he muttered a prayer to Pachamama.

And then she did her thing.

The ground shook with such complete violence that another six feet of cliff edge crumbled away, and the last thing Yupanqui and De la Cruz saw as they fell to their deaths were the glaring eyes of the enemy.

Out of sheer shock and total panic, the kid shoved Kane forwards with all his strength, inches from death himself, and it was impossible to keep their balance with the ground shifting in such aggressive spasms. Kane teetered, the boy shoving and grabbing at the same time, and in the instant Kane thought he might make it, and a quarter of a second before Sonco grabbed his arm, they tumbled over the edge.

Hiram Kane was gone.

The Fallen

Sonco fell to his knees.

Hiram Kane was dead, and it was his fault. He had let his friend down again, and now Hiram was gone. Forever gone. In those first few seconds it took all of Sonco's effort of will not to throw himself over the edge too, such was the weight of his despair. But thoughts of his family pulled him away from the edge, and he laid on his back, oblivious to the bucking ground.

The poor young Quechuan kid had died too, too young and brainwashed to know what he was dying for. He was barely sixteen, and now he was dead. Sonco had failed him, and he had failed his people. The magnitude of his failures broke Sonco Amaru's heart.

Several minutes passed, and at last the power of the quake lessened, until, after a few more shallow, shimmering ripples, it ceased altogether.

Ridley, Craft, and Haines stood and checked themselves over, amazed to learn they were more or less unhurt. Banged up, maybe, and covered in cuts and bruises. But considering what they had just experienced they were in good shape. *Small wonders*, thought the old professor who had a distinctively ominous feeling about things. He wasn't quite sure what it was he felt, but the odious thoughts wouldn't leave him.

They had all seen Kane and Sonco head off after Yupanqui and De La Cruz, and began their own search for their friends. The tremendously altered landscape now meant a somewhat easier passage through the devastated city, and in just a few minutes they emerged out onto the new cliff edge. As one they gasped, because the view that greeted them was stunning. The valley spread out before them, and the sun shimmered across the distant peaks. It was beautiful, and for just a few seconds the three of them basked in that beauty.

And then they saw Sonco, and Professor Haine's heart skipped several beats.

Sonco sat near the edge of the newly formed cliff, *a little too near*, thought Ridley, and they hurried over to him. The usually stoic Quechuan clutched his knees to his chest and his arms wrapped tight around his legs. It was almost inexplicable to Alex, but Sonco was crying. She knelt beside him, a knot tightening her guts.

"Sonco? What is it? Are you hurt?"

There was no response from the sturdy guide, and his tears continued, painfully unabashed. Sonco could not look her in the eye, and a hollow feeling settled in her stomach. John Haines stepped forward, followed by Craft. They looked from one to another, and all three feared the worst.

"Sonco, dammit, where's Hiram?" demanded Haines.

Still no response.

"Where the hell's my friend?" cried Evan as he grabbed Sonco's shoulder.

And then, in a moment that simultaneously shattered three hearts, Sonco pointed over the edge.

It was as if the air was forced from his lungs. "No!" was

all Evan could manage. He flung himself to the ground and looked over the side, nausea threatening to take over. His eyes darted right and left, searching for any sign of his friend, but he saw nothing. Not a trace. It was at least a thousand foot vertical drop to where the cliff sloped, and another thousand to the valley floor. No one could survive it.

When Evan's forehead dropped to the ground, Ridley's legs buckled. She knew the truth, felt it in her bones. Kane was gone. Her soulmate, the only man she'd ever loved, was dead. Ridley didn't cry. She was in shock, and had lost loved ones before. She sat on the floor, and like Sonco wrapped herself in her arms. John Haines took a seat beside her and draped an arm around her shoulder. There was nothing he could say, to Ridley or to any of them.

The man they all loved was dead.

Suddenly Evan's head jerked up again. It was so silent around them now that the sudden movement startled Ridley. Evan shuffled along the cliff a few yards, arching his neck out over the void. Some sound, a noise from beyond the reach of his view, had caught his attention, and through tears he scanned the cliff face. When, after a minute's silence, he looked back over his shoulder at the others, their eyes widened in shock. Evan was smiling. But the smile lasted only a second, and when he spoke, it was with authority. "We need to move. Now."

Fifty feet below the edge of the cliff, Hiram Kane clung on to the exposed roots of a fallen tree as if his life depended on it. It did, and not only his. Clinging to his legs was the young Quechuan, just a few strands of cloth from certain death. It mattered nothing to Kane that the kid had held a gun on him moments before. He would save the boy, or he would die trying. But his strength had sapped, and he couldn't hold on much longer

Kane looked up, trying to locate something more sturdy to grab. He saw a thick, gnarled root five feet above his head, but beyond that, he saw something altogether more shocking; the face of his oldest friend.

"Hold on," Evan shouted, "We're finding rope."

Relief flooded through him, but it was short lived. The terrified kid struggled, each movement weakening Kane's grip on the roots. "Mana wichay." No climb. "Manaraq!" Not yet! The boy seemed to calm a little but clung tighter still to Kane.

"It will be okay," he said to the youngster. "Just a little more time. We can do it. Kay sinchi." Be strong.

The boy's shame was evident in his falling tears. Sixteen years old at most, yet the kid had experienced more drama in a few days than many would in several lifetimes. His grip was strong, so strong in fact that he was endangering them both. Suddenly the tree roots slipped a few inches, jerking them down the cliff another foot. They barely held on. Kane had lost his kid brother many years ago. He had made mistakes that day, but he wasn't making one now. He would not let this kid fall to his death.

Kane looked up and shouted to his friend. "I can't hold on much longer. Five minutes tops. Hurry."

"You do like to make things difficult," came the sarcastic reply, but if there was one person Kane wanted coming to his rescue it was Evan. The two had been best mates for almost three decades and would do anything to save each other. Not in their wildest dreams, though, had they ever imagined a scenario like this.

With extreme caution, Evan lowered himself over the edge, and slowly, one hand after another, he lowered himself down the rope. Evan wanted an adventure. But this was further out of his comfort zone than he ever wanted. They secured the rope above through a combination of Sonco and Ridley, and the sturdy trunk of a polyepis tree, one of the last still standing. Hoping with all his heart that the earthquake had finished, Evan descended, inch by inch, foot by foot, until he closed in on Kane and the kid.

"Almost there," he shouted, and his confidence grew.

The boy was flagging, and so was Kane, their exhaustion threatening to send them to their deaths. Kane glanced about, frantic to find anything that could help, and he saw a thicker root, tantalisingly close but a yard out of reach. If he could just grab hold of that, then he knew they could survive, but if he let go with one hand he would not have the strength to hold both their weights with the other. He gripped with every last ounce of his energy and waited for Evan.

After what seemed like endless minutes, Evan was at last within reach. "Listen. I'm going to rest my feet on this small ledge, and attach myself to this large root. Once secure, I'll hand you the rope. Can you let go with one hand to grab it?"

"I don't know," Kane sputtered through laboured breaths, the veins on his forehead bulging from the strain. His arms shook, exhaustion winning the battle. He was seconds from falling. "The kid's finished," he gasped. "But I will... not... watch another die. The rope. Now!"

Secured to the tree root Evan lowered the rope for Kane. He took a few deep breaths, focused his mind, and mustering the very last reserves of his strength he took a glance down at the terrified face of the kid below.

But it wasn't the Quechuan boy that looked back at Hiram, but his missing brother Danny. The complete shock of it almost cost Kane his life. He blinked, the tears immediate, and blinked again. *Save me*, the face pleaded, *please save me*. Kane shook his head. He knew that shock and altitude and stress and a million other things had caused him to see his brother rather than the boy.

Kane had never accepted the disappearance of his brother, and despite the protestations of his family, excluding his father, Hiram had always blamed himself. But seeing the image of Danny now changed something. It galvanised him, gave him strength.

He would not let this kid die.

Kane braced himself hard against the cliff face, and summoning all his will and strength, he let go of the root with his right hand and reached for the life-saving rope.

He missed.

The momentum of the swing forced them away from the cliff, and they almost fell. But gravity somehow forced them back to the cliff in time to clasp the first root. Kane gritted his teeth and closed his eyes. He swung again, this time with a desperate lunge, and he snagged the rope. *Okay*, he thought. *Almost*. "Hold on, Danny," he shouted.

Just a few feet above, Evan froze. Did he say Danny? But it took him only two seconds to understand Kane's inspiration.

Kane lowered himself and ordered the boy to scramble up over his body. Now side by side, with supreme effort Kane fixed the rope around the boy's waist. A minute later, with the help of the combined efforts above, Evan clambered up the cliff, the tearful frightened boy right behind. Five minutes later Sonco was hauling Evan and the kid over the edge. To safety.

Kane breathed in deep, the effects of such physical exertion in the thin air almost beating him. But the image of his brother's face was still fresh. The illusion had seemed so real, so painfully real. But as he perched there, high above a valley in the ancient Andes Mountains, his imminent death still a possibility, Kane understood why his brother had appeared. Not, as he'd first thought, to inspire him to save the kid.

There was another reason. Danny was there to save Hiram's life.

His appearance in Kane's sub-conscience was to inspire Hiram to save himself, and in doing so, Danny had lifted thirty years of guilt from his brother's shoulders.

With this revelation came tears, tears that he had dammed for most of his life, and he gazed through those tears into the beautiful valley before him and knew he had to survive.

So this was it. Two innocent young Quechuans boys were dead, and Kane knew he would mourn their unnecessary deaths forever. He would visit their families, and with Sonco's help, do what he could to make amends.

The Pachacuti, the self-proclaimed Inca leader Yupanqui, was dead, and with him gone, Kane hoped the misguided Inca Uprising would die too. There was no doubt Peru needed to see changes, social reforms long overdue, but a violent movement was not the way to do it.

Also dead were Angelo De La Cruz and Howie Hooper. They were terrorists… they would not be missed. Maybe the Eagle Alliance would die too, though he doubted it. There would always be radical fundamentalists in all religions.

So many others had almost lost their lives too. Muddy Waters had not one but two narrow escapes. Kate Edgewood was seconds from becoming an Incan sacrifice. Umaq Huamani, the brave young kid who had saved her life. Evan had been shot, and risked his own life to save Hiram. The young Quechuan kid they had just saved. So many close to death. Too many.

And Hiram himself. It was the closest he had ever been to dying, and there had been many near misses over the years. He knew he had been lucky.

"Thank you," he whispered out into the void. "Thank you." He thanked Evan and the others for saving his life. He thanked Sonco for coming back, and for stopping a bullet meant for him. "Sulpaikee," he said, thanking Pachamama for her rage, though he would keep that thought to himself.

And last, but most important, he thanked his brother Danny. Not only for giving him the strength to save the kid, but for freeing him from the burden of guilt he had carried alone for so long. For too long.

Thank you.

Kane prepared himself for the final climb to safety. The sun appeared from behind the clouds for the first time in that most dramatic of days, and as he thought of the Sun God, Inti, and felt grateful for its warmth, he noticed his golden sun disc glinting outside of the neck of his shirt.

Hiram smiled. The gold.

Perhaps they would never know the truth about the gold. *Perhaps*, he thought, that was for the best. He swivelled to face the cliff and made his first careful move up the ropes.

Kane froze in his tracks.

Something caught his eye. Hidden beneath the giant, twisted root of the tree he held onto was an opening in the cliff. Kane shifted his position a little, and after a short struggle leaned his head into the gap. What he saw made his heart flip several somersaults. Stretching back into the cliff was an enormous cave, so far that he could not see its end. And within that cave, illuminated by the strong afternoon sun, was the most amazing sight Hiram Kane had ever seen.

Laid out before him, buried deep in a natural cave beneath the legendary Inca city of Vilcabamba, was the lost hoard of Atahualpa's gold. It was revealed now only thanks to the will of the Earth Goddess, Pachamama. Kane perched in his precarious position, exhaustion forgotten, and stared at the fabled treasure for what seemed an eternity. There was no possible way into the cave from that position, but what he could see was beyond even his imagination.

Several life-sized golden statues stood off to the left, and in front of those, three golden thrones. To the right, shimmering statues of animals sat surrounded by golden cast icons of birds and insects and jewellery of every kind; headdresses, bracelets, necklaces, and literally hundreds, perhaps thousands, of Inca sun discs, just like his.

Thoughts of Danny flashed once more in his mind, as well as the faces of his beloved grandfather and great-grandfather Patrick.

As he looked on in awe at the dazzling sight before him, the disappointed eyes of his predecessors faded into wide smiles, as decades of shame and regret transformed into happiness.

But the last face he saw while gazing upon the gold with wonderment was that of the revered explorer, Hiram Bingham. It was Bingham who had bought the wonder and mystery of the Incas out of the Andes and to the world's attention, and it was Hiram Bingham who had inspired in his family a lifetime of adventure and exploration.

But Hiram Bingham had never found Vilcabamba. And it was clear now that no one had ever found Atahualpa's lost gold.

The long lost Inca gold.

But Hiram Kane had.

Kane secured his grip with his left hand, and with his right grabbed the sun disc. He lifted the leather necklace over his head and held it out in front of his eyes. Kane stared at the tiny yet beautiful object, his most prized possession, for many seconds. Finally, he placed it against his lips, then said, "For you, Danny. And forever." He placed the disc into the cave's narrow entrance, and at last turned his eyes from the magnificence before him.

Looking back out at the equally spectacular valley it took him only a second to make a difficult but momentous decision…

The location of the lost Inca gold was a secret Kane would keep to himself.

Kane looked up to find Alex Ridley's beautiful face looking down at him. Then he spotted Evan, grinning like the cat who'd just found the golden cream. Professor Haines waved, and one by one all the remaining people at Vilcabamba smiled down at Hiram from above. It was Ridley who broke the silence.

"Everything okay down there, Mr Kane?" asked Ridley, who couldn't hide the expectant look on her face. "What's going on?" She knew Kane and recognised that look on his face.

He'd seen something down there, she was sure of it.

Kane grinned back but said nothing, lowering his face and focusing on his footing before beginning the difficult task of hauling himself to the top of the newly formed cliff.

"Come on mate, almost there," called down Evan, awash with relief that this was almost over. "Trust you to be last. Old habits die hard, eh?" Banter aside, Evan couldn't hide his pride and relief at the way his best pal had handled what had been a traumatic and unimaginable series of events. A tear crept into the corner of his eye as he reached over the edge to help Kane scramble to safety.

"Grab my hand mate," he said. "That's it... a few more inches."

"Reach down a little more," Kane grunted, his energy depleted. He paused a moment longer, giving his legs a few seconds rest before the final launch upwards. He gazed up and saw both determination and relief in his old friend's eyes. They'd been through a lot together over the years, but this was a whole new level.

They locked eyes, love and respect between the two men patently clear to any witnesses, and Kane nodded, the hint of a grin more pertinent in that moment than a thousand words.

"Ready?" asked Evan.

"Ready."

"Okay... on three... 3... 2... 1."

Kane leaned back, and with all his strength swung his left arm upwards. Evan grasped Kane's wrist and locked his grip tight. Inch by inch Kane pushed with his legs, and he soon had one arm over the cliff edge.

"That's it... almost." Evan said, breathing hard.

"Reach down... hook your arm under mine," Kane said "...

just a little more…"

Evan stretched, straining every sinew to find the extra inches needed to grip under Kane's armpit.

"Got it," he yelled. "I've got you, buddy."

And then in a moment none present would ever forget, the edge of the cliff gave way and Evan Craft tumbled over the side, his body cartwheeling wildly out of control until it smashed into a rocky ledge hundreds of metres below.

Lifeless.

Dead.

XI

Epilogue

Tribute

Kane placed down the fresh tray of drinks but didn't retake his seat at the table. He grabbed his pint. "I'll be back in a minute," he said, and wandered away from the pub's beer garden, taking a seat on the grassy bank overlooking the beautiful Norfolk Broads.

The Commodore was a pub with a view that never got old, and one Kane always revisited every time he returned to his native England. It was three o'clock on a Saturday afternoon, and as always on rare sunny days during the English summertime, The Commodore's beer garden was crowded. But there was something special about today's crowd. Most of the drinkers were drinking to toast the life of a great son, brother, uncle, and friend. Evan Craft.

After the tragedy in Peru a couple of months before, and after Kane had accompanied Evan's body home, a funeral had taken place just a week later. However, it was decided by the Craft family to wait until today, on what would have been Evan's 40th birthday, to have a memorial party. Not one to shy away from the attention of his adoring family and friends, Evan would have approved.

Kane estimated there were at least two hundred such people crammed into the pub and its broad-side garden, and though technically a sombre occasion everyone was in great spirits. Evan wouldn't have had it any other way.

Kane had taken the loss hard. They'd been best friends since primary school, and though they both had other close friends–most of them attending today–it was with Evan whom Kane had shared their most memorable occasions. One of those times was Peru, regardless of the horrifying way it had ended.

Gazing out across the passive water of the Broads, Kane cast his mind back to an incident that happened just several hundred yards from where he now sat. He took a sip of his beer and smiled. They were just kids when Evan had hauled Kane from the water after he'd fallen in and almost drowned. And it was Evan who was trying desperately to haul Kane once more to safety when he himself had fallen to his death. *Why is it always the good ones who die young?* he thought.

A kingfisher sitting on a nearby branch suddenly dove into the water, the flash of blue catching Kane's attention. It stirred another memory. As a kid Hiram's brother Danny had loved drawing the electric blue and red birds, a skill not shared by Hiram. Danny's image often appeared to Hiram at random moments, and just as it did while saving the life of the Quechuan kid on the cliff face in the Andes, Danny's image appeared to him now. Danny's eyes were wide open, and Kane couldn't read them. *Sad? Happy?* It was hard to tell. Of course, Danny had known Evan too, and perhaps it was Danny's way of giving Hiram a hug? Kane wasn't a spiritual person, not even close, but a small part of him wanted to believe that wherever they both were now, they at least wouldn't be alone.

314

Were they in a better place? Probably not. But he imagined they were anyway.

"Hey." Ridley's voice startled Kane, and the image of Danny faded away. It was probably for the best. Kane didn't want to get caught up on that downwardly depressing spiral of guilt, at least not today.

Alex Ridley had left the table of friends to join him by the water's edge. "It's a fitting send-off, isn't it?" She slid her arm around his waist and leaned into his chest.

Kane nodded, words unnecessary. But it was the perfect way to honour their friend's life. Many of the old gang were there. Lee, Jo and PG, Jon and Kim, Clare, Robbie and Callum, and countless other friends and family all devastated by the terrible loss but grateful to have shared their lives with a man so genuine and full of love.

"Coming back to the table? I've something to show you."

Ridley led Kane back to the table, and Kane's old mucker Lee couldn't keep the grin from his face.

"We thought you might want to see this," he said. "Hot off the press." He handed Kane a magazine, the unmistakable yellow border causing Kane's own smile to reappear.

"National Geographic," he muttered, and took a seat.

Lee nodded, before adding: "Read out the headline."

Kane looked around the table at his and Evan's friends. They all smiled their encouragement. Kane cleared his throat and read out the first few lines:

> **"The Lost City of the Incas: Vilcabamba**
> *Words by Leslie P. Moore.*
> *Photos by Evan Craft."*

A tear formed in the corner of Kane's eye. He continued:

"After more than a century of searching for one of the most enigmatic and mysterious sites in the history of exploration, the puzzle has at last been solved. A mystery no more, and Vilcabamba has been found. Legendary explorer Hiram Bingham failed. As did Gene Savoy, and numerous others over the long decades of the Twentieth Century. But in what is surely the most poignant moment of exploration history, none other than the great-grandson of Bingham's assistant Patrick, and a man named after the fabled Harvard scholar himself, Englishman Hiram Kane has finally located what so many others before him couldn't."

Kane shook his head, bashful as ever.

"Go on, mate," said Jo, "Keep reading."

He did. "Kane found Vilcabamba, and perhaps even more amazing, he located one of the most sought after finds in all history; the lost Inca gold. Expertly hidden in a natural cave, far from the greedy hands of the Spanish conquistadors, Kane found Atahualpa's treasure horde after an earthquake forever changed the landscape. During the process, Kane bravely saved the life of a young porter. Unfortunately, during the rescue attempt, expedition photographer Evan Craft lost his life. We at Nat Geo would like this special edition be a fitting tribute to a good man and a brilliant photographer."

Upon those words Kane wasn't the only one at the table to wipe away the tears. Kane either didn't want to or couldn't continue, and Lee took over.

"After several days of deep deliberation Mr Kane declared his discovery of the gold to the world. The now infamous expedition had been infiltrated by two separate terrorist groups, the Condor Uprising, led by deceased leader Yupanqui Atoc, and The Eagle Alliance, a little known Catholic terrorist group led by Spaniard Angelo De La Cruz, also deceased, and Ferdinand Benedix, a Dutch professor of antiquities with no previous known links to terror. Benedix currently stands trial in The Hague, accused of plotting terrorist attacks and inciting hatred and murder."

Lee paused and looked at Kane. They shared a smile, before Lee continued. "Each fundamentalist group was determined to claim the riches and wage war on their enemies, using Hiram Kane and his alleged map to locate the gold. But through amazing courage and no shortage of skill, not only had Kane located the lost city and the gold, but in doing so managed to prevent a religious conflict that would have spelt disaster for the entire continent of South America and beyond. The gold, estimated to be worth a staggering ten billion dollars–way more than previously speculated–is now being evaluated by the Peruvian government, who informed us they have paid Kane an undisclosed amount of money as an official finder's fee. Though he has repeatedly refused to comment, it's believed Kane has donated every penny of the massive sum–thought to be in the region of $5,000,000–to help the impoverished Quechuan populations, not just in Peru, but throughout the Andes."

Lee put down the magazine and stood, then climbed onto the pub table, his beer count evident by the ungraceful ascent. Grabbing a spoon, he tapped loudly on his pint glass. "Ladies and gentlemen, boys and girls… friends, family. May I please have your attention. I'd like to propose a toast… well, two toasts, actually. First, the main reason we are here today is to celebrate the life of our dear friend Evan, the life and soul of any party and a kinder, more lovable man you couldn't wish to meet. Perfect in every way… except those awful shirts, obviously. Please, raise your glasses… To Evan, the shortest of us, yet with the biggest of hearts."

Tears of joy and sadness fell in equal measure as the gathered hordes remembered their wonderful friend.

"Thank you, everybody," said Lee, scuffing away his own tears. "And now a second toast. To Hiram… finder of lost Inca gold and preventer of wars. Our friend. Our hero… our very own, Hiram Kane."

The clear skies over the Broads were aglow with the fiery orange of a sinking sun. Kane and Ridley once more stood at the water's edge, and watched as a pair of swans flew elegantly across the stunning scene. "They're beautiful," said Ridley.

After a moment, Kane replied. "They are. And so are condors."

Ridley chuckled. She knew it was true.

Across the other side of the world, deep in the heart of the Peruvian Andes, at that moment a pair of condors had also taken flight across their own magnificent vista, soaring effortlessly on thermals and oblivious to the chaos recently caused in their name.

The condors had indeed risen. It was true, and it was spectacular.

Most importantly, the condors had risen in peace.

Six Months Later

The violent Inca Uprising, labelled the Condor Uprising in the press, had for now been stopped. Its self-appointed leader, Yupanqui Atoc, was dead, and the uprising had received unanimous vilification from all sides, not least from the newly formed and peaceful Quechuan People's Party, and their recently elected leader, Sonco Amaru. Sonco was a national hero, albeit a reluctant one, and though the word would never be mentioned, not on his watch, Sonco was looked upon by all Quechuans as the real Pachacuti, their one true Inca leader.

In Europe, much like the Condor Uprising, The Eagle Alliance was finished. Its leader Ferdinand Benedix was in jail for life, the Dutch government finding him guilty of, among other charges, inciting terror, corruption, and manslaughter. They'd pushed for multiple counts of murder, but settled for the lesser charge of manslaughter provided he was never released from prison. His attorney agreed, but last month guards had found Ferdinand Benedix hanging from the bars in his jail window, a torn up copy of the St. James Catholic Bible beneath his swinging feet.

Umaq Huamani was alive and well, his guilt laid to rest by the wise words of his mentor Sonco. Umaq's poor family were one of the first to benefit from the newly formed charity, the Kane & Craft Foundation. His parents were finally receiving the treatment their poor health required, and his sister Miski was excelling at her new school. Umaq himself was currently applying for a place at the College of Hospitality and Tourism Management in Cuzco. It had always been his dream to attend university, and thanks to Kane he was about to fulfil that dream. The course would give Umaq previously unattainable opportunities, but if you asked him honestly what he wanted to do when it was over, he'd say, Andean trekking guide.

Katherine Edgewood had returned to England in shame and immediately turned herself into the police. She had told them everything she had planned to do, and was willing to accept whatever punishment the courts handed her. However, after some sterling character testimony from her former mentor Professor John Haines, she was given a suspended sentence and warned about future conduct. She then wrote a letter to Kane, begging him for a chance to be involved with *The Kane & Craft Foundation*, and was now living in Peru and working as a volunteer at its Cuzco office. Umaq Huamani was a frequent visitor.

After the trauma of the Andes John Haines had finally retired from his jet-setting life of adventure and much sought after speaking engagements around the world's most prestigious universities. He was devastated to learn of the sudden death of his friend and colleague, Muddy Waters, and was quick to visit the professor's family. Muddy had been recuperating at his Boston home, when after a series of sickening headaches, brought on as a result of the terrible head trauma he'd suffered at the Andean waterfall, out of the blue he slipped into a coma, and a week later he passed away.

Rather than share with them details of Muddy's alleged accident, his good friend Haines cheered them up with tales of the life and joy he had brought to that expedition, and other happy memories ha had of working with the brilliant archaeologist in the past

Both men were enormously popular in their respective worlds, and both would be sorely missed. John was now writing a posthumous biography of the great man, sure Muddy himself would have approved of the working title, Keep on Digging.

Kane wasn't surprised to learn that the Spaniard Angelo De La Cruz was a direct descendent of Francisco Pizarro, the most notorious of conquistadors. De La Cruz had lost, failed in his mission. Pachamama had seen to that, and for Kane it was just another example of nature trumping Man, and his imagined religions.

As for Howie Hooper, despite his grisly demise no one had given him another thought.

A Good Plan

November 5th

Somewhere above eastern Europe

Ridley and Kane snuggled up close on their flight to Asia. Several months had passed since the expedition to Vilcabamba, and much had changed. As predicted, Kane's discovery had put the name Hiram Kane on everyone's lips, and he was sought after for interviews and TV appearances the world over. But that wasn't Kane's style. He'd appeared on a couple of shows, but refused to talk about the actual expedition. Rather, he focused the attention on the lost city itself, and the amazing legacy of Atahualpa's gold and the fantastic good that had come of its discovery. He did mention his charity, *The Kane & Craft Foundation*, and the great work its staff was doing to help the disenfranchised people of the Andes, the Quechuans, and their modern day leader, Sonco Amaru.

Besides, it wasn't in either of their natures to sit still, and Kane and Ridley were ready to explore somewhere new. Thus, they were on a flight to India, a place they'd each been once, but never together. And they were an item now, Ridley finally letting her heart rule her stubborn head, and letting Kane claim his rightful place by her side. They were happy. Despite everything that had happened, they were ready.

And they were on a mission. Their late friend Evan had always admired the Dalai Lama, and they were on their way to visit His Holiness in Dharamshala on Evan's behalf.

It was a solid plan, a nice idea to visit such a peaceful part of the world in order to forget the events of Peru and put it all behind them.

It was a good plan.

But Kane's plans had gone wrong before.

THE END

Get the First Book in the Series Free

Building a relationship with my readers is my favourite thing about writing. I occasionally send newsletters with details on my new releases, special offers, and other bits of news relating to the Hiram Kane series. I also share stories about my travels and research trips around the world, and often give you the opportunity to discover other exciting new authors and their free and discounted books.

And if you sign up to my mailing list, I'll send you a no-strings-attached copy of 'The Samurai Code: A Hiram Kane Adventure Book 1, absolutely FREE. Here's the blurb:

One lethal storm. One deadly criminal. One ancient code.

Expedition leader Hiram Kane is in Japan when the storm of the century hits. He joins the rescue mission as flash floods cause chaos, death and destruction.

Yakuza boss Katashi Goto is retiring from the mob. Before he does, there is one more thing to achieve: revenge over a centuries old enemy.

When their two very different worlds collide, Kane is forced to make a choice. He has always known honour is worth fighting for. When challenged by Katashi, he has to decide if it is also worth dying for.

Sound like something you'd enjoy? Then simply go to this website, and get involved today:

www.stevenmooreauthor.com/get-your-free-book

Your Review Can Make a Big Difference

Reviews are easily the most powerful tools I have for getting attention for my books, and they give me both the platform and the confidence to continue doing what I love. As an independently published author, I don't have the luxury of being backed by a big publishing house, but I do have something way more effective than that, and it's something those publishers would kill to get their hands on:

A committed and loyal bunch of readers

Your reviews help bring my books to the attention of new readers. So if you enjoyed 'The Condor Prophecy' I'd be very grateful if you could spend just a couple of minutes leaving an honest review on the book's Amazon page (it can be as short as you like). Just go to your county's Amazon store and search for: The Condor Prophecy.

Thank you very much,
Steven

Author's Note

Hello there, and thanks for reading The Condor Prophecy.

I often get asked where my story ideas emanate from. The simple answer? From my extensive travels and wonderful experiences around the world. I first left my home country of England aged nineteen, and I've been travelling ever since—that's almost twenty-five years—and I've been fortunate enough to have visited some incredible places and met the most inspiring people. Combine this with real world events, historical characters, exotic locations, current social issues, my own interests and passions, and a large slice of imagination, and I have some pretty motivating material.

How about my protagonist, Hiram Kane?

Well, he's a guy I would love to be more like. Hiram has an archaeology degree, as do I, but just like Mr Kane I didn't follow through with my studies, instead choosing a different path. I've been on many similar adventures to Hiram, and have visited all the countries that will feature in the series, from Peru to Egypt, to India, and beyond. Also, like Hiram, I've found myself in more than a few dicey situations. I actually live in Mexico, so inspiration for exciting action and adventure in mysterious, enigmatic settings is never far away.

Once again, thanks for taking a chance on this book, and I hope you'll stick around for the next instalment, **The Shadow of Kailash**, coming very, very soon.

Also by Steven Moore

Steven's debut novel was a haunting literary coming of age adventure. Though a very different genre to his Hiram Kane action series, almost two hundred reviewers on Amazon have given it 5 stars. Here's the blurb:

England. 1960s. A cold, harsh autumn.

On an isolated island, an abusive man forces his wife to run for her life. Their son Tristan, young and afraid, also flees the island and sets out into the world to escape his demons and find his mother.

Hitchhiking beneath the backdrop of a wild and loveless November, Tristan encounters every possible character, from the genuinely kind to the inherently wicked. Beaten, robbed and stripped of even hope, Tristan finds himself on the gritty streets of London's East End, where everything he thought he knew about life starts to shatter and crumble around him. With all hope seemingly lost, a young boy even questions the futility of life itself.

But when he learns that there are others who share his torment and understand his pain, can Tristan find the courage to make it through his darkest hours?

Tristan's tale is a grim exploration into his own conscience. As he discovers the unique ability of humans to do such heinous things both to themselves and to one another, it's all he can do to keep control, as his passage of internal discovery takes one dark turn after another and sends him to the edge.

This dark, edgy and painfully honest coming-of-age tale packs a powerful punch. If you always root for the underdog and want to follow Tristan's trials and tribulations, simply visit your country's online Amazon store, and buy *I Have Lived Today,* today!

Bonus Chapter: The Old Rectory

April 1st, 1989

Hiram Kane was just fifteen years old when he bunked off school with his little brother Danny, who was barely thirteen. They didn't get in trouble in class, and both got consistently good reports. It was only the second time Hiram had ever played truant. Danny's first.

Every day on their cycle to school they rode by the abandoned and derelict Old Rectory off Christmas Lane, with its boarded up doors and smashed upstairs windows. They'd only discussed it a couple of times, but both knew the other's thoughts; it was just a matter of time until Hiram broke inside to explore. It seemed harmless enough, and even though there had been rumours flying around at school–the usual ones, that the Old Rec' was haunted by a long-dead vicar, or some drug addict squatters lived inside–Hiram was determined to investigate.

Hiram inherited his adventurous traits from his family. His great grandfather, Patrick, was the closest friend and most trusted assistant of legendary American explorer, Hiram Bingham. Hence, Patrick's son, grandson, and great-grandson were all complimented with the same name. And since anyone in the Kane family could remember, the youngest Hiram, like his forebears, was curious about everything. The mysterious

Old Rectory was no exception.

Hiram and Danny attended Benjamin Britten Secondary School, a ghastly faux-modern monstrosity in Suffolk. Its construction was so poorly executed that since it had opened in 1976, the building had literally been sinking into the ground. The local composer the authorities named the school after was probably turning in his grave. Of course, the students hoped it would hurry up and disappear.

So they wouldn't be missed from their classes, they met at the bike sheds during lunch break. Hiram beamed with excitement, but Danny, the younger, more timid of the Kane boys, did not share his enthusiasm. Nevertheless, Danny looked up to his brother and would follow Hiram anywhere. Anxious not to get caught skipping school and later face the wrath of the headmaster and their parents, it didn't take them long to leave the school gates behind. They pedalled furiously for a couple of miles, first through the village of Gunton, after which they sped down the hill at Woods Loke, and then along the notorious, never-ending stretch of Sands Lane, that, despite the season and whatever direction one was heading in, always seemed to resist you with a powerful headwind. When they at last reached the quietude of Christmas Lane, from where the narrow path to the Old Rectory began, they felt exhausted.

Shaded by a stand of brooding, ancient horse chestnut trees, they discarded their BMX bikes by the rusted cow gate, and paused. Hiram had been anticipating this moment for a long time, but now they were there it seemed somehow scarier, and away from the busy roads, everything had settled into an eerie quiet. The brothers shared a nervous glance, though soon followed up with grins. Only Danny forced his. Their hearts pounded, but they would go through with it. More than a little reluctant, Danny kept his fear to himself.

They strode along the secluded trail, their legs powering them on in long strides that seemed confident though were anything but, as the thick silence seemed to creep along behind them. Then a noise, and their heads shot around. Nothing there–or no one–but despite the isolation, they weren't convinced. The trees swayed, dark and ominous, their branches leaning down as if in warning. Stop, kids, they whispered, but they couldn't. They were close, the warm, sun-bathed trail drawing them along.

Ten more minutes, and they stopped. The boys had arrived. Hiram and Danny looked around, imaginations ripe and hearts racing, not from exertion, but from the looming forest and the unseen eyes watching from the shadows that made their breaths come fast and unbidden. But they made a choice, fear inspiring progress into the unknown, and pushed their way through the rotting, crippled fence beside the wide gates, the overgrown ivy a feeble barrier to determined kids. With a last glance back down the trail to make sure they were alone, they drifted with caution towards the infamous old building.

Spring had blessed them with a warm day, fat beads of sweat tickling their skin after their long cycle ride. But despite the heat the air inside the Old Rec' grounds felt cool. Goosebumps broke out on Danny's slender arms. Little light broke through the giant conker trees above, and nothing stirred in the placid air. Hiram wouldn't admit it to Danny, but he was on edge.

In keeping with the massive, decaying edifice, the grounds were vast and neglected, and it was a scrambling walk to the main entrance. Dotted around and shrouded in thick layers of green moss were a defeated army of grey and lifeless statues, sinister in appearance under the circumstances. Danny could have sworn the crumbling figures watched them as they passed.

They walked on in torpid silence. The only sounds were the soft, hypnotic crunch of disturbed gravel and a gentle spring breeze whistling in the treetops. From behind a statue of a fallen angel a pair of inky ravens took flight, startling the boys, who looked at each other and uttered nervous chuckles to conceal their shame. But a malevolent atmosphere hung all around them, and though brave, Hiram questioned if going inside was a good idea.

But they were so close to the building now, the broad and weather-beaten stone steps up to the boarded entry just yards away. They stopped again, appraising the situation–and with discretion, appraising each other. There was no use denying their trepidation, and they hesitated. Despite their taut nerves, though, Hiram was keen to push on. And rather than being labelled a chicken, Danny swallowed down his fear.

Looking about for the easiest access inside, they each tried peering through the cracks between the plank covered windows, Hiram to the left, Danny to the right, but the first couple of windows for both boys gave no obvious entry point. Danny turned the corner of the house, and the second window he came to along the east side of the former Rectory looked promising. With a deep breath, and determined to prove to his brother he was no coward, he pulled at the boards.

Hiram's first two windows offered no chance of entry, but upon his third, which had a wider gap between the boards, he peered into the darkness. Movement. Alarmed, he jerked his head back as visions of a shadowy, headless vicar flashed in his mind. Quick to accuse his heightened imagination, though, he blinked and looked inside again. This time, nothing. Weird, he thought, certain he'd seen something. Now perturbed, he turned back to Danny.

"I'm not so sure this is a good idea, Dan—"

Danny was nowhere to be seen. Hiram turned the corner and his heart skipped a beat as he spotted his brother halfway through a window.

"Danny, stop! Don't go inside," he called.

"Why not?"

"I don't think we sho—"

"Don't worry, I'll be fine," Danny replied as he disappeared into the darkness.

Hiram registered the soft thud of Danny's shoes hitting the ground, and a moment later, heard, "It's fine. Come inside."

"No, we're leaving. Come out now, Danny. Please?"

"It's okay, come on," he called back. Then a long pause. "I dare you."

Hiram looked around. The entire place appeared deserted, and seemed to have been that way for eternity, despite the rumours in school. He took a deep breath. With reluctance, and against his better judgement, he stepped to the window. "Wait there. Don't go anywhere without me."

"Sure thing," came the muffled reply, but Hiram heard the fading echo of footsteps retreating from the window. His throat went dry.

"Shit." His brother was a lot smaller than him and had edged through the gap with ease. Unnerved, he tugged hard at the planks to make room for his wider shoulders, but they wouldn't budge an inch. Panicking, Hiram heaved with all his might on the stubborn boards while calling out unanswered to Danny. At last, and with an almighty crash, the central plank gave way and Hiram sprawled to the mucky ground. Now, not only was he worried, but he was seriously pissed off.

He scrambled through that window in seconds and found himself in almost absolute darkness, the only light the angled spears of sun that filtered through the boards and highlighted the twisting swirls of dust.

Hiram paused to catch his breath and allow his eyes time to adjust. He crouched on one knee and stifled a sneeze. He noticed his pulse quickening with excitement.

Hiram stood up tall. This is what he'd been imagining for months, thinking about in all those hated maths classes.

Despite the disquiet he felt about his brother, Hiram Kane the Third was in his element.

"Where are you? Wait for me."

Hiram's voice echoed around the large and empty room. It still went unanswered. Climbing back into the window, he braced himself on the inner frame and smashed out the remaining planks with the sole of his foot, the heavy kicks and cracking wood fracturing the silence. The idea was to let in more light, but despite the immediate results, the rays illuminated what he didn't want to see–footprints in the dust leading deeper into the Old Rectory.

Though considered the sensible one, Danny was quite a character; witty, funny, and always playing practical jokes on Hiram. But dashing off by himself into a creepy old building? It was out of character.

The trail of fresh prints at least showed Hiram Danny wasn't just hiding in the shadowed recesses of that room, ready to pounce out and scare the shit out of him. On the flip side, it meant he must have ventured into the dark interior of that massive edifice alone, and the thought made him shudder. He paused a moment, listening for telltale sounds of movement, but heard nothing. He nodded. It meant nobody else was in the Old Rec' with them, despite the movement he thought he saw just a few minutes ago. "Only a pigeon," he whispered.

Breathing a little easier, Hiram left that room and moved onto the next, each footstep resonating in the now silent interior. He walked into a large sitting room that had once been grand but now lay dilapidated, a cobweb-laden chandelier evidence of years of neglect. Kane knew whoever had last occupied the Old Rectory had abandoned it long before his birth, and it seemed he and Danny were the first people inside those decaying walls in decades. He hoped it was true.

From out of nowhere the sound of footsteps thudded across creaky floorboards above his head, causing a surge of adrenaline to tingle his fingertips. *Wait... was that two sets of footsteps or one?* Hiram's pulse rate kicked up several more notches, and he listened as the thuds faded to nothing. *No, just Danny*, he thought, and let out a long, slow breath. "You're gonna get a punch on the arm for this," he whispered. But Hiram was still on edge.

He hustled in search of a staircase and found one sweeping upwards to the left just beyond the sitting room. Composing himself, he climbed, ears strained for the slightest sound. Other than his own echoing footfalls and heavy breathing, he heard nothing.

"Okay, Danny, that's enough," he called, trying to sound bored. "Time to come out." Hiram was tired of his kid brother's game now, and even though it was the first of April, he was no fool. "Come on, Danny, let's go. Dad will be home from work soon, and we need to be there first." He tried to sound calm and keep the irritation from his voice. He knew he'd failed.

There was still no response. In fact, there was no sound at all. Danny wasn't known as a brave kid, so this was very unusual. Hiram himself was unsettled inside the vast and swallowing darkness of the abandoned mansion, ashamed his little brother was showing him up.

He walked on, opening doors and looking behind curtains, each time with the same result. Nothing. He forced open a few upstairs windows, allowing more light to help locate more of Danny's prints in the dusty surface, settled even thicker upstairs. But that was the strangest thing; Hiram couldn't find footprints anywhere. It was as if his brother had simply disappeared. He ran back down the stairs, certain Danny couldn't have slipped past him and back outside, his pulse galloping as he ran.

"Where the hell are you?" he shouted as he reached the front door, and with considerable effort roused by anger and escalating fear, he forced that open too. The harsh infusion of daylight startled a dozen pigeons from their perches, which flashed by him and through the door, causing Hiram to duck. "Okay, Danny, it's not funny anymore. If we're late, dad will kill us. And if he doesn't kill you, then I will." He listened. Silence. "Where are you?" he shouted.

But something felt very wrong.

Hiram rushed down the stone stairs and turned in a full circle, eyes wild and frantic and searching for any movement, but the only thing that moved was the stirring treetops and fleeing pigeons.

Total silence again, both outside and in, and he didn't know how silence could seem so loud. It roared in his ears, and grasping his head in his hands, Hiram fell to his knees.

Acknowledgments

A quick note from Steven:

I don't know any author who can finish a book of any kind without a lot of help and support, and I'm certainly no different. The assistance I've received for this novel and the entire series of books has been both necessary and invaluable.

So, a quick shout out to these lovely folks—I couldn't have done it without you:

John Hopton, John Bowen, Kevin Partner, and of course, the one and only Leslie Patrick Moore, my unstintingly supportive wife.

Also, I owe an enormous debt of gratitude to my Advanced Readers, cheesily labelled The Condors. Your early feedback, general advice and grammatical corrections have proved invaluable, and were so gratefully received. In no particular order, a huge thank you to:

Daisy, Manie Kilian, Jenny Parrott, Tony Crewe, Mark Richards, Roger Bailey, Edward Kim & Ron Torgerson.

Thank you all,

Steven

Ps: As ever, an extra special thank you to John Bowen for the amazing cover.